Advance Reviews for *Elixir*

"Read this book, and get your mind blown."

~ Aditi Saha, Goodreads #1 Top Reviewer

"Read - no, devoured - *Elixir*...and loved it."

~ Rodger Nichols, News Director, Haystack Broadcasting

"An exhilarating read that was unputdownable and totally riveting from beginning to its glorious end."

~ *Housewife Blues and Chihuahua Stories* blog

"Combines...love and action in a well-written package."

~ Steve Anderson, Executive Editor, *The Anderson Agency Report*

"Character dynamics that are astounding. A captivating read."

~ Melissa McComas, CEO, Tsunami Worldwide Media

"A thriller with suspense and relatable characters."

~ *Examiner*

"A great book."

~ *The Secret Bookshelf* blog

"A brilliant debut novel."

~ *Aoibh Reads* blog

"I adored this book."

~ *The Reading Wonderland* blog

"Galdi has done a masterful job."

~ Chuck Rounds, Editor, *Callback Entertainment News*

"It is tightly bound in terms of plot structure and the characters are well created...you'll certainly not have a dull moment, that I can assure you."

~ *The Book Worm* blog

"Galdi incorporates real issues with a sensational story."

~ *Motherhood Moment* blog

"Wild ride of a novel that moves at breakneck speed."

~ Jeff Cox, author of 20 books

"Galdi...shows the power of love in the most unimaginable of situations."

~ *Crazy for YA* blog

"Incredibly intriguing and so thrilling to read."

~ *My Fantabulous Bookshelf* blog

"Action packed."

~ Paul Sciria, Managing Editor, *La Gazzetta Italiana*

"*Elixir* is a debut book that is not only unique, but also compelling."

~ *Much Loved Books* blog

"Until the very end you wonder what else will happen."

~ *Tom Law Book Reviews*

"A real page turner."

~ Susan Henderson, Publisher/Editor, *Mountain Views News*

"An entertaining and provocative read."

~ *Scared Stiff Reviews*

"I thoroughly enjoyed this novel."

~ *What 'Cha Readin'?* blog

"A thrilling adventure."

~ *Pure Politics*

"It's a race against time and a battling journey to the finish line."

~ Sandra Lopez, author of *Beyond the Gardens*

"An extremely well-written action thriller...which will keep you gripped from start to finish."

~ *Bookwormed Reviews*

Elixir

By Ted Galdi

ISBN: 098985079X
ISBN: 978-0-9898507-9-7

To Mom and Dad.

ELIXIR

That Kid From *Jeopardy!*

"This mythical hero stole Hippolyta's girdle as one of his labors."

"Who is Hercules."

"Correct."

Sean is sandwiched between Melinda, "a mechanical engineer originally from Roanoke, Virginia," and David, "a tax attorney originally from Spokane, Washington," on the *Jeopardy!* stage. Melinda, forty-one, and David, forty-seven, have scores of $600 and $200 on their podiums toward the end of the second round. Sean, eleven, stands behind a $42,500. "H Names for two thousand please," the kid says, head slumped to the left.

"In Genesis Sixteen this handmaid of Sarah flees the household."

"Who is Hagar."

"Right."

Glancing at his opponents, he thinks about all the faces in their spots over the last eight weeks, then says, "Country Time for four hundred please."

"Nepal's western, eastern, and southern boundaries are with this country."

"What is India."

"Right."

"Country Time for eight hundred please."

"What was long ago called Cush, part of Nubia, is considered to be this African country today."

"What is Ethiopia."

"Correct."

He peers at the studio audience through the glare of the hot lights. He notices a few people pointing at him, whispering to their neighbors. One person waves a sign saying "Sean Malone Is a Mutant." Another laughs in amazement. Listening to the applause, he wonders why he hasn't met an intellectual equal during the last eight weeks. He figures something must be wrong with him.

College Boy

Three years later Sean is jogging across the Southern California Technology Institute's palm-tree-lined campus with a Pittsburgh Pirates cap pulled low. He's fourteen now, a few inches taller than he was on the game show. Sliding his phone from his pocket, he checks the time. 2:17 PM. He picks up his pace.

He goes down a flight of stairs and trots to the Computer Science Building, a stone structure with a red door. Pushing the handle, he wanders inside, then climbs to the second floor, flooded with undergrads. Shoulder on the wall, he walks to the side of the foot traffic. He crosses the hall, bumping into a bulky student, losing balance for a moment. "Sorry kid," the guy says strolling off. Sean steps to an office labeled "Dr. Steven Merzberg – Dean of Computer Science" and knocks.

"Come in," a cheery voice says.

He twists the knob and enters, the room blanketed with plaques and trophies for academic achievements, including a framed Fields Medal, the world's highest honor for mathematics. "Sorry I'm late," Sean says to the professor, a pudgy, bald man in his sixties with dimples.

The instructor is sitting behind his desk with tweezers, poking at the inside of a transistor radio. "I like your shoes," he says, nodding at the boy's neon-green skateboarding sneakers.

"Thanks. They're new."

"How do you think I'd look in a pair of those?" he asks with a touch of sarcasm.

"Slick," Sean says, matching his joking tone. "I'd have to teach you how to skateboard though."

He chuckles. "So what do you have for me?"

He hasn't even started the independent study he's doing with the professor and decides to tell the same small lie he's been babbling since the semester began. "It's a tricky one. It's taking me a while to decide how to approach it."

"Have a seat." He sinks into a thick-cushioned chair opposite the desk. "The Traveling Salesman Problem has caused many sleepless nights for many brilliant people." With a sigh he sets down his tweezers. "There's a reason it's the biggest enigma in computer science. Quite the undertaking. Even for you."

"I'll have something next Wednesday. Promise."

"I certainly don't expect you to solve it in the formal sense. But if you can document a strategy we can review, it would be a useful exercise. I was hoping by today you would've at least gone through those papers I sent you that my colleagues wrote on the topic, and commented on their techniques." The professor appears disappointed. He admires the fourteen-year-old's towering intellect and was hoping they'd spend the session yakking about math formulas and algorithms and the like.

"I'll email you. Soon."

"All right. We're already three weeks into the semester. I'll be waiting." He starts toying with the radio again. "How was that new burrito place you were telling me about last time? Did you wind up going with your aunt?"

"It was awesome." Sean's expression brightens, the subject of burritos much more exciting to him than computer-science problems. "They have this sauce called El Widow Maker. It was as hot as the ad said it was. I couldn't get down a bite without coughing."

"You're absurd with that spicy food of yours. How can you even enjoy the meal when it's that hot?"

"I love it. Kind of a challenge."

"I prefer keeping my challenges confined to number theory and combinatorics," he says, aware of how nerdy he sounds. "No coughing required."

Sean grins. He likes the professor, beneath all his talk of theorems and proofs and his Fields Medal is a family man not all that serious in the way he takes himself. Each week, Sean glances at a photo on the desk of him and his wife on a boat at Niagara Falls in blue ponchos, water soaking them while they laugh.

Tapping his thighs with his palms, Sean says, "I've got another class on the other end of campus, and I need to stop at the library for a book I forgot, so—"

"Yes, yes. You can go. Just make sure you email me that outline."

He gets up and adjusts his Pirates cap. "Cross my heart."

"You better," he says, doing a bad job trying to seem stern. "If you don't, next Wednesday I'm keeping you the full hour." He stabs the air a couple times with the tweezers, then smiles and gestures toward the door. "Get the hell out of here. You can't be late for two courses in a row."

He snickers. "See ya Dr. M."

The next morning Sean scurries down the stairs of his house in Pasadena, a suburb of Los Angeles, nothing on except pajama pants, eyes still sleepy. He turns into the kitchen, his Aunt Mary at the counter sipping coffee and reading the *Los Angeles Times*. "Morning bud," she says, attention on the paper.

"Morning." Running a hand through his messy hair, he walks to the refrigerator, grabs a gallon of orange juice, and chugs from the bottle.

She realizes what he's doing just from the noise. "What did I tell you about that? Get a glass you animal." She holds a stony look on him, but he can sense she doesn't mind deep down. Living with her the last ten years, he's accustomed to every line and curl in her expressions and their meanings. He decides to have some fun and test her. He swigs again. She rolls her eyes, then says, "Me and my friend from book club are going bowling a little later. Want to come?"

He feels a hint of accomplishment knowing she wasn't going to question him again about drinking from the bottle. "I've been putting off that independent study. The Traveling Salesman thing I told you about." He takes another gulp. "I want to get it out of the way. I feel bad for the professor. He thinks I've been working on it."

"Oh yeah, I kind of remember. You need to find the shortest distance between all the cities a salesman has to visit on a business trip?"

"That's the one." He puts the jug away and knees the refrigerator shut. "Nobody's been able to come up with a formula to automatically do it."

"Ever?"

"Not one that would work in any case."

"Jeez. My head would explode trying to figure that out." She folds the paper to the Opinion section. "Chicken on the barbecue okay for dinner later?" she asks, skimming a column about violence in videogames.

"I'm gonna eat at Kyle's. His parents invited me over." He opens a cabinet and snatches a bag of M&Ms.

She hears the crumple of the package and asks with disappointment, "That's your breakfast?" With a smirk he scampers out. She groans and returns to the videogame article.

He goes up the steps and into his room, passing an unmade bed with a *Die Hard* poster above, scattered clothing on the rug, and a brown dresser with half the drawers open, half shut. He scoops his laptop from the floor and sits at his desk.

He closes Netflix, *Family Guy* episode paused on the screen, then creates a new Microsoft Word document, titling it "Solving the Traveling Salesman Problem: Computing the Least Cost Cyclic Route Through All Nodes of a Weighted Graph in Polynomial Runtime."

He grabs his phone and scrolls through its music library, selecting the album *Siamese Dream* by The Smashing Pumpkins. He fishes his headphones from a drawer and plugs them in. Wrapping them around his ears with one hand, he hits play with the other.

As the first song starts he tears the candy pack with his teeth and pours some in his mouth. Chewing, he empties fifteen or so pieces on the carpet by the chair, situating them a few inches from each other.

He pictures each M&M as a city a salesman could visit on a trip, envisioning all the possible paths connecting them. Closing his eyes, he pumps his right knee to the rhythm. The large studio-grade headphones cover the full of his ears, giving them a toasty feeling as his mind rips through mathematical questions that have dumbfounded the world's top scholars for decades.

In an hour or so he stops the music. He figured it out. The whole thing. He doesn't appear excited, rather, disappointed. He cracks his neck and begins typing the answer in the Word document.

Derailed

Slouched on a bench next to his Aunt Mary the following day, Sean spins his watch bezel back and forth as their train rumbles through the Los Angeles subway. "It looks funny from the previews," she says in an optimistic tone. "I hope the producers didn't get lazy though because it's a sequel. It happens a lot in comedies."

"It'll be hysterical with that cast," he says with confidence. "Even if the plot's a little loose, I'm sure there'll be three, maybe even four scenes you really remember. With a comedy that's all I care about. Just give me a few parts that make me piss myself and it's fine if the plot is…whatever."

"Don't get me wrong. I'm excited to see it. Let's pray the story's not too silly though. Like that last one with the main actor." She stares out the window at the flashes whizzing by from the lamps on the underground walls. He looks at the mild crow's feet by her eyes. She's transitioned into her forties with grace but still shows natural signs of wear. Her hair is a different shade of brown than it used to be too, lighter since she's been dying it to hide the grays. He thinks about how much he likes doing movie night with her every Thursday but wishes she'd cancel once in a while to go on a date, been about five years.

"You look familiar," a girl about his age says in a soft voice from the seat across, grabbing his attention. "Do you go to Jefferson High?"

He surveys her, Lady Gaga T-shirt, cute face, a little too much eye shadow. "Nah, I go somewhere else."

"You look so familiar," she says, leaning closer, inspecting him. He's sure she recognizes him from *Jeopardy!* but hates when people associate him with the show. Playing dumb, he shrugs. "What school do you go to then?"

"It's in Pasadena, but not Jefferson."

"Barish? The private one."

"It's private. But not Barish."

A few moments go by. "I'm Cindy." She points at her friend, next to her in a different Lady Gaga top. "We're going downtown for the concert. You too?"

"We're just getting something to eat." He nods at his aunt. "Then the movies."

"Oh. Okay." Her pal whispers in her ear and they giggle. "My friend wants to know if you have a girlfriend."

He grins. "Your friend couldn't just ask me?"

"She's shy." More laughter. "A few of us are chilling by all the shops and restaurants near the arena when the concert's over. You should come say hi. When you're done with your movie." His aunt pretends to be oblivious to the interaction but listens to every word she can make out above the sound of the tracks, absorbing as much juice as she can.

"Cool," Sean says to the girl. "I'll see."

"Here," she says, motioning toward herself with two fingers. "Give me your phone. I'll put in my number." He hands it to her, she types it in, and passes it back. "Cindy."

"I didn't forget. Sean. And your friend's name?"

"Amanda," she says for her.

"Nice to meet you Amanda," he says looking at her with a smile. Blushing, she grins, then turns away. He finds it funny how shy she is. He thinks about the girls on the college campus and how different they are from ones his age. He wonders where between fourteen and eighteen they grow up. He's not sure but hopes he'll figure it out someday.

Wheels screeching, the train coasts to a halt. Riders stand as the doors split. "Have fun," he says to the Lady Gaga fans as they walk off in the station.

Hands buried in his pockets, he moseys toward the shine peeking from above ground, the smell of mold lingering. He hears his aunt's distinct patter of shoes behind him. Glancing over his shoulder, he notices her weaving toward him. He braces himself for an interrogation. Sure enough she says, "They were cute. Did she give you her number?"

"What're you spying on me?" He doesn't mind chatting with her about stuff like this but decides to mess with her anyway. With a smirk he speeds up, distancing himself from her in the pack of commuters.

She swerves her way back to him. "Are you going to call her?"

"I don't know."

"What do you mean?"

Climbing the steps, he says, "If anything I'll text her. People don't call each other anymore when they first meet. I'd look like a big weirdo if I did."

"That's not true. Calling is still more popular."

"Not for kids my age. The average teenager sends sixty-three texts per day I read somewhere."

"Calling is so much easier. I'm not a big texter. Takes me forever to type out what I want to say. How long are the messages usually?"

"I read in the same article the typical text is like ninety letters. Mine are around there I guess."

"That comes out to how many button clicks a day?"

"Fifty-six hundred seventy," he says, doing the math in his head in an instant.

"So in a year it—"

"Two million sixty-nine thousand five hundred fifty," he says, processing the second calculation in a snap as well.

"Boy." She mulls over all that thumb activity as they emerge on the street, skyscrapers towering above on all sides, cold air wrapping around them, throngs of nine-to-fivers spilling out of the downtown buildings toward the subway entrance. "What were their names?"

"Get out of here. I'm not talking about this with you anymore."

"Am I being annoying?"

"A little. I forgive you though." He pats her shoulder a couple times. "I know you can't help it when it comes to me and girls."

"Just curious," she says with exaggerated sadness, trying to be funny.

He chuckles, then blows in his hands. "Man. When did it get so cold?"

"I should've brought a real jacket." She rubs her arms over her thin purple sweatshirt.

"Where's the restaurant?" he asks, spotting black clouds on the horizon. "It's gonna pour. We should get inside this place." As she scans her phone for the address, his own vibrates in his pocket. Pulling it out, he sees a missed call and voicemail from an unknown number. Assuming it's a telemarketer, he puts it back.

"This way," she says, pointing left. Following her, he feels it vibrate again. He thinks about ignoring it but decides to answer. "Hello?" He listens for a few moments, struggling to hear on top of the rush-hour car horns, plugging his ear with his index finger. "Dr. Merzberg?" He cuts across the road into an alley away from the street noise. "Is everything all right?" His expression shifts from confused to surprised. "Now? I'm...out with my aunt." He sighs. "Fine. I'll meet you at the campus. You're sure? Fine." He hangs up.

"You okay?" Aunt Mary asks, bewildered.

"I have to go."

"Where?"

The disappointment on her face upsets him. He realizes how much she looks forward to this night every week. "Dr. Merzberg. You've met him. My professor from school...he said it's an emergency. He needs me to see him."

"For a class? Where?"

"He didn't want to talk about it over the phone. Whatever that means. Wanted to do it in person. He said he needs me to come to his office. Right now." He's quiet for about five seconds, pondering the professor's possible motivation. "I'll fill you in as soon as I know. We'll see the movie another day. I'm sorry."

About an hour later he knocks on the professor's door in the Computer Science Building, the tap of rain outside, water droplets dancing on the hallway windows. "Come in," he says from the room, not upbeat like usual.

He enters, noticing a half-empty bottle of Absolut Vodka on the desk. He examines his squinty-eyed, red-cheeked teacher and asks, "Are you drunk?" He doesn't reply. "What's this about? And why couldn't you just tell me over the phone? I had to leave my aunt for the night to come—"

"Because someone could be listening in on a phone dammit." Standing, he pulls a plane ticket from a drawer and extends it to Sean. His expression is grave. "We're going to DC. A car's outside ready to take us to LAX Airport. The National Security Agency is expecting you."

Shreds of Doubt

A thirtyish woman rocks a screaming infant on a grounded aircraft, Sean and the professor one row behind. Sean stares out the window at three men in orange vests loading luggage on another plane, sky still dense with rain. He sticks his hand in a bag of spicy Doritos, pops a couple in his mouth, and chews, the crunch muffled by the wailing child.

"You need to shred every copy of the paper and erase the file from your computer," the professor says in a hushed yet frantic voice from the middle chair. He glances to his right, making sure the guy in the aisle seat isn't listening. He's not, bobbing to music in his headphones. "I destroyed the one you sent me after I emailed it to the NSA."

Sean regrets the lie the professor made him tell his aunt about why they were going to DC, a math conference at Georgetown they "couldn't miss." The guilt of it has been weighing on him. "I still don't get why the freaking NSA cares so much. Don't you think this is a little extreme? A cross-country trip? I can't even tell my own relative where we're going?"

"The existence of your algorithm and the involvement of the NSA must be kept a secret. Family included. If not, there's a chance word can get out that it's a reality and people will hunt you down for it. Bad people. What you've created has catastrophic potential. If someone without the purest of intentions got access to it the world as we know it could change."

"Because of a math formula?" He bites into a Dorito.

"It's more than a math formula."

"If you knew it was gonna be such a big deal why didn't you give me a heads-up before we even started the independent study?"

The professor peeks over his shoulder to see if anyone is eavesdropping, an oblivious overweight couple playing Angry Birds on iPads. He says to his student, "We never discussed you doing something as...significant as this. I thought you'd analyze the historical approaches to the Traveling Salesman and maybe make some marginal gains in its runtime. I didn't expect you were going to exponentially alter the fabric of it." He taps his fingers on his knees for a while, eyes jumping around. "You do realize how encryption works, don't you?"

"Sort of. I was gonna take the class last semester, but it was full." He tosses two more chips in his mouth.

"Well...you should've registered earlier," he says with a trace of frustration. "All sensitive information, whether it's confidential government documents or credit card numbers, gets scrambled when it crosses the internet so people can't steal it. Hackers and what not. Hard-to-solve math like the kind in the Traveling Salesman Problem is used by the good guys to do the scrambling." A pause. "Do you see the issue?"

"So if you had my paper you could hack anything that was encrypted by the problem?"

"Not only the Salesman. But any one even similar to it."

He bangs his hands together a few times, knocking the Doritos dust off. "How much encoded info is in that…group?"

"Pretty much all of it."

Sean leans back, the gravity of the situation sinking in. He's quiet for about half a minute, the crying baby the only noise between them. "Sorry."

The professor lets out a nervous laugh. "Oh Sean, oh Sean." The screens mounted to the rear of the headrests glow and a welcome message plays from American Airlines. A perky stewardess recites a safety announcement over the PA system. Passengers flip up their tray tables and power down their phones.

Sean stuffs his chips in the pouch in front of him. He lost his appetite. The more he thinks about this all, the more it bothers him. He contemplates how he'd deal with the guilt if an evil person obtained his work and did something terrible with it. He's not sure he could.

In a bit they begin crawling from the gate. "Why the hell did you tell them about it in the first place?" he asks.

"I'm aware this is a bit vexing. And I do apologize for that. But I had no choice. If they found out someone in my position didn't report this after his own student created it, it would look awfully suspicious. They'd have me barred from teaching computer science in every American university."

"What do they even want from me when we get there?"

He tucks his copy of *MIT Technology Review* between his armrest and potbelly and says, "I of course already explained to them you didn't foresee the impact this would have. But they need you to sign some things…affirming you'll never share the file. Ever."

"They can force me to do that?"

"It is the truth of course. You won't be speaking of this… or using it." A pause. "Right Sean?"

"Yes. Jesus. I don't want to steal people's credit card numbers or whatever. I just want this to be over with."

"Then sign the papers and it'll be done. Easy. If you don't, then well…they'll hawk over your every move. Whether they admit it or not. This is the NSA we're dealing with." He leans in, so close Sean can smell a hint of the Werther's Original caramel candy he had two hours ago in the car. "They don't like operating with any shred of doubt. None."

"I got it, okay?" Sean's brain pulls up all the information it's ever absorbed about the agency. Involvement in wars. Meddling with popular consumer web companies. Spying on US citizens. He doesn't like how his life is now crossed with it. He has a bad feeling a simple signature on a page won't be the end of this new relationship.

The engines roar. He yanks his seatbelt tight. His pulse throbs against the side of his throat. The plane bullets down the runway and ascends into the stormy sky.

Hearing Things

A taxi buzzes along a service road, Sean and the professor inside viewing the dreary morning in Fort Meade, Maryland, bags under their eyes, neither getting much sleep between last night's flight and today's early alarm.

They approach two large block-shaped buildings, no signs or writing on either. The cab stops in the eighteen-thousand-spot NSA parking lot, the professor sliding his wallet from his pocket. As he pays, Sean gets out, fixating on the black reflective windows, staring back at himself on the surface.

The professor steps on the curb, wraps his trench coat snug around his chest, and nods at the main facility. They wander toward it, Sean eyeing the faces of NSA employees as they walk by, emotionless expressions, whispered conversations.

They enter the lobby. Sean peeks through the one-way glass at the sea of cars outside. "We're meeting by the memorial," his teacher says, veering toward a hall. "This way."

In a short while they're at the end of a corridor. Hands in his pockets, Sean inspects an eight-foot-tall triangular memorial dedicated to fallen American codebreakers, "They Served in Silence" engraved above one hundred seventy-one names.

A fit woman in a dark business suit approaches, click of her high heels echoing. "Welcome gentlemen," she says with her palms up. "I'll show you to Mr. Goya's office."

In a bit she's escorting them across an upper floor lined with wide black-rimmed monitors, interactive graphs and charts on each. They thread through a couple dozen bustling workers, stopping at a door labeled "P. Goya – Technical Director." She cracks it and says, "He should be just a few minutes. You can wait on the couch until he's back."

"Thank you," the professor says as they slip inside the corner office. Sean soaks in the personal touches, on the wall an encased Philadelphia Eagles jersey, on the desk a picture of a man posing with the CEO of a multi-billion-dollar software company, next to it another of him with his wife, son, and daughter in front of Disney World's Cinderella Castle.

The professor settles on the edge of the U-shaped leather couch, fingers tapping his knees. Arms folded, Sean leans by the football jersey. The muted morning sun oozes through the Venetian blinds in faint strips, streaking across his body and the jersey's glass case next to his head. His teacher starts humming a song he can't make out. "Staying Alive" by the Bee Gees? The room is silent other than the off-key tune.

In some time the man from the photos strides in smiling. He has energetic green eyes, much more colorful in person than in the photos. "I appreciate your patience," he says, shaking the professor's hand. "Nice seeing you again." He grips the kid's. "Patrick Goya."

"Sean."

Patrick gets comfortable in his ergonomic chair and says to the professor, "I can't thank you enough for contacting me. What you did was the absolute right choice." Then turns to

Sean. "You've definitely complicated my life here, that's for sure." He has a sip of coffee from a blue cup with the NSA seal on it. "That being said. I've been at the agency for seven years and worked in the private sector at a handful of major tech companies for fifteen years before that. In no position have I ever seen a discovery made as inventive as yours. It took me a while to even understand what you did. It's unlike anything I've ever been exposed to. In any kind of math."

"I didn't think it was gonna cause so much trouble. I probably would've done another problem if I did."

He laughs. "Come on. That's the King Kong of problems. Trouble aside, you must be thrilled you were able to…wrangle it. The sense of accomplishment with something of that magnitude has to be incredible." Sean shrugs. "I'm sorry we have to keep this classified. You deserve the notoriety."

"Notoriety is the last thing I want."

Patrick looks confused. "It was an achievement up there in the field with…the invention of the personal computer. You don't want the public to know you did it?"

"Man. I'm glad you guys want to keep it a secret."

He rocks back and forth for a few moments. "Why'd you try to solve it then?"

"I wanted to see if I wouldn't be able to."

"What do you mean?"

"Everyone at school said it was the hardest one out there. I thought maybe I'd…hit a wall trying to figure it out."

"You don't hear that a lot at the NSA." Patrick chuckles, so does the professor. "Why would you hope for…failure?"

"It would be a change I guess."

"From what?"

"It feels weird." He rubs the back of his neck. "How easy stuff like that is for me, compared to…things other people say about it."

Patrick absorbs this. "Ah. It must be lonely at the top. I get it. Not a bad thing though. Being at the top." He has some more coffee. "How much did you win on the game show again? A mill and a half?"

"One point seven," he says with reluctance. He's always been embarrassed to admit he became a millionaire from answering trivia questions, aware of how hard the average American has to work for a paycheck, like his aunt, a dental assistant for twenty years before they got rich.

"You could've won a hundred million. Me and my wife used to watch you. Why'd you step down?"

"It was time."

"You're crazy. If I were you I would've milked that as long as I could've." He studies Sean from head to toe, Pirates cap, wrinkled shirt, neon sneakers. "I can't say you're not interesting Malone."

"He certainly is," the professor says with a slow nod. "With an IQ of two hundred and fifty, he definitely has the ability to surprise."

Patrick stands and saunters to a chrome-edged table in the corner, refilling his mug under a Krups machine. "You're a Pennsylvania boy I hear?"

"Yeah," Sean says. "Shipville. I saw your Eagles jersey on the wall. You too?"

"Lay a finger on it and there'll be hell to pay. I know you guys in Shipville are all Steelers fans." The boy smirks. True, he does like the Steelers. "Don't let the suit fool you. I'm a North Philly kid at heart." He pours a dash of milk in his drink and stirs it with a thin red straw. "How're you liking California?"

"It's cool."

"You're a little young for the dorms, right? Did your parents move west with you?"

Over the last ten years Sean's gotten good at showing no outward signs of pain when the word "parents" is mentioned but hasn't made much progress with the inward reaction, the bottom of his stomach dropping. "My aunt. My parents passed away."

"Sorry to hear that."

"It was a while ago."

His gaze tilted down, Patrick waits for the awkward moment to dissolve, then says, "We'll meet with the rest of them in a bit. You guys want a bite before? I can have my secretary put in an order for us."

"Pizza would be good," Sean says, excitement in his voice for the first time all day. "Maybe with peppers? Spicy ones. Not the yellow banana kind."

"Professor?"

"I've never said no to pizza. But please, only the hot stuff on half. I'd have indigestion for a month if I came close to a habanero."

"Done," Patrick says, glancing at his gold watch on one hand, lifting his phone with the other. "We'll need to eat quick.

The people we're meeting with aren't exactly the type who tolerate bad punctuality."

A short while later Sean is twisting back and forth in a swivel chair in an underground conference room, brown-oak paneling, dim track lighting, agency logo mounted on the far wall. He has a bad cramp in his left leg, the result of a six-hour plane ride and lack of sleep. The professor sits next to him at the shiny table, Patrick at one head, four government men among them. In the center is a stack of confidentiality documents all seven just signed.

"He's on his way down," Patrick says as if warning everyone.

In a couple minutes the door opens, a brawny man in his sixties entering, some others tensing in his presence. Sean recognizes him from press conferences on TV, the United States Secretary of Defense.

He grasps the non-disclosure contracts, then advances with slow strides to the empty head seat and descends his six-foot-four frame into it. He thumbs through the sheets of paper, grunting in approval as he counts each signature. Once done with all seven, he looks up and says in his baritone Southern accent, "None of you have any business telling anyone outside this circle the formula exists. Wives. Kids. Priests. Anyone. If you do, I'll personally see to it that my friends in the Justice Department throw every punishment outlined in this agreement down on you to the letter. Are we clear?"

"Yes sir," Patrick says in the sort of tone employees use with their bosses. "All seven of us are fully aware of the stipulations."

The Secretary glances at him for a second, then sweeps his gaze across the other four federal officials. "The fact that something like this is out in the world changes how each of your organizations has to go about its business. Forever. But your staff will carry on without a whisper of it. From the janitor all the way up to your second-in-command. If you have reason to believe this algorithm leaked, you're to discuss it strictly with the four other reps sitting here. Assess the problem with them, then trickle the orders down to your staff. If your subordinates ask questions, you tell them it's classified. If they keep asking…you send them to me. And most importantly, if you have a suspicion anyone else in here is responsible for a potential leak, you tell me before you find the time to take your next breath. Is that understood?" They all nod. He pivots his stare to Sean, cracks the knuckles on his right hand, and asks, "Do you know who I am?"

Sean's brain retrieves all the information it's ever read about him, birth date, pounds of tobacco his wealthy family's South Carolina farm produces every year, rank when he fought in Vietnam, position he played on the Cornell football team, name of the Middle Eastern dictator the defense contractor Peltex Industries was accused of selling weapons to when he was the CEO ten years ago. All he says, "You're the Secretary of Defense. Paul Pine."

"That's correct." He lingers on the boy's neon sneaker, jutting out from the side of the table. "Now, you interrupted the lives of the leaders of the most important bureaus in this country. I hope you're aware of that. They can never operate in the same capacity again with this…variable in the mix."

Head down, Sean says in a low voice, "I'm sorry. I didn't think it was gonna be this...big of a thing."

"It's bigger than a big thing. All right. And for what? The thrill you could do it? Knowing you have the power to hack something?"

"Sir, to clarify," Patrick says. "Sean's intentions were innocent, never about hacking. This began as an academic exercise at the Southern California Technology Institute he was doing alongside his instructor Steven Merzberg, who's with us too." The professor gives a clumsy wave. "There was never any goal to hack into one of our data centers, or any other. As soon as Dr. Merzberg found out, he escalated it to me immediately."

"That's a hell of an assignment you handed out professor," Pine says.

A few seconds pass. "That's all it was ever intended to be," the professor says, a thin layer of sweat on his bald head. "An assignment. I planned for him to analyze the nature of the Traveling Salesman Problem, and possibly make some slight efficiency gains in the time it takes computers to process it. Even a minor improvement would've been considered a momentous feat." A pause. "But I never thought he was going to come up with a formula to turn it on its head, and decrease the runtime by an order of magnitude. In my field, doing what he did is essentially considered impossible. This...outcome of his never crossed my mind when we began the independent study." He glances at Sean. "In hindsight though...I probably shouldn't have made that assumption about the boy. He's not a...typical student."

"How do you mean?"

"Well." He folds his hands in front of him. "I've been around academic professionals my entire adult life. Brilliant men and women. Harvard, Stanford, MIT, Oxford, Cambridge. Everywhere. I've seen the reaches of the human IQ spectrum. The small group at the far-right corner of the bell curve. To be honest, I'm considered one of those people myself." His face contorts into a ponderous expression. "But Sean, see, he's different. Statistically speaking, at any given time, there is someone who isn't in any group. By definition you can call that individual the smartest person on Earth. Based on my knowledge of the minds out there in the most distinguished realms of academia, my own mental abilities included, and comparing that to what I've observed of the boy since he's been at the school, I would say there's a good chance he would be just that. The smartest person on Earth. In terms of raw intellectual firepower, he surpasses anything I've ever come across." He pauses. "By a landslide."

Hearing this speech, a few people at the table glimpse Sean, a flash of wonder in their eyes they're trying to conceal out of professionalism. The Smartest Person on Earth. He hates that title, been called it three times before. Once over a decade ago by a child cognition specialist who gave him an IQ test. Once backstage at *Jeopardy!* by a physicist from Poland he rendered scoreless. Once by their mailman in Pasadena, a big fan.

Not only does the label itself draw the sort of attention he doesn't like, such as the stares he's getting right now, but it has implications that bother him at a deeper level. Without a mind on the planet superior to his, there's no line of defense between him and those hard, almost otherworldly, questions that have baffled humanity for ages. Why did nature create any of us in the first place? When it did, how come it made us so different from each other? Now that it has six billion versions of us on this giant floating rock in infinite space, what are we all supposed to do?

As gifted as he is he can't answer any of these. The universe scares him. Knowing he's our best hope to make sense of it scares him even more. The Smartest Person on Earth. He didn't ask for that title. He asked for it just as much as someone asks for bad vision or an inability to digest certain foods or crooked teeth. He was born with it.

Pine reclines, his large build flattening the leather cushion. "I realize he's not normal," he says to the professor. "I remember him from *Jeopardy!* a few years ago." He shifts to Sean. "How old are you now?"

The cramp in Sean's leg tightens. Rubbing it, he says, "Fourteen." He doesn't like the way the Secretary is looking at him. He detects an animalistic hostility in his eyes, veiled beneath a shallow disguise of civility from years of boarding school and the Ivy League, summers at country clubs, hobnobbing at political fundraisers, and all the things that come along with the others.

Pine lets out a sarcastic belly laugh. "We're sitting on quite possibly the generation's biggest threat to national security and we're trusting the secret to a fourteen-year-old?"

"If I may," Patrick says. "Sean signed the same agreement as the rest of us. His age makes him no more likely to leak it than anyone else. The probability of disclosure is equal with everyone at this table.”

“No Goya,” Pine says. “I’m the least likely to let it out. Because ultimately this all boils up to me. Can you wrap your head around the political nightmare that’ll happen on my watch if this was exposed? Imagine what the President would do.”

One of the other attendants, the chief of the Drug Enforcement Administration’s Intelligence Division, says to Pine, “It’s important to consider that this is not only a burden, but an opportunity. Yes, in the hands of foreign intelligence many of our systems would be vulnerable.” He raises his index finger. “However, with the algorithm on our side those fortunes flip. The math can be used to crack the codes that have been holding back our more…stubborn… DEA initiatives.” He looks at another face. “I’m sure the same is true with the CIA.”

“Of course I’m aware of the opportunity aspect,” Pine says. “I advise you all talk about ways it can be used in each of your branches. The possibilities I’m assuming are…bountiful.” He turns to the DEA representative. “Do you see it having an immediate impact anywhere?”

“Absolutely. In fact, earlier Goya and I were talking about it in the context of Operation Golden Bear down in Mexico. If the NSA could break that code we’d have enough information at the DEA to bring the mission to…completion.”

“I see,” Pine says, gathering the seven documents. He bangs the bottom of the stack on the table to square it off. “Get to it then.” He rises, marches to the exit, and leaves.

The federal employees grin, invigorated by the chance to apply the formula in the field. Sean seems bothered by this though. He thought they were just going to bury his work. Nobody ever mentioned using it.

Strike Three

The next day Sean swings and misses in an indoor batting cage back in Pasadena, ball thumping a chain-link fence. He bangs the head of his bat on the rubber plate, then lifts it, eyes on a pitching machine sixty feet away. The metal arm spins, scooping up one more and hurling it at him. He takes a cut, no contact, another thud behind.

His coach, a fit black guy in his late thirties, says from the other side of the fence, "All right Malone. Let Stutzel get his rips in."

Aluminum Louisville Slugger dragging, Sean flips the gate open and exits while a husky teammate with shaved red hair enters. "What's the matter?" the hefty kid asks in an insulting tone. "You couldn't write a physics formula to show you where to swing?" He laughs, along with a few other players waiting their turn.

Glaring at him, Sean says, "Eat shit Stutzel."

"Watch the mouth Malone," the coach says. He motions to Sean with his clipboard. "Get over here." He wanders to him. "What's going on? You're dropping your shoulder when you swing. I didn't catch you do that once all last season."

"I'm rusty I guess."

"You look like you got something on your mind. You hardly said three words all practice."

"I'm fine." He's not, still anxious about everything with the NSA. After the Defense Secretary left, the meeting ended, Sean and the professor escorted out of the building without any additional information about them using the algorithm.

"First game's only two months away. Now's not the time to lose sight of the fundamentals. Stand in front of a mirror tonight and do a couple dozen practice cuts." The coach grips a pretend bat. "Check out your reflection." He points at his own eyes with his index and middle fingers. "See if anything breaks. You're smart enough. You should be able to fix it." He gives the brim of the kid's hat an encouraging slap. "All right?"

"Yeah coach." Peeling off his batting gloves, Sean walks to his equipment bag, in a heap with a dozen or so others against the cement wall.

Kyle, another boy on the team, Sean's best friend, smacks him on the back. "Yo," Kyle says, shaking strands of his pin-straight black hair from his face.

"Hey."

"Stutzel's an asshole."

"Whatever. What're you doing later? Can you hang out?"

"Yeah definitely. Pizza?"

"Your mom's not making dinner for you guys at the house?" Sean asks, surprised.

"She is. But...I'd rather get pizza."

"Why?"

"What do you mean? It tastes good. I don't know. We'll go to Gino's."

"Gino's is cool for a couple slices, but your mom makes a feast. And your dad's funny." Sean's expression glows. "I liked that story he told about that one guy at work. The one who goes to New York a lot and forgets to reset his watch when he gets back to California and is always super early to meetings."

"Yeah he's pretty funny. For a dad I mean. Try living with him though. He's a pain in the ass."

"Come on. He's pretty cool."

"Do you want to go to Gino's or not dude?"

"You sure you're not gonna eat with all them?"

"Let's get pizza."

"All right man. I'll text you after I get home and shower and stuff."

"Solid."

About an hour later practice is done. Sean pushes open the front door of the facility and steps into the February air. He crosses the parking lot, kneeling at a bike rack, twisting the combination on his lock. He stuffs it and his chain in his equipment bag, climbs on his ten-speed, and pedals off the property.

He cruises along a sidewalk, cracks every few feet, blades of grass protruding. The sun is setting, goose bumps running up his forearms as the night takes hold of Pasadena. He advances for a couple blocks, thinking about the NSA, wondering what it's going to do with his algorithm.

His thoughts are interrupted when his handlebars start shaking and his front tire kicks to the side. Squeezing the brake, he skids to a stop. Spinning his head behind, he sees five spots of blood on the gray cement leading to a sparrow on its back.

He throws down the bicycle and sprints to the wounded bird, a gash on its yellow coat, wings fluttering as it hangs on for life. He yanks the zipper on his bag, grabs his mitt, and scoops the animal in it, crimson specks dotting the leather. He mounts the bike and pedals, one hand guiding the handlebars, the other supporting the glove, sparrow wobbling inside.

About twenty minutes later he rides up to the Pasadena Animal Clinic, a one-story brick building with a paw-print logo on the front. He chucks his bicycle to the asphalt and dashes toward the entrance, mitt steady in front of him. Stare on the bird, he notices its wings aren't moving anymore. Panicking, he bolts inside and up to the counter. "I need help," he says with urgency to everyone in the place.

A curly-haired woman wearing a white lab coat over jeans saunters to him and glances at the sparrow. She slides a rubber glove on each hand and pokes its chest, then wings, then head. "It doesn't appear he made it. I'm sorry."

"What do you mean? All you did was touch it. How do you know?"

"It's pretty…apparent…you can…see yourself." He can't look. He sticks his hands on his hips and takes a few anxious breaths. She taps her knuckles, getting his attention. "When people lose pets we usually put them in receptacles they can bring home and bury. I can give you one free of charge." She studies his face for a couple seconds. "Do I know you from somewhere?"

"No."

In two hours or so he's in his backyard, a flat-tip shovel in his clutch, the sun down, air much colder than it was before. He jams the head in the ground, rips it out, dumps the dirt onto a pile, and repeats for a while. Soon a hole about three feet deep is in front of him.

His phone, on the grass by his feet, lights up and vibrates. He notices "Kyle" on the screen. Reaching down, he clicks a button on the side, ignoring his best friend's call. He digs some more, then grabs a black container about the size of a shoebox. He places it in the ditch with care, then begins pouring dirt on top. "Sean," Aunt Mary says from behind, confused.

"What?"

"What the heck are you doing?" Stepping to him, she spots the hole, eyes widening. "You're ruining the lawn."

"I'm burying something. You bury things in lawns."

"Burying what?"

"A bird."

"A bird?"

"Yes."

A couple moments pass. "You don't have a bird."

"I ran one over coming back from practice. I killed it."

She watches him fill the pit for about a minute, a light sweat on his forehead. "It sounds like an accident. Animals die a lot from coincidences like that. Wrong place, wrong time."

"That's not how things work," he says, sure of himself. "I was there. I wasn't paying attention. And I hit it. And I couldn't save it. It's my fault. So just let me bury it, okay?"

"Things aren't so black and white," she says in a soft voice.

"They are. It's logic."

She doesn't speak for about ten seconds, then in an even softer voice says, "Maybe you're being a little too logical right now."

He dumps another mound of dirt inside. "No such thing."

As she processes this all, a trace of understanding gleams on her face. Based on certain things from his past, as strange as this scene is, it makes sense to her in a way. "I'll be inside," she says retreating toward the house, no reply from him, noise of the shovel persisting.

Strike Four

A black limousine with federal-government license plates idles in front of the Pentagon the following Monday afternoon in Washington, DC. Patrick and the DEA's Intelligence head from Sean's meeting, both in suits and wool overcoats, approach from the curb, winter wind cutting into them. The driver, wearing dark sunglasses and an earpiece, steps out and opens the rear door, nodding as they climb inside.

Heat on high, they take their jackets off. Secretary of Defense Paul Pine, only other person inside, sits across immersed in a piece about an Iraqi election in the *Washington Post*. "I have a press conference with the Vice President in an hour," he says, attention still on the article. "This better be as urgent as you said it was."

The DEA representative unclips the latches on his briefcase and takes out a manila folder. Leaning forward, he hands it to Pine and says, "My team on the ground took that last night. We have reason to believe Carlos Salinas has been hiding inside."

Setting down the newspaper, Pine opens the folder. He examines a night-vision photo, a grainy image of a white mansion with closed shutters, a man in front with an Uzi, mountains behind. "How confident are you he's actually here?"

"With the…new mathematical tool we have at our disposal…we were able to decrypt the code he uses to communicate with his lieutenants. Nearly all the thumb-drive messages we retrieved trace Salinas to Taxco, an old mining town in central Mexico. I sent three of my best surveillance experts down there yesterday. They got a visual on one of his security men. They tracked him back to that compound."

Pine shuts the folder and tosses it on the seat, the late-afternoon sun coming through the window glimmering on his pockmarked neck. Reaching to the mini bar, he grabs a bottle of bourbon and a glass. He unscrews the top with slow spins, pours, and sips, the limo filling with the smell of liquor. He makes eye contact with them for the first time, jumping between each. "So," he says. "What's the plan?"

"The Mexican Federal Police are ready to pounce on this prick," the DEA man says. "They'll make a move when I confirm the intel. I wanted to of course notify you first since this would be an official engagement brought on by…a certain academic paper you have a vested interest in."

Patrick doesn't seem comfortable. He hunches forward and says to Pine, "Though we're confident about the intelligence, we're not entirely sure what kind of muscle and arsenal Salinas has in the compound. I'd expect it's not light. We need to keep in mind he's in a residential neighborhood. We can't make a war zone of it."

"This drug-lord piece of shit has been making a war zone of South Texas for the last three years," Pine says.

"I want him just as bad as you, but we should maybe consider luring him out of the area first, then apprehending him in a more stable location."

Pine swirls the bourbon for about ten seconds. His squinty brown eyes locked on Patrick, he asks, "How many enemies did you kill when you fought in Afghanistan?"

"None sir." He pauses. "I wasn't in the war."

"How many when you were in Desert Storm?"

"I wasn't in that war either."

"How many in any other wars?"

"I was never in a war sir." A long pause. "As you know."

"I killed seventeen men in Vietnam," Pine says with pride. He turns to the DEA man. "How about you?"

"Ten."

Pine looks back at Patrick. "Twenty-seven dead enemies of the United States between the two of us. None from you. If I have a question about a computer, I'll ask you. If I have a question about eliminating a threat to the nation in a real, physical way, I'd prefer if you kept your mouth shut. Is that clear?"

Patrick doesn't speak for some time. "Clear."

"Good." Pine shifts to the DEA man. "What's your call?"

"He's a sitting duck in that compound. Baiting him out is only a risk. I say we mobilize our friends south of the border tomorrow morning and put an end to Operation Golden Bear inside the house."

"That's what I figured you'd say."

Early the next day machine guns ring through the misty hills of Taxco, Mexico. A black Cadillac Escalade with tinted windows speeds out of the garage of the mansion in the surveillance photograph, turning onto a quiet mountain road with a screech. An unmarked white van follows, three Mexican federal officers in body armor inside, one driving, two hanging out pointing assault rifles.

The chase rumbles down to flat ground, where dozens of people are strolling among shops and restaurants. Everyone turns to the commotion. Pedestrians dive out of the way as the vehicles roar by at about eighty miles per hour.

A policeman blasts the rear right tire, hollow-point lead ripping through the rubber, sparks dancing around the hubcap. The incapacitated truck destroys five cafe tables, then slams into a brick restaurant front. Smoke rises from the wreck, no more than a few blocks from the Santa Prisca Church, an ornate cathedral towering above town. Bystanders rubberneck from the periphery.

Salinas the narcotics kingpin and a bodyguard with an AK-47 stagger from the Escalade bleeding from their heads and arms. The underling lunges in front of the boss to defend him, spraying his weapon at the van. The cops roll out and crawl behind, metal-on-metal bangs rippling through the streets as the siding gets pummeled.

One of the policemen slides around the bumper, pumping two cover shots. A second slips around the other end, capturing the henchman in his crosshairs, discharging a round at him. It enters him about an inch under his right eye, a rope of blood squirting as his body crumbles to the asphalt. Still alive, he sweeps for his gun but goes lifeless when two more slugs pass through his forehead.

Salinas is terrified without his human shield. He fumbles under his jacket for a pistol but can't get to it in time. The cop sticks three bullets into his chest, knocking him ten feet back while he chokes on his last breaths.

As the officers pile into their vehicle, onlookers scream, four riddled corpses on the pavement, two belonging to the criminals, two to a young man and woman killed by stray fire from the AK-47.

Return Policy

Sitting cross-legged on his blue bedroom carpet, Sean pours crackers on a paper plate. He's in a better mood today, the bird predicament almost behind him after a few days of talking it over with his aunt. His best friend Kyle eyes the saltines between them. "One minute," Sean says. "The whole thing."

"Come on," Kyle says as if his buddy's been lying to him. "It's not that much."

Smiling, Sean claps a couple times. "All right then hotshot. Go for it. Twenty bucks if you do it."

"You've got the money?"

Sean walks to his desk, pulls a ten and two crumpled fives from a drawer, and drops them on the rug. "It can be yours in sixty seconds."

"You're telling me nobody can do it?"

"I'm not telling you anything other than if you eat six of them in a minute you get twenty bills."

"How you timing it?"

Sean points at a digital clock on the wall by his *Die Hard* poster. "As soon as the minutes change you start. You got until they do again. Cool?"

"Easiest twenty bucks I'll ever make," Kyle says, arrogant. He extends his hand, Sean shaking it. They watch the clock,

Kyle brushing away strands of his straight black hair. In a few moments it flips from 3:07 to 3:08.

"Go," Sean says, leaning forward.

Kyle downs the first. "That's one," he says, grabbing a second. He takes some bites and finishes. On the third, his chewing slows.

With delight, Sean sees his expression go from cocky to distressed. "How're those gums feeling champ? Nice and moist?"

"Shut up," Kyle says with a mouthful, speech muddled. He gropes at the plate for another.

"Time," Sean says with a celebratory slap on the floor.

Crumbs all over his lips, Kyle gawks at the clock. 3:09. "No way that was a minute."

Sean snags the cash and sticks it in his pocket with a smirk. "Want some water?"

Kyle nods, gnawing what's left in his mouth. "Still can't believe it."

"You saying I rigged it somehow?"

"No…just…I don't know." He swallows. "Whatever. I need some Goddamn water."

"Kitchen. Come on." They stroll out, then down the stairs.

Sean opens the refrigerator and fishes out a bottle of Poland Spring and a canister of Tropicana. Kneeing the door shut, he tosses the water to his buddy. He heads to the living room with the orange juice dangling from his hand, noticing Aunt Mary and a heavyset lady in a denim jacket on the couch watching a soap opera. "Hey," Mary says to him.

"Hey," he says, admiring the sultry blond actress on the TV.

Gaping at him, the other woman on the sofa says, "Hi there."

"Sean, this is Babs," Mary says. "Babs, Sean. She's my friend from book club. We're heading over there in a bit." He raises the jug as a hello gesture.

"I'm a huge fan," the lady says. "I saw every episode of you on *Jeopardy!*."

"Oh yeah?" He rubs the back of his neck.

"Malone's such a common name, but when I met Mary I had a feeling you two were related. Same...face shape. I thought maybe your mom at first. Then we got to chatting one day and sure enough...not mom, but still blood."

"We are," he says. He turns to his aunt. "We're gonna ride our bikes to the mall. Came in to let you know."

"Okay. I'm making pork chops for dinner when I get back. Say around—"

"How do you remember all that stuff?" the woman asks him, cutting off Mary. "It just doesn't seem possible."

"What stuff?"

"From *Jeopardy!*."

"I don't know," he says, a tad defensive. "I just kind of do." He unscrews the juice.

She inspects him as he drinks. "I pictured you'd have a bigger head in real life. To store it all." She pauses. "Your head's pretty normal-sized."

"Yeah," he says in a flat way, lowering the bottle.

She pulls her phone from her purse and visits Wikipedia. "Let me try to stump you," she says with excitement as she types.

He rubs the back of his neck again. "I think we're leaving soon."

"Hold on," she says, oblivious to his discomfort. "I got one. What's the capital of Uganda?"

"That show was years ago—"

"Did I stump you?"

"I guess."

She pumps her fists in triumph, jean jacket squeezing her excess arm weight. "The girls at work aren't going to believe this." She peeks at his aunt, expecting her to be happy. Mary is straight-faced, aware of how much her nephew hates stuff like this. Sensing an awkwardness, the woman says, "I'm going to freshen up in the bathroom before we hit the road."

"No problem," Mary says. The lady lifts her big body off the couch with a groan and lumbers toward the hallway.

As soon as she's out of sight Sean says, "Kampala."

"What?" his aunt asks.

"The capital. Of Uganda."

"Why didn't you say it before?"

"I wanted her to leave me alone. She would've kept asking me stuff if I got it right."

She laughs, so does Kyle. "Well played," she says, surfing the channels. "Sorry about all that."

"Ready to go bro?" Kyle asks.

"Yeah." As Sean returns to the kitchen a newscaster's voice on the television grabs his attention. His brow creases. He turns to the screen, a live image of Mexico's Church of Santa Prisca plastered all over it with the headline "Drug Lord Gunned Down Outside Mexican Cathedral." He steps closer. "Don't change it," he says with alarm, a chill tingling his skin.

A newswoman in a red blazer says, "…Who governed a narcotics empire estimated to generate north of four billion dollars a year. Salinas was anonymous for nearly eighteen months, no visuals or hints of his whereabouts until today. Multiple eyewitnesses confirmed the presence of three Mexican federal policemen engaged in gunfire this morning with him and associate Bertram Velasquez. Deaths have been verified for both of the men, with no reports of any police injuries. We've also learned however that Fernando and Natalia Flores were pronounced dead at the scene as well. Fernando was thirty-two, Natalia twenty-eight. A husband and wife from Taxco with no apparent connection to Salinas or his criminal network."

A photo of the Flores family appears, the victims standing in the Pacific Ocean swinging their young son above a wave. "According to Mrs. Flores's mother, the couple was walking to church around the time shots broke out," the newscaster says. "Local authorities determined they were struck by stray bullets from Velasquez's automatic weapon. When the shooting took place Mrs. Flores's mother was at home with the couple's two-and-a-half-year-old son, Mateo."

"What a shame," Mary says in a deflated tone.

Sean marches to the kitchen, the reporter audible behind him, everything spinning, the Tropicana label, the fake plant his aunt keeps next to the sink, her copy of today's *Los Angeles Times* on the dinette table. "Dude what's wrong?" Kyle asks, confused.

Sean clamps his eyelids as tight as he can, his buddy foggy in his ears. In ten seconds or so he says to nobody in particular, "I'm going to the school."

"You have class on Tuesday?" Mary asks from the den, noticing his tense expression through the entryway, growing concerned. "I thought you guys were going to the mall?"

As they stare he trots outside. The chilly air hits him. Rubbing his bare forearms, he crosses the lawn onto the blacktop. He charges up his serene, tree-lined suburban street, a neighbor mowing his front yard, US Postal Service truck making its daily route, the rhythm of a basketball getting dribbled.

He freezes as the screech of brakes fills the block, a silver BMW X5 stopped a few feet from him, angry middle-aged man honking inside. "Watch where you're going asshole," the guy says behind the windshield. Sean's brain is so fixated on the news story his heart rate doesn't even rise from the near collision. He catches the driver's eyes for a moment, then tilts his head down and keeps moving.

In about twenty minutes he passes under an arch that says "The Southern California Technology Institute" in big orange letters. He cuts through a busy courtyard and jogs down the stairs. A kid from his "Advanced Methods in Applied

Statistics" class from the semester before last calls out to him to say hi, but Sean ignores him. He stomps to the Computer Science Building, pushes the red door, and runs up the steps.

He weaves through his older, taller schoolmates toward the professor's office. He twists the knob and barges in, his teacher standing in front of a whiteboard lecturing five grad students on the finer points of the Chinese Remainder Theorem. Everyone stops what they're doing, staring at the boy. "I need to talk to you," Sean says in a demanding way.

"Can it wait?"

"No."

The pupils glance at each other, then the professor. He nods. They close their laptops, zip them in their cases, and file out, avoiding eye contact with the fourteen-year-old. "What is it?" the professor asks, examining the twitching muscles on his face.

Sean shuts the door, turns on the television in the corner, and flips through about thirty channels to CNN, two commentators discussing the shooting. "Is that Operation Golden Bear?" he asks with hostility.

"Operation what?"

"From the meeting at the NSA. The guy from the DEA mentioned something called Operation Golden Bear in Mexico."

The professor glimpses the TV. He's beginning to understand what he's implying. "I haven't spoken to anyone at the NSA since we've been back. I don't have any clue what this is about. Why don't you sit down and we can—"

"Call Patrick Goya."

"Please, relax first. You're upset and you're not thinking with a clear head."

Sean slams his fist on the metal desk, filling the room with a rattle. "Two innocent people are dead. You don't have any blood on your hands. But if that's Operation Golden Bear, and they used my algorithm, then I have blood all over mine."

The professor lingers on the Flores family photograph on-screen. "What're you planning on asking him? Patrick."

"I want to know if they did or didn't use my paper for this. That's it."

"It's their business, not yours," he says in a soothing voice, patting his shoulder. "You personally have nothing to do with this, no matter how it may be related." He shrugs. "Even if it's related at all."

"It's my business after they stole the work I did. Call him. Now."

By the emotional look on Sean, the professor can tell he won't give this up. "Fine. I'll dial him for you. Just, please try to calm down." He slides his cell phone from his pocket. "Don't lose your temper with him. I've been a colleague of his for a long time. He's a good man. He absolutely did not intend to put you in any circumstance—"

"Just call him, all right?" In a few seconds he keys a number, hits send, and nudges the phone across the desk.

Sean clasps it and walks to the corner. He holds it to his cheek as it rings, eyes on the CNN reporters. Patrick answers and the kid says, "No it's not Steven. It's Sean. Malone. Mexico. All over the news. Was the US behind this?" He listens for a few moments. "Did you use what I did for it?" He's still for a while, then dips his head, Patrick confirming the suspicion in a slow, hesitant voice. "Put the Secretary of

Defense on a conference line with us. I want to talk to him too. Do it dammit."

The professor grasps a bottle of Xanax in a drawer and pops the cap. "Sean—"

"You heard me," the boy says into the phone.

The professor takes a pill with a sip from a thermos. "Why don't you hang up? You and I can figure out a better—"

"Mr. Pine, it's Sean Malone." He listens for a bit, then asks in a challenging tone, "What're you doing to make things right for the family of the two bystanders in Mexico?" Pacing, he bites his lip, teeth clamping so hard they almost break the skin. In a dry voice Pine says a few things in the earpiece. Reacting, Sean kicks the wastebasket into the wall, trash pouring all over. "Because reaching out to relatives isn't your policy?" His face shades to a deep red. "How about I hack into the database of Peltex Industries and dig up all the company files when you were CEO there? I have a feeling I'd find some interesting things about a certain dictator who paid a lot of money for your products under the radar. I'll print everything out, wrap it in a bow, and walk it over to the *Los Angeles Times*. They can do what they choose with the info. How does that sound? Or would that not be part of your policy either?"

Panicking, the professor lunges at him. "Sean, enough."

"I'm done." He hangs up. "I got nothing else to say." He flings the phone into a cushion on one of the chairs and storms out, slamming the door.

Photo Finish

Kyle rides a BMX bicycle up Sean's street a few days later, his red backpack hanging a couple inches above the rear tire. He hooks into the driveway, tosses the bike down, and strolls to his friend's stoop. He knocks. No answer. Then once more.

Mary opens the door, surprised to see him. "Oh. Hi Kyle."

"Hey Ms. Malone." She looks a tad frazzled, no makeup concealing her crow's feet, a few astray light-brown hairs.

"He's upstairs. Come in." He enters. "I didn't know you were stopping by. What do you guys have planned today?"

"Nothing really. Just chilling."

"I made cookies before. Sean said he didn't want any." She points at the doorway to the kitchen. "I have a bunch and can't eat them all myself. Hungry?"

"Man, I knew I smelled something good. Yeah, I'm always hungry."

She leads him inside, a basket of twelve fresh chocolate chip cookies cooling off on the counter. "Sit. I'll get you a dish." Removing his backpack, he hops on a stool. "You want anything to drink?" she asks, plopping a paper plate in front of him.

"Nah. I'm fine."

"Help yourself."

He grabs a big one from the top, rips a piece off, and chomps into it. "Mmmm. That's legit."

"It's the sea salt you're tasting."

"I can't tell you what it is, but it's delicious. You got to send my mom your recipe." He finishes with a couple bites and goes for a second.

She leans toward him, elbows on the counter, chin on her folded hands. It seems like a lot's on her mind. "Sean didn't even want one. Can you believe that?"

"I don't know what that boy's thinking sometimes."

"Have you noticed anything weird about him? Say, in the last three days. Since he randomly went to the school the last time you were over."

"Yeah, the school thing was kind of weird. I know his classes are like super-strict and stuff though. He probably was late dropping off a paper or something. Weird other than that? Ugh, not really." He takes a bite and says with a full mouth, "Well, he's been kind of quiet at practice. Coach has been on him lately. He hasn't been hitting good."

"Did he mention anything to you about a problem with a certain class?"

He swallows. "Nah. Not to me."

"Well. He hasn't been himself. Not talking much. Not eating much. Not even watching TV much."

"That is strange."

"If you do hear anything, do me a favor and let me know."

"No worries." He gobbles the last of the cookie, wipes his fingers on his jeans, and climbs off the stool. "I'm heading up. Thanks for the cookies."

She collects the crumb-filled plate. "Glad you enjoyed them."

He slings his bag over his shoulder and leaves the kitchen. He barrels up the steps and knocks on Sean's door. "Yo. It's me." He goes in. "Sup man."

Sean is on the edge of his bed in baggy gray sweatpants and an old Pittsburgh Steelers sweatshirt, hair matted and unwashed, eyes vacant. "Do you have it?" he asks without looking at him.

Kyle checks the hallway to see if Mary is around, then closes the door. "I asked my brother to get what you said. He knew exactly what it was." Kneeling, he unzips the front pouch of his backpack, takes out a see-through medicine bottle with a brown tint, and rattles it.

"OxyContin, forty milligrams?"

"Scope it." He lobs it to him. Sean examines the eight tiny yellow pills, then slips them in his pocket and opens a desk drawer. He grabs three hundred twenty bucks, in sixteen fresh-from-the-ATM bills, and hands the money to his friend.

"What do you want them for anyway?"

"Just wanted to try it."

"Cool," Kyle says with a trace of doubt, cramming the cash in his purple-and-gold LA Lakers wallet.

"Is that not okay with you bro? If it isn't, give me back the money and you can keep them."

"Whoa man. I'm only asking. Your aunt was grilling me about you downstairs. I just want to make sure you're cool." Kyle inspects his unkempt appearance. "My brother said the forty milligrams are pretty strong."

"I'm...fine dude," Sean says, yanking his sweatshirt sleeves down, hiding his hands inside.

"Enough said." Kyle shimmies two DVDs from his bag, flashing the covers with enthusiasm. "I got the new zombie one and the one with that hot British chick."

"I can't do a movie today. I'm really tired."

"Sure homie?"

"Yeah. Maybe tomorrow."

"All right." He jams the film cases back inside, between his ninth-grade Math and Social Studies textbooks. He extends his hand, Sean sliding his from the sweatshirt and meeting it with a halfhearted slap. "Hit me up tomorrow." Kyle loops a strap over his shoulder and exits.

Sean closes the door, then goes in the dark bathroom and flips on the sink, only a few dabs of light from the falling sun making it inside through the bedroom window. The sound of running water in the background, he lifts the OxyContin container from his pocket, twists the cap, and shakes a pill into his palm. He observes the small yellow circle, hoping it'll get rid of the terrible panic attacks he's been having the last three days like online forums said it would.

Popping it in his mouth, he levels his head with the faucet. He sips, some water splashing across his face into his left eye. Standing, he gazes at himself in the mirror, droplets trickling down his cheek. He swallows.

He returns to the bedroom, glancing at the digital clock by the *Die Hard* poster. 4:23 PM. He figures it should kick in around 4:43. He counts the seconds in his head. He wonders what it's going to be like, having never experimented with OxyContin or any other recreational drug before.

In a short while the muscles in his neck ease. The same happens with the ones in his shoulder blades, lower back, and legs. He sits on the floor and stares at the blue rug fibers. His thinking slows. He enjoys it, an escape from the intensity of his mind for the first time in his life. He doesn't budge for a while, other than to blink.

A rush of blood dizzies his head as he pushes himself to his feet. He wanders to the closet, tossing towels and a suitcase out of the way, grabbing a dusty green photo album. Setting it on the carpet, he lies beside it with his stomach flat. He's surprised he let himself near the album, been years since he had the courage. He guesses the OxyContin must be working, taking off some sort of edge.

The plastic jacket sticks to his fingertips as he peels open the cover. He glances at a photo of himself with his parents in front of a fireplace at a ski lodge in the Poconos when he was three, both adults in their early thirties. They're all drinking mugs of hot chocolate, smiling. His parents were good-looking, mom with high cheekbones and silky brown hair, dad with a strong build and warm eyes.

Studying their faces, he remembers the moment the picture was snapped, its slice of space and time in the universe. He recalls the musty smell of his father's ski jacket and the corny joke his mother told a lady the next table over right after the camera flashed. He finds it strange how happy they are in the photo, as if they should somehow all be aware of the plane crash killing the two adults in a few months.

His anxiety spikes. He peeks at the clock. 5:16. He realizes he's not supposed to have another pill for a few hours but feels he should regardless. Heading back to the bathroom, he turns on the sink. Gripping the brown bottle, he decides he might as well do two to be positive. He rests both on his tongue, leans to the faucet, and swallows. He puts the medicine container in a drawer and closes it.

He paces, waiting for the additional dose to hit. Twenty minutes seem an eternity, the drug fogging his perception. The cold sensation of the tiles on his bare feet isn't like the one he's used to. It's muted, as if he was wearing socks he thinks. The voice in his mind sounds the same way, muted. He doesn't recognize the person he is right now. And likes it. A goofy grin spreads on his face. He stops moving, looking at himself in the mirror.

He spots his shower in the corner of the glass and convinces himself to take one, curious how the touch of the liquid will be on his skin in the state he's in. He pulls off his Steelers sweatshirt, tugs open the polka-dot curtain, and runs the water. Waving his hand under it, he gauges the temperature. A little hot. He nudges the knob, then checks again. Lower a bit still. Good. He wiggles out of his loose cotton pants and steps in.

As he's drenched he notices he was wrong about the heat, his whole torso filling with goose bumps. He turns it up. Now too high. Then down again. While he fiddles with the handle his neck starts to lose feeling, his head seeming disconnected from the rest of his body. The fog in his brain thickens. His eyelids get heavy, the three pills in his system combined with only an hour of sleep last night creating a conking effect. His legs weaken.

He's nervous now. It becomes hard to breathe, Sean gulping for air but only absorbing bits in his lungs. To support his weight he gropes for the stainless-steel-wire basket hanging from the showerhead. The shampoo and soap bottles plummet to the wet surface with a smack.

He starts wobbling, then his world goes black, his knees giving out, his fingers slipping from the metal rods. He smashes into the wall and topples to the tub facedown. Water keeps dumping on his motionless, unconscious body.

Things on My Chest

A faint beeping noise repeats every couple moments. Sean's eyelids flicker open, a blurry hospital room in front of him, a mess of lights and colors. He blinks a few times, vision getting better. He looks left, an EKG machine measuring his heartbeat, then down at his chest, three round white sensors attached to his skin, then at the window, black outside. "Sean," Mary says from the foot of the bed in a relieved tone, wrapping her arms around his legs. "Thank God."

It's a comfort to hear a recognizable voice. He tries to speak but can't, his mouth too dry. Squeezing his stomach muscles, he pushes spit up his esophagus, a tad of moisture coming to his tongue. "What the hell is this?" he asks, raspy.

"You fell asleep in the shower." She circles her hand on his thigh in a gentle motion. "You banged your shoulder pretty hard, but the doctor says you're okay." She points up. "I heard the water running upstairs for an hour and knew something was wrong. If you landed on your back you could've drowned for Christ's sake." She hugs him again. "Oh thank God."

Memories start clicking in his head, the polka-dot shower curtain, the faces of his parents in the photos, the yellow pills. "Hi Sean, I'm Rebecca," a tall, tan, fortyish lady says in a Midwestern accent. She strides toward him, hospital-employee badge dangling from the top of her knee-length skirt. She turns to his aunt and touches her forearm with familiarity, seems like they've already been talking.

Mary nods, then says to him, "I'm stepping outside to get a cup of coffee. Rebecca is going to chat with you while I'm gone. It's very important you listen to her. Love you."

"Wait—"

"You two need to talk." She closes her eyes and holds up her palm. "I'll be back in a little." She gathers her purse with nervous hands, then walks to the doorway, lingering on him before she leaves. He doesn't like the way she's looking at him, reminds him of how she appears when she watches a sad movie in the theater and fights the urge to cry in public. She exits, silence other than the chirp of the EKG.

The lanky woman drags a chair by the bed and sits. She rests a clipboard on her lap with a stack of documents attached. His body begins emerging from the numb trance it's been in. The aching is unbearable, his head, shoulder, and back throbbing. He wishes he could just be unconscious again. "Not a fun place to wake up, huh?" she asks.

He tries to peek at the text on her top page but can't get the right angle. "How do you know my aunt?"

"I met her tonight, an hour ago maybe. She loves you very much. All she wants is for you to be happy. More than anything in the world. She's concerned, obviously." She slides a pen from her jacket pocket. "I am too." She twirls it for a bit, then clicks the button and jots a couple things down. "I'm here to help you get through this. I have conversations with people at the hospital, especially young people like yourself, who've made a bad decision with drugs or alcohol. Do you want to tell me what was on your mind earlier?"

"Doesn't matter," he says, gazing out the window.

"Well Sean, all addictions start somewhere," she says, voice slowing with dramatic intention on "somewhere." Still attempting to meet his eyes, she lurches over the mattress. "Understanding why you did what you did can prevent a potential dependency from developing. That's what we need to get from this conversation. An understanding of the motive."

"Let me chill out for a little. I just got up. Okay?"

She flips through the papers on her clipboard, stopping five down. "I have your medical history here. I understand this isn't the first time you've spoken to a psychiatrist."

"Once." He pauses. "Wasn't even my idea to go. I got forced into it."

"Why do you think the court made you go?"

"I guess they thought I had anger issues or something. Who knows."

"How about you tell me in your own words what happened that day?"

"I don't get the point."

"According to the record, it seems like anger wasn't the problem. More guilt. Your aunt actually thinks your issues dealing with guilt are still there. She mentioned one thing that took place recently she didn't like very much. Feelings about a bird you came by while you—"

"Why do I have to talk about all this now?"

A few moments go by. "She realizes you took an excessive amount of OxyContin. She found a bottle in your room, and it came up in your blood test. That's not a light substance to toy with. If I can't give her a clear explanation of your behavior, she'll push you into counseling until someone else can. You're going to have to face this one way or another. She's... scared of a potential drug problem. Imagine how hard this is for her."

He runs his hand through his hair. "Jesus Christ, fine," he says as if surrendering. "What do you want to know?"

"I don't see us figuring out what caused today's incident unless we get down to the core. Previous incidents are the best place to start." Legs crossed, her right foot bobs in anticipation. "Why don't you give me your story about that day five years ago?" He's quiet for a bit. "Sean?"

He clamps a patch of the bed sheet and says, "I was playing basketball at the park with a few kids from my neighborhood back in Pennsylvania and I got into an argument with this jerk over whether or not the ball was out of bounds. He said something to me and I broke his nose. That's the story."

She writes a few notes down. "What did he say?" No reply. "I'm aware these memories tend to be a little uncomfortable to discuss. But the only way we can learn about things they trigger is if we have a conversation."

"It's probably in your file. Why do I even need to say it?"

"I have an overview in here." She scribbles some more, eyes intense. "But I always like hearing it from the patient directly. Reading off a piece of paper is...like looking at a painting from a distance. You can see what's going on, but you can't appreciate the details. The brushstrokes. If that makes any sense."

He clenches the sheet even tighter. "He told me if I wasn't such a freak my parents would still be alive."

A couple moments pass. "Why would he say something like that?" she asks in a sympathetic tone.

"Just read it in the file."

"It's not all in there." She gives the mattress by him a soft tap. "And like I said, I'd rather hear it from you."

He's silent for a while. "When I was really young my mom and dad wanted to put me in school. This special private school for kids that…were…smart or whatever. They found one in Maine. They dropped me off at my aunt's house and flew up to see it. They were planning to move us there if they liked it." His heart rate escalates, the beeps of the EKG closer together now. "It was in some rural area and they needed to take one of those little planes. It was winter. And the pilot misjudged the weather, and shouldn't have left…and…they crashed. Okay?"

"That's terrible." Hands folded, she stares at the tile floor. "I'm sorry."

"Nothing to do about it now."

About ten seconds go by. "Do you believe him? This other boy. What he said."

"He shouldn't have said it. That's why I kicked the crap out of him."

"I realize he shouldn't have said it. But do you believe it?"

He observes the wires protruding from the sensors on his chest for a bit. "If I was normal there'd be no need to visit that school and they wouldn't have gotten on that plane. You can give me a million reasons why it's not my fault and all that other garbage. The last shrink tried to do the same thing." He locks eyes with her. "But the truth is, if I was like everyone else, they'd still be alive today. That's a fact. No matter how you slice it. It's logic." She writes some more things down, Sean watching. "What're you putting on there?"

Unresponsive, she keeps sweeping the pen across the paper. "Your aunt mentioned to me you haven't been yourself the last few days. It's a...mystery to her. She feels something may have happened at school. Did someone make a hurtful comment about your parents recently? Another student? Is that what's causing this behavior with you?"

"Can we not talk about them anymore? I already told you a lot."

She tilts her chin to the side, staring at his face. "She also told me you were very bright. The school you attend is... world-class. I of course know its reputation. To be there at your age is...well...it's quite an accomplishment. I don't follow the show, but she also said you were on *Jeopardy!*. That's all extremely impressive. I'm sure you're smarter than every one of my other patients. I'm sure you're smarter than me." A few moments pass. "But the mind has many facets, not just the intellectual one. I've been around a lot of smart people who were never able to figure things out emotionally. Those two pieces of the brain don't necessarily work hand in hand. In fact, the smarter the person, the deeper emotional problems can cut. The intelligent mind tends to dig into itself when it's unhappy. It's harder for bright people to put things to rest. Often—"

"I recognize life is crappier for people like me," he says with a huff. "Can we be done with all this now?"

"You can't just brush this aside." She sets the pen down and looks at the ceiling. "Think of your mind like a glass table and the difficult things in your past dishes. I can put a heavy dish on and it's fine. No change to the table. I can put on another." She mimics stacking a plate. "Fine. And another, and another, until I have say twenty on it. The glass is the same with twenty as it was with none. Perfectly intact. Now I put one more plate on. And the weight of that twenty-first is too much. In an instant the table shatters. Permanently broken. Unrecognizable. It was impossible to tell it was going to crack a moment earlier. I've had that happen to patients who kept piling things on without taking any off. They accepted the pain without doing anything to change it. It's not sustainable. If you view yourself as a victim you won't be happy. If you do it long enough you'll reach a breaking point where you'll never let yourself have a chance at happiness again."

He analyzes her grave expression, then the EKG device, then the creases in the ruffled blankets. He's not convinced that by just talking about a memory the pain of it can go away. Thinking about all the terrible things in the story of his past, he begins experiencing a loss of control in the face of history and its permanence. Wanting to convince himself he has a chance to be happy in the future, he decides to say something he hasn't told anyone else, a fantasy he's had since he was orphaned. He just wants to hear it out loud right now. "I have a plan you know?"

"What do you mean?"

"An attempt at being…content…happy…whatever you want to call it."

"And what does this plan entail exactly?"

"I'm gonna have ten kids one day," he says, optimism in his voice, subtle grin on his face. "Six boys and four girls. We're gonna live somewhere really faraway. Where nobody knows me. Probably Asia. I might even just change my whole name. And I'm gonna work with my hands designing stuff. Maybe boats because we'll probably be in a fishing village. And I'm gonna sell them in town during the day. And come back up to our house at night. It's gonna be high in the mountains. Kind of like those temples in kung fu movies. I'll hike it up there after work. No driving. And we'll have dinner together every night. All of us. Me, ten kids, and my wife. When the kids get older I'll build them all a house in the area. Same mountain. Not too close, but not too far. I'll be really good with my hands by then so building them won't be a problem. I'll have help too. And they'll move in with their husbands and wives. But we'll all do dinners at my place at least once a week. With my kids and whoever they marry and then eventually their kids. My grandkids."

She smiles, moved by what he said. "Six boys and four girls, huh? Why not five and five?"

"So the boys can look out for the girls. When we're not around. It'll be easier if there's more boys. Me and my wife are gonna make sure we teach them stuff like that really young. Watching out for each other and sticking together and all. My wife is gonna be cool. I know exactly what she's gonna be like. I picture her a lot."

"That definitely is a big family. It's terrific to have goals. Especially family ones. I'm sure you'll make a fantastic father and husband one day." A pause. "But I'd really like to get back to the event today, so—"

"I told you I don't want to talk about it," he says, now annoyed. "I thought I'd let you know about my plan because I could tell you're worried about me. I figured if you heard it you'd think I might wind up fine. But I'm done talking about all this today."

"I need a few more minutes," she says. "We're only on the surface."

He'd love to get the stress of the NSA incident off his chest but knows if he does the existence of his algorithm could surface to the public. The therapist would be sure to tell his aunt. Mary would be outraged the government took advantage of him. She'd want to go after the people involved, flying to DC herself or hiring a lawyer. Not only would his contract with Paul Pine be violated, but he'd also become a lifelong target of cyber-crime gangs hunting him for the information in his head. He figures his only option is to continue repressing the pain.

He rips the sensors and covers off himself, climbs out of bed, and says, "I'm gonna take a walk or something. Not trying to be rude. I just…want to move around." He steps toward the door with his hospital gown, boxer shorts, and bare feet.

"Sean. Come back." He turns the knob. "Sean," she says standing, chair legs screeching. He slips into the hallway.

Hacked

Patrick bangs his knuckles on his gold watch the next Monday, standing a few feet from the Lincoln Memorial in DC. He unhooks it from his wrist and inspects it, no tick, needles frozen. Dead. With a sigh he shoves it in his pocket, pulls out his cell phone, and checks the time. 11:59 AM. He looks around, a teacher reciting facts about the memorial to a fieldtrip of grade-schoolers, a dozen or so tourists snapping photos.

"Goya," a deep male voice says.

He turns left, noticing an Asian man in his late thirties, blue suit under a tan raincoat. "Hey Lee," Patrick says, shaking his hand.

"You look like you lost a couple pounds," the guy says, eyeing his midsection.

"I've been assistant coaching my son's basketball team. Running around with the young bucks a few nights a week."

"How's Pat Jr. doing?"

"He's great. Almost as tall as me now."

"No?"

"I'm telling you."

"It's been a couple years since I saw him." He looks up, tapping his chin. "You brought the family out to that fundraiser at the aquarium."

"Yes. You wouldn't even recognize him now. My little girl too."

"Crazy how time goes. Me and Marissa are almost married ten years. Five more months."

"Wow. Is that right?"

Nodding, the man peeks at his watch. "I'm sorry Goya, but I've got a deposition I need to be at in forty-five minutes. I don't have a lot—"

"That makes two of us." Patrick points at a staircase a short distance away. They weave through the pack of students toward it.

The man looks over his shoulder, assuring nobody is in hearing range, then leans close and says in a hushed voice, "I'll give Pine points for creativity."

"It doesn't sound good already."

"It's not." They walk between two massive white pillars and descend the steps toward the National Mall Park, a brisk wind hitting them once they leave the confines of the monument chamber. "My colleague in the Justice Department heard Pine's angling to pin him with hacking and willful communication of classified intelligence."

Patrick buries his hands in his jacket pockets, confused. "Malone didn't do either of those."

"He'll make it up. He's going to say he hacked into a government database and is planning to sell information to a ring of computer criminals in the Ukraine."

He thinks for a bit. "How will he prove it?"

"The Justice Department has one of the lower-level members of this Ukrainian crime gang on some online credit-card scam. He's looking at a pretty hefty fine. They'll cut him a break on the bill if he says Malone reached out to him with an offer."

"Jesus. And Pine has a contact at the DOJ willing to go along with the lie?"

"The real insiders seem to all agree Peltex did do business with those Arabs when Pine was CEO. There was just never a smoking gun. If the truth gets exposed and he goes down, a bunch of other well-connected people that came up with him will get dragged in too. The Navy, Army, CIA, you name it… former Peltex executives in a lot of top spots. They all have friends at the department. I'm sure it wasn't difficult for a good ole boy like Pine to find one's ear." His brow wrinkles. "I'm curious, why did this Malone kid threaten him in the first place?"

"I wish I could discuss it, but…it's one of those things. If I told you I'd ironically be committing willful communication of classified intelligence myself. Just…just realize their paths crossed with some NSA business." Wind intensifying, he wraps his scarf tight around his neck. "We threw the kid into a pretty intense situation." He watches the trembling water of the Reflecting Pool as the wind blows, a hint of guilt on his face. "He was just…venting on the phone. It was an empty threat. But…Pine obviously took it literally."

"Glad I was able to get this on your radar."

Letting out a long exhale, Patrick stops, right hand extended. "Thanks again Lee. I didn't expect a backlash like this." They shake.

"When I heard your boss was going after a teenage hacker, I figured you'd be intrigued."

"I owe you a favor."

"Please. I still owe you seven or eight. I built a legal career putting away cyber criminals you and the NSA fed me."

"Hopefully I'll be sending you a bunch more. But this kid isn't one of them. He was only...blowing off steam."

"Reputation is everything in this town though. You know that. The Secretary isn't taking it lightly. And he's acting fast. I wouldn't be surprised if the accusations went public by the end of the week." He folds his arms. "Are you considering helping the kid somehow?"

"If not me, then nobody." His expression turns solemn. "But at this point there's only one thing I can think of."

Silence for a while, then his associate nods, appearing to realize what he's referring to. "That one. Yes. Well, it does work."

"It usually does." To be polite Patrick forces a smile even though he's not in a smiling mood. "Take care. Tell Marissa I say hi."

"You too PG. Send my best to Allie." They walk off in opposite directions.

Shot

That night Sean is on the edge of his bed staring out the window at three malnourished-looking crows in the driveway, glow from a streetlamp illuminating part of their bodies, rest of them in shadows.

The birds pried open a corner of a trash bag and are picking at the remains of cheeseburgers Mary made last night. Watching them go at the scraps in desperation, he contemplates death. He's never been able to arrive at a confident answer on the afterlife, something he's wrestling again with now.

Though he's not certain, he hopes the soul lives on, maintaining crystallizations of the moments on Earth that defined a person. Sort of like photos. He tries to convince himself of this, but can't help thinking that maybe the experience of death is the same you have before being born. Nothing. No good. No bad. Nothing.

He glances at his closed closet, sensing the presence of his family photo album buried in the corner, thinking about the flashes of the past captured inside. He envisions the faces of his parents in all those photos, preserved in slices of space and time, unaware of the gruesome destiny to come of them. The muscles in his shoulders and neck tense as he pictures himself as an agent of death, responsible for putting people in the ground. First his mom and dad because of a flight they had to take because of his intelligence. Then two innocent people in Mexico, his "gift" the cause of that as well.

He imagines his mother crying and hyperventilating as their plane was nosediving, his father trying to appear strong for her in the next seat even though he was horrified himself. He visualizes his dad clasping his mom's hand and telling her how much he loved her. Then the impact. His mother, at least seventy pounds less than his father, dying right away. His dad watching the life sucked from her face, alive another two minutes or so himself as the flames overtook him. That's how it always happened in his nightmares at least.

He watches the feeding birds for a while longer, then gets up and walks to the bathroom. Urinating, he looks at the empty bottle of OxyContin in the trashcan by the toilet, Mary flushing the remaining five pills. He enjoyed them before he passed out, feeling like someone he wasn't, escaping his mind. He pulls up his gray sweats, presses the toilet handle, and wanders back to the bed.

Visiting Netflix on his laptop, he puts on an episode of *Family Guy*, his favorite show. He doesn't laugh. The characters don't even sound like he's used to, his entire sensory toolset skewed. He figures it's because he's depressed, things once fun now stripped of their flavor. His whole world feels barren, no excitement from anything.

He turns to a knock at the door. Aunt Mary is in the hallway, a wide beam of light behind her cutting through the darkness across the floor and up the mattress and over him. "Hey bud," she says.

"Hey." She comes in, sitting next to him. He puts the computer down and grasps a wooden slingshot from the night table he had since he was a little boy, a worn, chipped look to it. "What do you need?" he asks, no mood for chitchat.

"Instead of cooking, maybe we can try that burrito place again. The new one you like."

"I don't want to go outside. It's cold."

"Come on. It's not that cold. You're used to way worse in Pennsylvania." Ignoring her, he catches his reflection in the mirror on the bathroom door. He aims the unloaded slingshot at it, stretches the band, and lets go, a snapping noise accompanying. "I'll even try some of that super-spicy sauce this time," she says, pushing his arm in a joking way, scanning him for a smile.

He remains devoid of emotion. "I'm not hungry anyway."

"You need to get out of this room," she says, expression shifting from playful to concerned. "One way or another. I'm going to annoy you until you do. Get rid of me quick or draw it out. Up to you."

He fires a blank at his reflection in the glass again, then with reluctance says, "Fine."

About an hour later a middle-aged waitress balances a tray as she maneuvers down a crowded aisle of the Dapper Devil Burrito Shack, approaching the Malones' booth. "All righty," she says. "Tilapia for you, no sour cream." She slides a combo basket toward Mary. "And coffee." She places a mug in front of her with the place's logo on it, cartoon devil in a tuxedo. "Large Coke for you." She sets a plastic cup of

soda by Sean with the same logo, no food for him. "Enjoy."
She scurries off.

Mary scoops some guacamole with a tortilla chip and eats
it. Going for a second, she asks her nephew, "Want some
guac bud?"

Slumped against the wall on the vinyl bench across, he
doesn't answer, his filthy boots on the cushion, elbows on his
knees. He looks around, a man in an Oakland Raiders jersey
eating at the counter, a couple fighting two tables over, their
waitress lighting a cigarette outside the backdoor. He turns
to his aunt and says in a casual tone, "I'm dropping out of
school."

"You're what?" Shocked, she freezes while raising the
chip to her mouth.

"I'm done."

"Sean. How—"

"I made up my mind. Nothing you can do to change it."

"You thought of this now?"

"I've been thinking about it."

"Why?

"I'm not getting anything out of that stupid place."

"Please. Pause for a minute." She pats the tablecloth by
him. "You never loved it, but you never considered dropping
out before. I don't understand the sudden…change of heart."

"Feels right."

"Sounds wrong." She rubs her forehead. "That's not the
type of decision you…just make."

"I already made it."

"Does this have anything to do with you running out of the house to go there last week? I find it a little too much of a coincidence Sean. What were you so upset about then?"

His eyes dart away. "It's...I felt like this for a while. All right?"

She glimpses her untouched fish burrito, then him, and in a concerned-adult voice says, "I wanted to give you your space for a few days. I know you needed it. But in light of this...revelation of yours...I think it's time to find you a good counselor. Someone you'll be comfortable talking to—"

"I'm not going to some shrink, okay?"

"Why? Because you've been so mentally stable recently? Overdosing on hard drugs in your shower and almost drowning? There's obviously something...going on with you you're not telling me. With that college. You need to talk about it with a professional, and work it out. If you don't, you're bound to buy more of those Goddamn pills. I will not let that happen again. You understand me?"

An urge runs through him to confess all his secrets to her, the NSA stealing his algorithm, the dead couple in Mexico, the contract he was forced to sign. But then he considers the possibility of her leaking it, and pictures leading the rest of his life with one eye over his shoulder in fear of criminals who want what's inside his head. His foot starts tapping, specks of dirt flaking off.

"This is not up for debate," she says. "I'm finding you a therapist on our health insurance first thing tomorrow and booking the next available appointment. I'm forcing it as your guardian."

"Fine. I'll go. I got no choice I guess. But you can't keep me at SoCal Tech. It's college, not elementary school. You can't force me to stay. I can leave on my own whenever I want."

"If I don't have legal authority to keep you in I'm going to press you as a…loving family member then. Who cares. I think it's a big mistake."

"Going was a big mistake."

"Going was a once-in-a-lifetime opportunity," she says, her voice elevating, neighboring patrons staring. "You got a full scholarship to the best technical university in…well the world. As a twelve-year-old. Are you aware how many people would kill to have that chance?"

"I only went there because I thought I'd meet someone… you know…smarter than me or whatever. Same reason I went on *Jeopardy!*."

She weighs that comment for a few seconds. "I'm sorry you didn't find what you were looking for." He flicks the straw in his Coke, knocking it into the cup rim, watching the black liquid swirl. She eyes his disheveled appearance, stained sweatpants, crooked baseball cap, messy hair peeking out. "Finish out the semester and see how you feel then."

"Why go back at all?" he asks in a challenging way, swinging his right hand through the air.

"Because you have a gift," she says, stress on the last word.

"People gawking at me on national television like a circus act? Doesn't sound like much of a gift to me." He flicks the straw again. They don't talk for a while, loud rock music from a nearby speaker consuming their booth.

"You leave, then what?"

"Then...I'll figure it out."

Leaning forward, she pushes away the salsa bowl between them and grabs his forearm. "You've had this ability your whole life so you've never been able to see it from the outside in. Don't waste it. You have the power to do...so much. So much good."

He breaks away from her grip. "If I was so smart I should've realized the plane mom and dad were getting on that morning was gonna crash. How come I didn't know the weather was gonna change? I can answer ridiculous questions about meaningless facts, but I couldn't figure that out."

"You had nothing to do with that flight," she says as if she told him countless times before. "Jesus." She presses her fingers tight against both temples, then pulls them off. "The fact that you're still stuck on that..."

"Being...how I am...doesn't mean you can do anything that matters. Like predicting a disaster and saving someone's life. It just makes you some novelty. A trivia-show spectacle. Or a number cruncher other people take advantage of."

"That is so not true Sean."

He fixates on the cloud of smoke around the waitress out the window. He starts torturing himself with thoughts, the inside of his chest burning. He wonders why he was born so different than the six billion other humans on the planet. With so much pain engraved into his past, he considers if it's possible he can ever be happy again, the way he was in the picture of him and his parents in the Poconos. Or if moments like that are lost on him forever, just as dead as Billy and Jenny Malone. He feels in all likelihood they are.

Killing Sean

A few evenings later Mary sits at the kitchen counter picking at leftover pasta, the only light the glow of the TV from the den, *Seinfeld* rerun playing, no one watching. It's Thursday, movie night, but Sean didn't want to go this week, two in a row. His pill mystery and dropping out have been weighing on her. There's a physical tension to her movements, how she's chewing her macaroni even, her jawbone protruding with each nervous chomp.

The bell rings. She wonders who could be visiting at almost ten o'clock. She wanders through the shadowy house to the front door and opens it. "Can I help you?" she asks, staring at a man she doesn't recognize.

"Good evening ma'am," Patrick says on the stoop in the chilly weather, five o'clock shadow, jetlagged eyes. He's not in a suit like usual, rather, jeans and a North Face jacket. "I know your nephew and I need to talk to you both," he says with urgency. "It's extremely important."

About twenty minutes later they're huddled in the living room, the two Malones on the couch, Patrick in a chair across. Nursing a vodka tonic, Mary looks out the window, dry tears on her cheeks. Patrick and Sean just filled her in on it all, the algorithm, the real reason for the flight to DC, Operation Golden Bear, the Peltex threat to Paul Pine, the fake accusations about to land from the Justice Department. Everything. The pieces make sense to her now, why he rushed to see his professor during the news report, the OxyContin, withdrawing from SoCal Tech.

"So let's say it works," she says, voice hollowed and raspy from crying. "And they lie and accuse him of hacking and willful communication of so and so. Then what?"

Patrick sticks up his index finger. "For starters they'll probably throw him in some hellhole juvenile detention center." He extends his middle finger. "Then when he gets out they'll limit where he can work, people he can associate with." Last his ring finger. "To boot he'll have a black mark hanging over him. An American traitor. Forever."

"What's the point of putting him through all that?"

"The conviction would destroy his credibility. So if he were ever to come out with information against Pine and Peltex in the future, nobody would pay much attention to it. They'd dismiss Sean as some…crazy anti-American hacker, spinning lies so he could get back at the Secretary for busting him on the sale of government data to the Ukrainians. It's a dirty, old-fashioned political move."

A few moments pass. "So we just hang around and wait for him to do whatever he wants?" she asks. "We have money from the game show. We'll hire a lawyer. The best."

"A lawyer is one route," he says, setting his drink on the coffee table, using her *Good Housekeeping* magazine as a coaster. "But if you want to take this to a public court and fight Pine's lie with the truth, you have to keep in mind the truth can come back to bite…maybe even worse than the lie. If it gets out that a fourteen-year-old kid was able to get the attention of the United States Secretary of Defense with a formula, it would be pretty apparent this was some special formula. Every cyber criminal in every hole around the globe would want to know the math Sean does so they can use it. He'd be a walking bull's-eye for…kidnap, extortion, you name it. For the rest of his life."

The room is hushed, Sean and Mary both in a daze, the bleakness of their options sinking in. Patrick taps his knuckles on the table, capturing their attention. He swings his green eyes to her, then Sean. With an undertone of optimism Patrick says, "There is something else though." A pause. "It's not conventional and you don't have to go along with it. But in situations like this…it does work."

"What?" she asks, shrugging.

He reaches under his coat, sliding out a thick white envelope. He places it on the glass table. "You disappear." The overhead lamp shines on it, throwing a soft-edged rectangular shadow on the tan carpet below.

"Disappear?"

"I explained the situation and Sean's innocence to a buddy of mine in the FBI. I convinced him to put together profiles for both of you. The papers inside cover everything. New names, backgrounds, all of it. Obviously, Sean's the only one that needs protection, but with him being so young, I assumed you'd want to go too. As opposed to him getting paired with a foster family."

"It's a completely different identity?" she asks, fingers raking through her uncombed hair.

"A fresh start."

"This is the only way around it?"

"If you stay, when the charges hit, Sean's life as he knows it will be turned on its head anyway. He'll be stamped a US enemy. Someone who exposed secret government files to foreign fugitives. And since he's a public figure from *Jeopardy!*, the media will have a field day with it. He'll still end up with a new identity. An ugly one. If he goes with the FBI program on the other hand, yes, he'll still have a different identity, but it'll be one for him to craft at his own will. No black marks." He puts his hands in a praying position and shakes them at her, urging her to heed his words. "My friend from the Bureau can guide you through the whole process. His number is inside. I suggest you both discuss this tonight, think about it, and if you want to move ahead… give him a call tomorrow. Don't wait any longer than that."

"Where would we live?"

"Most people go with Europe or South America. The choice of cities they can relocate you to is phenomenal. You have a lot of places to choose from."

"If we did it…and that's a big if…what will become of… Mary and Sean…here?"

"To assure Pine drops it completely, you'd need to be gone. Gone, gone. They'd say you two were killed in a car crash. On your way to a camping trip in Arizona. It's all planned out."

The thought of their real names associated with death makes her face turn an even lighter shade of pale. She takes a couple deep breaths and asks, "How would we support our-selves? Once we wind up in our new...home."

"All the *Jeopardy!* money, and anything else you have, will be transferred into an overseas bank account. Not to men-tion, you can get any job you want."

She lifts her glass to her lips and gulps, finishing it. She stands and starts pacing on the rug with her bare feet. "This whole thing sounds ridiculous," she says in an anxious tone to nobody particular. "A new life? To just re-root like that? All because of a crime he didn't even do?"

"It's the only way to protect him without a doubt."

For Sean the idea of avoiding Paul Pine's allegations is comforting, but he sees a new identity as something with much larger potential, a shedding of the labels he's had his whole life, an escape from the story of his dark past. A thrill courses through his chest. He picks up the envelope and tears it open.

Finding a View

Four years later Fabrizio's dusty brown boots are banging against the cobblestones as he runs down an alleyway in Rome. "Stop," a chasing police officer says in Italian, arms waving above his head.

Fabrizio, eighteen and in shape, widens his lead on the cop, fifty-something and overweight. Fabrizio jumps over a tin trashcan lid in his way and continues down the shadowy path. "Left," he says to Sean, now eighteen too, about a dozen feet ahead in a full sprint. He's taller and more muscular than he was at fourteen, with a beard-stubbled face. He veers toward a train station, its lights twinkling in the night sky. His buddy follows, the policeman lumbering behind.

Sean twists through a herd of travelers by the entrance and trots inside. Fabrizio glimpses over his shoulder, then says with excitement, "I think we ditched him." They get a few weird glances from people passing, bright dabs of fresh paint on both their shirts. As they zigzag through the hundreds of passengers, Fabrizio pulls out his cell phone. "I know a girl in one of the apartment buildings not too faraway. We might be able to see it from her balcony. I'll text her."

"Yeah?"

"Let me check if she's home. What is it like eight? She should be there." As he flips through his contacts Sean shoulders an exit door and they step back into the chilly November air. They're on the backside of the terminal by a gated loading dock, nobody else around, the drone of faceless voices far off in the distance, a brick wall to their right with thick weeds at the base. They wander away from the station on a gravel path bordering the tracks, the little rocks crunching under them, lights growing fainter behind.

Fabrizio removes a pack of cigarettes and matchbook from the front pocket of his jeans, sparks one, then stuffs them back. Sean jumps on a train rail. He moseys along it, arms to the side keeping balance. In a half-minute or so he goes up on one foot. He skips ahead, swaying but not falling, then switches to the other boot with a thud on the metal. Glancing back at the noise, Fabrizio takes a drag and says with sarcasm, "Look at you."

"Hey," Sean says, teetering.

"Yeah what?"

"I'm in kind of a mood."

"What kind of mood?"

Sean doesn't speak for a while. "Let's go out tonight."

"Yeah we'll go out." He puffs again. "Saturday night." As he exhales, his phone vibrates. He slides it out, peering at the screen through a cloud of smoke. "I told you," he says with enthusiasm. "She's home." Wind cuts across the tracks, Sean blowing in his hands, nothing on but a T-shirt, temperature high-forties at best. He hops down from the metal beam, soles digging into the gravel, then jogs toward his pal. They walk side by side as he texts her back.

About ten minutes later they're inside an apartment complex on the eighth story, Fabrizio thumping the gold-plated knocker on one of the units. A pretty brunette opens up. She moves her lips to say something, but before she can get a sound out he grabs her waist and lifts her. *"Ciao bella,"* he says in a jovial tone, twirling her through the doorway as his wavy black hair bounces. She lets out a squeal as he carries her across the floor. Setting her down, he squeezes her cheeks and kisses her forehead.

"Hi to you too," she says in Italian, adjusting her red sweater. She looks at Sean, still outside, half his body visible to her in the hallway. She motions him over. "Come in." He enters, thumbs in his jean pockets. She surveys him, then turns to Fabrizio. "I don't think I know your friend."

"My apologies," he says in Italian, gripping Sean's shoulder, pulling him close. "Alegra, this is James. James, this is Alegra."

"Hi," Sean says in the same language, fluent. "Nice to meet you." He shakes her hand. "James."

"You too. Sorry for the mess." She nods at the dining room table, filled with a heap of fabric samples and a couple textbooks from fashion school.

Grinning, he shrugs. "Whatever. It's cool."

A pause. "Are you American?"

"Originally. I live here now."

"You look it. Where in America?"

"New York."

"I always wanted to go," she says, a longing to her voice. "Manhattan seems so cool. For shopping at least."

"Not New York City. New York State."

"Oh. What's the difference?"

"New York City is just one city in a state also called New York. I'm from one of the other ones."

"That's kind of confusing." She notices Fabrizio walking along the wall flustered, flipping every light switch he passes.

"Come on, come on," he says. "How do you get the damn balcony ones on?"

She nudges back some drapes, another switch below. "Chill. Under here." She presses it, a flood of light pouring onto the terrace.

Tugging the sliding glass door, he goes outside, wide view of the city square before him. He leans forward with his palms on the brass railing, analyzing the skyline, tapping his fingers. "Ah ha," he says, pointing at a four-story brick building in the distance. Sean and the girl step to his side, eyes on a colorful piece of graffiti art on the front wall, a streetlamp shining by it. "It's a beauty," Fabrizio says, clapping.

Sean peers at the painting, a man in a suit with a kitten head, briefcase in one hand, Tommy gun the other. Fabrizio grabs his shoulders and shakes him, Sean smiling as he wobbles back and forth.

Fabrizio starts snapping pictures of their creation with his phone. "That's one of your better ones," the girl says to him. "I still can't believe you've never been arrested."

He circles his arm around her lower back. Humming a waltz song, he takes her hand in his and dances. She chuckles, going along with it. "Arrested?" he asks, spinning her. "Don't ever doubt me. Don't ever doubt James."

As the other two dance around, Sean climbs on the ledge where the railing meets the complex wall and looks at the cityscape, first a few old Renaissance-era buildings, then the modern-styled office they spray-painted. He's quite a ways up from the street but doesn't seem scared at all, his leg dangling off the side. "The green worked," he says, gaze on some streaks in their piece.

"Hell yeah, it did," his graffiti partner says, dipping the girl. "Me and James are going out to celebrate another clean getaway," he says to her. "Joining?"

"My parents are making me go to church with them tomorrow," she says, dispirited. "Early. I can't go hung over."

He lowers her again, her long brown hair almost grazing the floor. "Your loss." He hoists her up to him. "Things are about to get crazy."

Face It

The headlights of Sean and Fabrizio's motorcycles cut through the dark sky, Sean on a black Triumph, Fabrizio a red Ducati, T-shirts blowing behind them, engines howling. They hook a right into a busy nightlife district, weaving between honking cars, then coast to the side of the road and park. They get off, hang their helmets on their handlebars, and make their way up the sidewalk.

Veering left, Fabrizio trots to a fountain in front of a posh hotel and jumps on the ledge. Kneeling, he dips his fingers in the water and runs them through his wavy black hair, a couple pedestrians glancing over. He climbs down and heads back to the walkway. He pulls out his smokes and matches, lights one, and takes a drag. Pointing at an alley with one hand, he slaps Sean's shoulder with the other and says, "Up there."

"Cool." Though Sean's mastered the local way of speaking, he still prefers English and uses it around Fabrizio and others he's close with.

Wandering ahead, they spot a line of at least a hundred people, high heels and small skirts on the girls, dress shoes and expensive shirts on the guys, excited voices going back and forth. Strolling parallel to the crowd, they approach a stone building that looks about a thousand years old, no windows, no signs, three large men in suits behind a velvet rope out front.

Fabrizio's cigarette burns close to the filter. He sucks the rest of the life from it and tosses it to the cobblestones. "Caprice," he says, signaling to an attractive woman in her late twenties with a clipboard. He locks his green eyes with her blues, holds up two fingers, and nods at Sean behind.

She taps the arm of one of the bouncers, about six foot eight, and whispers something to him on her tippy toes. As Fabrizio steps up, she says in Italian, "Hey love."

Leaning over the red barrier, he kisses both her cheeks and asks in the same language, "I'll see you inside huh?"

"Once it calms down out here." She glimpses the swelling line. "Probably a while. Have fun."

The security guard removes the blockade with his massive hand and the two guys saunter inside, the roar of the electro music hitting them. "Not bad right?" Fabrizio asks with a smirk, voice fighting the super-charged sound system. "Time to get drunk bitch," he says, shouldering through the swarm of partiers as his graffiti partner trails him. Sean takes in the place, one dark pipe-shaped room extending from the entrance to a DJ stage against the back wall, soles of his boots rumbling as the bass thuds, beautiful young people dancing all over.

"Yo asshole," a sarcastic male voice says in Italian somewhere to their left.

Fabrizio turns to a kid in a purple velour blazer standing on a booth, flailing his arms. "Hey man," he says to the guy in the same language, surprised to see him. "What's up?"

"I bought a table," he says, motioning them toward him. "Come on." Fabrizio smacks Sean's chest and points at the private booth. They slide through the throng of people on the dance floor and climb a couple stairs to it. Two bottles of Grey Goose are perched in a frosty bucket, carafes of club soda and cranberry juice on the side. Fabrizio hops on the red gator-skin cushion, hugs his acquaintance, and starts talking to him like it's been a while.

Sean situates himself in the corner. He scopes the others in their section, two guys and four girls moving to the fast-paced beat on top of the couch. Leaning forward, he clutches a glass and vodka bottle. He scoops the cup in the ice bucket, dumps some booze in, then some club soda. Swigging, he bounces his leg to the rhythm, the song an electronic remix of "A Rush and a Push and the Land Is Ours" by The Smiths.

Gazing at the dozens of faces in the place, he notices most are smiling. He wonders how many of them are happy and how many are just pretending to be to seem lively or inviting or whatever else to the opposite sex.

Based on what he knows of the world after eighteen years, he figures it's impossible for all of them to be as happy as they appear. Swishing a cold ice cube around in his mouth, he contemplates whether he's satisfied with life. He wouldn't say yes but also wouldn't say he's depressed. Since he's been in Italy he's enjoyed shedding the Sean Malone identity and the labels that came with it but still feels adrift. Starting over in Rome didn't have the magic effect he'd hoped. He's not sure why.

The condensation from his drink dampens his palm. Wiping it on his jeans, he thinks of a dream he often has where he's in blankness, white as far as he can see, a rope tied around his ankles stretching down to infinity, two others wrapped around his wrists going to endlessness on each side. The ropes don't hurt. They're just holding him in place and nothing more. In the dream, he has a sense he's waiting for something. He's doesn't know what.

"Yo James," Fabrizio says to him, Sean snapping from his daze. Fabrizio is pinching his apartment key at his hip, the groove stuffed with cocaine. "Want?" Sean sucks the crevice empty with his left nostril. Scanning for security, Fabrizio reaches in his pocket and pulls out a small clear baggie with more. He buries the brass key inside, raises it, and snorts. "Her tonight," he says in a vivacious voice as the drug hits his bloodstream, nodding at a brunette on the dance floor in a shiny outfit. Rubbing his nose, he watches her gyrate.

Sean angles his head between the people at the table. "She's cute bro."

"Give me a little time. She'll be coming home with me." With a chuckle Sean has some more of his vodka club soda. His pal peers at the girl with determination for about five seconds, then maneuvers down and shuffles toward her.

In a bit Sean's glass is empty. He shakes it, ice clanging, then goes for the Grey Goose. Refilling, he spots a cute girl at the booth grinning in his direction, toned legs, tiny black dress, straight hair the same color. He smirks back, then splashes more club soda in his cup. Dancing between two of her friends with an arm in the air, she keeps peeking at him. Their eyes catch. He sticks his tongue out at her, then sips his drink.

A couple hours later they're under the sheets in his apartment. She's asleep. He's awake. Her back is to him, her dark locks fanning over the white pillow. Glancing at her head, he realizes he can't remember what her face looks like. The details at least. The same thing's happened to him with every other girl he's spent the night with since he lost his virginity two years ago.

He wonders why he doesn't feel good right now, always thought eighteen-year-old guys were supposed to live for one-night stands with attractive girls. He pictures Fabrizio and how excited he gets when he does things like this himself. He attempts to channel that mindset. It doesn't work though.

The supposed laws of happiness seem so haphazard to him, almost anarchistic to the rationality of other things in the world. He's always been able to understand the rules around most things in life, no matter how complex, whether math or physics or languages or anything else. But not happiness. He can't deduce an underlying pattern. He rolls over, closes his eyes, and keeps trying to talk himself into experiencing joy.

The next morning he's jolted up at about eight o'clock by a mishmash of angry voices in the street outside the window. He peels his covers off and walks to the wooden blinds, enduring the pain of his hangover. Wedging his fingers between the slats, he watches a loud mob march down the road. Curious, he decides to check it out.

He rubs his forehead and glimpses the bed, the girl still sleeping. He grabs his balled jeans off the rug and steps into them. He slides his T-shirt on, slips his bare feet in his boots, then leaves the room and the apartment.

In a bit he walks out the front door of his building, right pant leg bunched around the rim of his shoe. It's colder than it was yesterday. Blowing in his hands, he peruses the bobbing picket signs, one a photo of a sixtyish man's face with a red X painted on top of both eyes, another a different image of the man with the term *"Assassino"* under it. Meaning "Murderer."

As the mob veers toward the financial district, he climbs down the stairs and wanders to it. Striding alongside, he tries to make sense of what the protesters are shouting about, but it's tough, just a wave of curse words and grumbles. "Excuse me," he says in Italian to a stout guy in his mid-twenties. "What's this all about?"

"Salvatore Costa."

"Who?"

"Remember a year ago there was that major car recall at the Blanto Motors plant in Turin?" he asks in the same language. "Engines were catching on fire?"

"Yeah, it was in the news."

"Costa is the CEO of KLI Partners, some investment firm that had a big stake in Blanto." He tightens the green scarf around his neck as they advance. "Turns out the car company knew about the mechanical problems for a while. Costa threatened them not to make them public."

"So the stock wouldn't go down?"

"Why else? If they called back the orders as soon as they found out, half the people that died wouldn't have."

"Jesus."

"They got all his emails. An employee leaked them." He removes a rolled-up *La Repubblica* newspaper from his jacket with a leather-gloved hand and slaps it against Sean's chest. "Keep it. I read it twice already."

"Thanks."

"*Prego.*" He scampers off.

Sean distances from the horde of people and sits on a curb in front of a closed butcher shop, poring over the lengthy front-page article. He reads the first half verbatim in about fifteen seconds, then flips to the middle of the paper and absorbs the rest in the same amount of time.

He ponders the horrific story, bothered by the loss of all those innocent lives. Running a hand through his hair, he stands. Jamming the paper in his back pocket, he jogs into the street and meshes with the group as a fellow demonstrator.

In ten minutes or so they all congregate by a big, swanky building, tinted windows, "KLI" in tall silver letters across the top. Five police officers stand on a ledge in front, holding their hands up, barking in Italian at the crowd of about three hundred. Sean sees a tomato fly through the gray sky, smashing into the office's dark glass wall, oozing guts. The group cheers. Another tomato sails above and splatters, then two more. Clenching a fist over his head, he cheers with everyone else.

In a few hours Sean bites into a chilly piece of pizza at the foot of the Roman Pantheon temple, his back to the others in the city square, pleasant conversations behind him. He tries to stop fixating on the newspaper article but can't. He's focused on the part about two grandparents and their three grandchildren burning in a Blanto vehicle on their way to the country for a weekend trip. He imagines the father, robbed of his children and parents on the same day. His appetite fades.

Gazing up at the Pantheon's two-thousand-year-old columns, he sets down his paper plate, half-eaten slice hanging off. He's consumed by an urge to make the situation right somehow. Though his life has been tainted by hardships, he still believes in the goodness of the world, memories of his mom and dad and the pureness of his early childhood fueling this. He hates when lives end too soon.

He turns to a swooshing sound, a hooded crow flapping on the rotunda, gray feathers, black wings and head. The bird looks at the dish for a while, then him. He envies the animal, the simplicity of its existence, its unsophisticated brain unable to perceive terrible thoughts like the ones of Salvatore Costa.

He grabs the cold pizza, breaks a chunk off, and tosses it in front of the crow. The morsel slides on the surface a few inches, then stops. The bird eyes it, then picks at it.

Sean feels a vibration on his thigh. Pulling out his phone, he notices a call from Fabrizio and answers. "Yo. Did you get my voicemail about the car-recall thing?" He listens for

a bit. "See if you can find this guy Costa's address online."
He nods. "Yup, I do have an idea. I think you'll dig it. This
asshole won't know what hit him. Meet me at my apartment
in an hour. Yeah. Bye."

Making a Mark

Late that night Sean and Fabrizio creep through a ritzy sub-urban neighborhood on their bikes, headlights off, road dark other than the shine from a few streetlamps in the distance, expensive cars parked on the side of the road. Sean marvels at the trees, an exotic flair to them, things he pictures in fairy-tales. He points at a shadowy nook off the main path.

They turn in and shut off their engines. They look around, making sure nobody is watching, then remove their helmets and sling them over their handlebars. Untying a twine rope around his chest, Sean frees a guitar case from his back. His graffiti partner flips open the cargo unit of his motorcycle, revealing a plastic bag of spray paint cans and a few other things. He situates it on the grass, pulls out two black ban-danas, and tosses one to Sean. They fold them into triangles, wrap them around their faces, and fasten the backs. Fabrizio lobs him a roll of tape. Sean breaks a few pieces off, sticks them on his shirt, then asks, "Ready?"

"Shit yeah."

"Come on." Holding the guitar case parallel to the ground, Sean advances into the street, his buddy following with the sack of spray cans tucked under his right arm. They walk for a while, then veer onto a block with multi-million-dollar homes peeking out behind elaborate landscaping. A noise to their side, they stop. Sean spots a cat's silhouette scuttling into the bushes and says with relief, "Just a cat."

"Yeah?"

"Yeah."

They progress for about five minutes, their footsteps as quiet as they can be, then take a left onto a cul-de-sac. Scanning the numbers on the driveways, Fabrizio points at a house. "Bingo. Costa's right there."

Sean scopes the property, a brick wall about ten feet high enclosing a mansion. Stopping on the manicured lawn, he lays the guitar case down and says in a hushed voice, "I'll go up first." He looks back at his friend's green eyes, wide and fiery above his bandana. "Bump me." Fabrizio sinks to a knee with a cradled grip, Sean stepping on top. He thrusts him upward.

Chest flying into the wall, Sean wraps his right hand around the ledge, the cold bricks scraping his palm. Grunting, he clamps with his left and heaves up his torso, then legs. Crouching on top, he glimpses the brown-and-gray-stone manor. Fabrizio passes him up the guitar case. Sean sets it down and gives him a thumbs-up. He tosses him a spray paint can. He catches it with give in his wrists, trying to soften any clinking noise, and rests it on the case. Fabrizio lobs him five more, Sean lining them all up with care.

Dropping to his stomach, Sean shimmies back. Pressing his thighs into the wall, he extends his hand down. Leaping, Fabrizio grasps it, Sean hauling him up to the perch. They stare at the mansion for a while, all the windows dark except one on the third floor. "Let's go," Sean says with a whisper.

He jumps off, boot heels spearing the soil on the other side. His buddy lowers him the cans and case, then hops down, landing next to him in a crescent-shaped shadow. "I'm thinking right there," Sean says, nodding at a chunk of house between two hedges styled into spirals.

"I like it."

"I won't be long." Sean pops the metal buckles on the case, opens the lid, and grabs a cardboard stencil they made earlier. He tiptoes to the space on the home between the hedges, adrenaline surging. Pressing the stencil against the wall with his left hand, he peels strips of tape off his shirt with his right, securing it.

He gestures to his friend when he's done. Fabrizio strides over, three paint cans pinned under each arm. He rolls them onto the ground, some pinging sounds as they nudge into each other. He clasps the blue and black ones and blasts the stones through the stencil, a steady aerosol hiss accompanying. He throws them down and snags two more, red and yellow. He sprays, then chucks them and grasps the last pair, white and green. He spatters in the remaining gaps on the stencil, drops the cans, and rips off the wet, colorful piece of cardboard.

They bolt toward the edge of the property. Sean hurls his right boot at the brick wall, pushing himself up, grabbing the top. He drags himself on, then attempts to help his pal up, his elbow straining as all Fabrizio's weight hangs on him. Groaning, Sean lugs him to the flat surface. Catching their breath, they observe their work, a pop-art-style man and woman in a burning car, pile of money in the backseat, hand with an "SC" ring for Salvatore Costa swiping the cash.

Fabrizio slides his phone from his pocket and snaps a photo, a flash streaking across their black bandanas. They jump off and sprint toward the street, four loud boots thudding through the mute neighborhood.

In ten seconds or so Sean's startled to only hear the rhythm of his own feet. Over his shoulder he makes out his buddy frozen in the headlights of a Mercedes Benz by the residence next door, a brawny twenty-something guy in a suit clenching his collar. "What the hell are you doing?" the guy asks Fabrizio in Italian, fixating on his suspicious outfit.

"Let go of me dick," he says back in the same language, struggling to get away.

Sean approaches with diplomatic open palms, rumble of the idling engine in the background. "Hey, leave him alone man," he says in Italian, voice relaxed. "We're leaving. We don't mean any trouble."

He surveys Sean. "What're you two doing, robbing that house?"

"We're not robbing anything. You got the wrong idea. Just let him go and we're gone dude." Sean hears a car door open. He notices a girl about his age stepping out of the passenger's side, the peripheral glow of the headlamps casting a soft light on her. Leaning against the hood, she crosses her arms, her alluring blue eyes swaying among the three guys. His gaze catches hers for a second, then she darts hers away.

"Go inside your house and call the police," her acquaintance says to her in a commanding tone. "These assholes are trying to break into your neighbor's place." She glances at the next home over and spots their bright painting through the iron-bar gate, realizing they're not burglars but graffitists. Amused, she grins as she brushes some blond hair from her face.

Fabrizio thrashes around but can't get free. "Let go of me scumbag."

"Stay put," he says to him, specks of spit on his chin. He shifts to the girl with an enraged expression. "Natasha dammit, call the cops."

Sean, not liking the way he's talking to her, is consumed by a strange urge to protect her. He's no longer calm, a steely determination about him. He locks stares with the kid. For less than a second both of them are still, then Sean cocks back his right fist and slugs him in the mouth.

As he stumbles to the asphalt Fabrizio escapes his clutch and races away. Jogging after him, Sean spins his head back, his focus on the girl. She peers at him as she wanders with little enthusiasm toward her bloody-lipped acquaintance. He keeps his eyes on her until she's lost in shadows.

He twists forward and dashes up to his accomplice. They cut onto the grassy area they parked and mount their bikes. Heart pumping, Sean fishes the key out of his jeans and struggles to get it in the ignition, his fingers trembling from all the adrenaline. In a few moments he starts it, ignoring his helmet, zooming up the road as it flaps on his handlebars.

Mixed Messages

Sitting on the narrow balcony of his second-story apartment the next morning, Sean lifts a cup of black coffee to his lips, pajama pants, beanie, and loose flannel shirt on. He didn't get much sleep going to bed so amped up from last night's events, still jittery processing everything that happened.

Sipping, he checks out the aching purple bruise across his right knuckles from the punch he threw. He thinks about that girl, remembering the details of her face. Every one.

He hears a thump inside. Looking into the living room through the patio screen, he notices the main door swung open, Fabrizio holding today's *La Repubblica* newspaper above his head, pride gushing from him. He marches outside, drops it on the glass table, and says, "Ta da."

Sean puts down his mug and grabs the paper, folded to an interior page with a photo of the mansion they spray-painted and the headline "Daring Graffiti Artists Target Salvatore Costa." He skims the article. "No way. We made the paper?"

"Rex Cassidy and the Moondance Kid are officially the hottest street artists in Rome," Fabrizio says in a loud voice over the terrace, a passerby gawking up at him from ground level.

"How did they find out about it so fast?"

"I posted the picture to that website Street ArtSenal as soon as I got back like I always do. We got ten thousand two hundred twenty-eight views already thanks to that article. Way more than any other post I ever put up. I've been getting messages all day. Everyone hates that prick. And they think the piece is dope too of course."

"It's anonymous right?" Sean asks with concern. "Our names and faces and stuff?"

"Totally. Nobody knows the real us. No cops."

A few moments pass. "Dude this is insane." Sean kicks his left foot up on the banister and slips his hands inside his flannel sleeves.

"Right? It's spreading more and more each time I check. Even if half the people that already saw it send it to say…three friends each, and then half of them send it to another three, we'd have…" Fabrizio takes out his phone and opens the calculator app. "Let's see, it—"

"Forty eight thousand five hundred eighty-three total views," Sean says in an instant, a quiet murmur, his subconscious doing the talking. As soon as he hears the number come out of his mouth he wishes he hadn't said it, assuming the rapid calculation would seem weird. He's right.

"Wait, what?" Fabrizio asks with a chuckle.

Wanting to change the subject, Sean stands and says, "I'm hungry as hell, let's get something to eat."

Ignoring him, Fabrizio taps the calculator buttons for a while. To his surprise he learns the answer is in fact forty eight thousand five hundred eighty-three. He gives him a funny look. "Whoa man. What the hell was that?"

He lets out a nervous laugh. "Lucky guess, I don't know." He nods down at the city square. "Some new place opened up two blocks away. You can see them making the sauce and stuff right from the counter. Big portions. I think you'd like it. Let's go." He approaches the doorway.

"You bet your ass that was a lucky guess. Damn."

Sean slides his right hand out of his shirt and slaps his buddy on the shoulder. "Come on. Let's grub."

Fabrizio spots his swollen purple bruise and asks, "Is that from last night?"

"Yeah," he says, relieved the topic changed. Though he's sworn off academics since the former him died in Arizona on his way to a camping trip, sometimes when he's around numbers, his mind can't help but try to pick them apart and make sense of them. Overwhelmed by all the trouble his intellect has caused him through the years, he represses this urge whenever he can. But it's still there, even if buried.

He rotates his puffy fist so his friend can observe the extent of the damage, hoping he asks him more questions about the punch and forgets about that accident with the math. "Damn," Fabrizio says, studying it. "You all right?"

"I'm cool."

"You knocked the shit out of him."

"Not bad for my first time punching anyone, huh?"

"I didn't expect you had it in you dude. I was like... yo." A pause. "You better ice that thing down today. We're celebrating our fame tonight." He scoops up the newspaper and waves it a couple times. "I got us a hook-up at that new club I was telling you about."

"Yeah bro. I'll be straight."

"Hell yeah."

That night they're at a trendy hotspot by the bar, the song "Talk Talk" by the band of the same name blaring. Vodka and club soda in his hand, Sean dances around, drink spilling a bit, his eyes squinty, cheeks red. "Let's do another shot," he says.

"Already?" his graffiti partner asks, checking out a pair of cute girls by them.

"Come on."

"You're really getting after it tonight James. Shit."

"I thought you said we were celebrating?" He pushes his shoulder.

"Screw it. Fine."

Lifting up two fingers, Sean signals to the bartender. He slides a couple tequilas in front of him, strong smell rising. He pays, passes one to his buddy, and says, "Cheers." They bang glasses and take them.

Fabrizio sticks out his tongue and gurgles. "Hot damn." He shakes his arms as the booze burns in his throat, then grabs his phone from his black-denim jacket and starts texting.

"I got to take a leak man."

"Do your thing."

Bobbing to the music, Sean wanders to the rear of the venue and pushes open the bathroom, one other guy inside.

Squaring to the urinal, he unzips his fly. He's drunk, swinging his head a bit as he does his business. The other guy leaves, Sean alone now, DJ muffled behind the closed door. He still feels jittery, same sensation since he woke up this morning. The alcohol is helping but not much.

He flushes, then flips the sink on and stares at his bruise as the warm water cascades over his skin. He washes up and tears a paper towel from the dispenser. Drying off, he looks at his reflection in the oval mirror. He conceals the part of his face below mid-nose with his hand, mimicking a bandana. He observes the image in the glass for a while, wondering what the girl from last night remembers about him, realizing this is all she saw.

He saunters out and meshes with the crowd on the dance floor, swaying to the rhythm. The left side of his T-shirt bunches in his jeans, a byproduct of twisting between so many people, a hundred or so packed tight around him, a lot of body heat. A girl rubs her hip against him, trying to get his attention. He glimpses her, then turns away, preferring to be by himself. He closes his eyes and keeps grooving.

The song "Ceremony" by New Order comes on. He muscles his way to the heart of the crowd. He has a slight hop in his step, sweat building on his face. Right hand above his head, he mouths the lyrics as he jumps around. *Oh I'll break them down, no mercy shown. Heaven knows, it's got to be this time. Avenues all lined with trees. Picture me and then you start watching.* He recollects a dream he had last night during the few hours he was asleep, considering what provoked it. *Letting me know. Forever.*

It started with him suspended in the middle of infinite blank space by three ropes, something he's dreamt about before. However, this time they didn't just restrain him. They tore him to pieces. First his left arm, then right. As they ripped, no blood came out, instead just noise. A buzzing rang from the holes where his limbs used to be, something he imagines a million bees would make if in one giant hive. As the third rope began severing his legs, he woke up. He tries to avoid thinking of it, but it keeps surfacing.

After a few more tracks, he weaves back to his pal at the bar, mid-chat with a pretty girl in thigh-high leather boots. "Hey Mike Tyson," Fabrizio says to him above the booming speakers. "You got a message."

Sean hears him but doesn't know what he's referring to. "Huh?"

He gives Sean his phone, an email opened on it. "Through that StreetArtsenal website, where I posted our pic. The blonde from last night." He reads the text on Fabrizio's screen:

Dear Rex Cassidy OR the Moondance Kid,

Not sure which one of you threw that right hook, but thanks. It was a surprisingly delightful end to the worst first date of all time. My dad showed me the article in the paper about our neighbor's house. He asked me if I saw anything. I told him no. Holy hell is Mr. Costa pissed. I can see his wall from my bedroom window. There are about 10 butlers scrubbing it as I'm typing this. You can hear him screaming inside. Pretty funny. I always knew that guy was a sociopath. Even b4 the whole car recall thing. Every time I saw him outside he would always say, "Hello Miss Vonlanden" in this really creepy voice, with this weird smile. Anyway, my hat is off to you for vandalizing his house. He deserved it. The newspaper mentioned you were on this website. Not sure if you actually check the messages from it or not. Nobody will probably read this, but I figured I'd send it anyway. Worth a try. Thx again for the punch.

-Natasha Vonlanden

His mind spins. He can't even hear the music anymore, all his mental capacity locked on the email. He rereads it, heart rate accelerating. "Can I borrow this for a second?" he asks, holding up the phone.

"I need it. Expecting a text from someone coming."

"I won't be long." He starts walking away with it.

"Where're you going?"

"A minute."

"Dude?"

"I'll be back." He fights through the crowd toward the exit, a few sweaty drunk girls sliding by, the combined linger of five or six different perfumes leaving an irritating fruity scent in his nose. He bursts outside into the square, the cool air refreshing on his hot skin. It reminds him of the briskness of the cranked-up air conditioner in Aunt Mary's SUV when she used to pick him up from baseball practice in Pasadena in mid-August.

He sits on the ledge of a fountain, marble angel in the center spouting water from its hands, a droplet jumping up and grazing the back of his neck every now and then. Clicking the reply button, he stares at a blank input box. He starts typing. Then stops and erases. He begins again. Then pauses and deletes. He looks around a bit, then writes:

Hey Natasha,

I don't typically go around town with a bandana around my face knocking people out. Kind of a bad first impression if you ask me. I'd like to have a try at a second. Want to grab a cup of coffee tomorrow?

-James

He hits send, then begins tapping his foot. Situating the phone in his pocket, he concentrates on the trickle of the fountain behind him. A long fifteen minutes later his thigh vibrates. He checks the screen:

Oooo, okay. Meet me at the Hotel Vanessa. Lobby. 2 PM.

He soaks in the response. Yes, yes, yes. He gets up and walks to a food stand, the attendant nodding at him. "Bottle of water," Sean says in the local language, his spirit so elevated his own voice sounds distant to him.

"That's it?" the guy asks in Italian.

"That's it." The man pulls a bottle from a cooler and passes it to him with a small paper napkin, stuck to the condensation. "Thanks." Sean peels some cash from his wallet and places it on the chipped wooden counter. "Keep the change."

"You sure?" he asks, estimating the generous tip.

"Yup. Have a nice night sir."

"*Grazie.*" Sean swigs. Water never tasted so good, his whole body on a natural high. He dabs some sweat from his cheeks with his sleeve, then takes another sip. He doesn't feel jittery anymore.

Memory Pool

The next day Sean cruises on his motorcycle, leather jacket blowing, Roman Colosseum in the background, sun nudging its way out behind long, thin clouds. He turns onto a street in a chic commercial district bordered by shops for Gucci, Valentino, Prada, and other luxury Italian brands.

A sign for the Hotel Vanessa is at the end, an inscribed marble block with a large gold "V" on top, sunlight glistening on the right tip of the letter. Nearing the property, he slows, dips his boot heels to the cobblestones, and walks the bike into the lot. He stops under a canopy, torches flanking the sides.

Engine humming, a kid about ten looks the motorcycle up and down, then glances at Sean with eyes envious and admiring. Grinning, he parks it next to a row of motorized scooters, then gets off, hangs his helmet, and approaches the front door. A bellman opens it and says, *"Ciao signore."*

Nodding, Sean enters, a few well-dressed thirtyish people checking in at the front desk, an antique copper espresso machine behind an oak bar, an ornate chandelier above everything. The place has a traditional Roman ambience but also appears to have been renovated no more than ten years ago, some modern flavor in the furniture and carpeting.

He sits on a white leather couch with bright-orange pillows. A few minutes pass. His right foot taps. A lady, about sixty, plops herself one cushion over. She waves at him, then removes a train schedule from her purse and analyzes it on her lap.

Ten more minutes go by. The wait makes him anxious, muscles in his neck and shoulders stiffening. He starts thinking about what he's going to say when he sees her, rehearsing three or four greetings in his mind. He feels silly for being antsy, no girl ever making him fret before.

"Thaaaaaat's you," a feminine voice says, Sean turning to it. Natasha stands by the sofa to his right, black leggings, white V-neck T-shirt, pink-rimmed Wayfarer sunglasses. She lifts her shades and rests them on her head, strands of blond hair falling around them.

It takes him a couple seconds to get his bearings, thrown by her not coming in through the front. Looking at her in the abundant natural light, he likes how her image is no longer clouded in his memory by the shadowy road the night he first saw her. She is everything he imagined and more, those blue eyes filled with energy and a dash of vulnerability, that button nose, those golden locks. "Yeah, it's me," he says in a soft yet confident voice. Folding her arms, she studies him. Rising to his feet, he presses his right palm to his face, mimicking a bandana. "Was it the top of my nose or eyes that gave it away?" he asks in a joking tone.

"The hand," she says, pointing at it. "It's bruised as hell." She speaks perfect English with a hint of an accent, doesn't sound Italian though, more German.

He glimpses his fist, black and blue. He chuckles, a flash of embarrassment on him. "Fair enough." He offers his left for her to shake instead. "Nice to meet you. Officially."

She twists her right thumb toward the floor and extends her hand to his. "Natasha." She smiles at the goofy upside-down grip she has on him.

"James." He matches her grin with his own.

"I don't really like coffee," she says as if letting him in on a secret. "Is it okay if we skip it?"

"We can skip it."

She pats her thighs. "Good." Her eyebrows spring up. "I want to show you something. Follow me." Her expression is mischievous and cheery at the same time. She crosses the lobby and veers down a hallway lined with faceless sculptures of the human body, Sean trailing. Turning her hip, she thrusts her tiny self into the metal bar on a door with the stairwell symbol, opening it and slipping through.

Catching it before it swings shut, he follows her. "Where're you going?" he asks, his heavy boots rumbling the aluminum-tread steps. The stair shaft lacks the elegant detail of the foyer, exposed pipes running along the walls, no curtains on the windows, an area visited most of the time by employees not guests.

"You'll see," she says down to him, a flight or so ahead. "Best kept secret in town." They go up a story. Then another. She moves with fast yet soft strides, not even making an audible noise to him. "Almost there." She's getting excited. They climb some more. At the sixth floor she spins her little self into an exit door, sunshine flooding in.

She walks onto the rooftop, Sean behind, a drained pool in front of them, nobody else up there. "They close it after summer," she says. "They don't lock it though. No one is ever up here in the fall. You can have the whole thing to yourself."

He stares at the eight-foot-deep concrete crater, then at a cabana next to it, windows boarded, dust in every crevice. There are no lounge chairs or towel stacks or anything else typical of a hotel pool. He feels there's a sadness to the place as if it were lost or forgotten, or both.

She leans over the railing along the edge, checking out the amazing view of the city. He stops a few feet to her side, gazing at the Colosseum in the distance. They take in the Roman skyline through the glare for a while. He puts on his sunglasses. She doesn't put on hers.

Squinting, she peers through the shine, nowhere in particular. She looks like she's thinking about something. A lot of things. He wonders how often she comes up here alone and does what she's doing now. About two minutes go by, neither talking. Then in a flat tone she says, "I like Rome."

"Yeah. So do I." He leans against the wall, playing with the zipper on his leather jacket, a hint of nervousness in his hand. "Did you always live here?"

"We're from Switzerland. We moved a few years ago. For my dad's job. You know how it goes." Hands on the banister, she sways forward, then back. "What about you?"

"Nah. States originally."

"I had a feeling." Her back to him, she saunters across the deck and skips onto the diving board. She rubs the sole of her leopard-print sneaker against the grainy plastic coating on the end. She jumps a few inches and lands. "So what do you do other than vandalize houses?" she asks, vibrating with the board under her feet.

He scratches his left calf with his right boot toe. Trying to be funny, he says, "Vandalize office buildings."

"Makes sense I guess." She doesn't laugh at his attempted joke. She hops again, her attention on the pit as the board pulsates.

He decides to change his approach and get a bit more serious, hoping it'll open her up. "Art's my thing. Especially the graffiti stuff. Me and my buddy, the guy from the other night, we tag all over town. I do some canvases too and sell them at a few of the local galleries."

"Which one are you anyway?"

"What do you mean?"

"Rex Cassidy or the Moondance Kid?"

He thinks for a moment. "To be honest with you, neither. Or, I mean, both. We never really talked about it. Or picked. We just wanted to come up with a cool name for the two of us. Like a duo." He rubs the back of his neck. "It's kind of cheesy I guess. People remember it though."

"You should be the Moondance Kid. I like that one better. I picture a dude in really big sneakers dancing on top of the moon with headphones on."

He chuckles. "Okay." He can't quite get a read on her.

She sweeps her vision over the city, the left of her body in sun, the right a shadow. "Hey, wanna bounce me?" she asks, turning to him.

"What do you mean?"

Holding out her hands, she motions him toward her with flicks of both ring fingers. "Here. Come up." He pushes off the wall, strides across the terrace, and steps on the board. She spins, the backs of her heels hanging off the front, then grabs his wrists and pulls him in. Being so close to her, he feels his heart speed up. "Okay. Do a really big jump and it'll shoot me in the air. It's fun."

Observing the ominous hole, he asks, "What if you slip?"

"Just catch me."

He finds it somewhat flattering she would trust him with such a thing. "You ever do this before?"

"In a regular pool. With water. Me and my friends used to do it in Zurich."

He takes another peek at the pit and says, more to himself than her, "I don't know."

"I won't fall. I promise."

"You're crazy." He scratches his head. "Fine." He adjusts his jacket collar, not sure why, maybe to give himself another couple moments before he has to do this. He meets her eyes. There's that expression of hers again from the lobby, part mischief, part cheer. He bends his knees, a rush of adrenaline pumping through him. He leaps and lands, board dipping about a foot, then launching her in the air. Arms in front of him, he follows her with his stare, her thin legs kicking in the sky. As she comes down, her sneaker bottoms scrape against the board and she tilts to the right. He clutches her. He can feel her heartbeat, just as fast as his.

She snickers against his chest as they teeter. "Nice. I was up there." She stands straight, pinches the corner of his sunglasses, and tilts them down. "What's your favorite band?"

"Smashing Pumpkins. What about you?"

"The Cure."

"Cool. I like them too." With a slight smile, she looks into his face.

"You ever go to the Happy Dragon?" she asks, tapping her fingers on her tight stomach as if she was playing a bongo drum.

"Happy what? No."

"Best karaoke bar in Rome. In Italy." She throws her arms up and says, "The world."

Chuckling, he rubs the back of his neck. "I'm not any good at singing."

"I'm terrible. It's fun as hell though. Let's go. We're going."

Glancing at her, he thinks about all the times he visualized her since the other night. She almost doesn't seem real to him, more like a collection of thoughts plucked from his brain and played back to him on a screen. But he can smell her perfume and notice how she narrows her eyelids a bit when the wind blows and see the way the shoelaces of her leopard-print sneakers flop as she steps. She is real. And he's glad he's real to her.

And he wants to hug her and tell her a joke she thinks is funny and watch a good movie with her and watch a bad movie with her and know what scares her and protect her from all those things and laugh about something silly she does in front of him and laugh about something silly he does in front of her and sit by a fire somewhere at night with her and eat something delicious with her and kiss her.

But he doesn't speak any of this. He just puts his hands in his pockets, looks at her with a grin, and says, "Sure, let's do it."

In ten minutes or so Sean swings a leg over his bike, knocks the kickstand back with his boot, and starts the engine. Natasha, a couple feet away, fastens the helmet strap under her chin. Gripping his forearm, she hops on the seat behind him.

"You good?" he asks.

"Good."

"Just kind of hold onto me."

She squeezes his leather jacket at the armpits. "Like this?"

He laughs. "No. Like around me. Like make a circle." She inches closer, wrapping her arms around him, interlocking her fingers on top of his chest. "Yeah. You got it." The engine roars. Eight or nine people in front of the hotel stare. The wheels spin and the bike accelerates across the pavement.

He drives down the street onto a main road, the Colosseum and other ancient landmarks zipping by in their periphery. "You doing okay?" he asks, his voice fighting the whip of the air.

"What?"

"You doing okay back there?" he asks, louder.

"Yeah. First time on one."

"I couldn't tell."

"Very funny."

They cruise for about twenty minutes. Bearing right at an intersection, he heads into a dumpy neighborhood with pieces of litter scattered on the road. He parks on the side of the street in front of a fortune-teller storefront with colored wooden beads in the window. The engine quiets. He jumps off, then helps her down. He unhooks the strap under her chin, slides the helmet off, and hangs it. "What did you think?" he asks, running a hand through his hair, putting it back in place from the windy ride.

She gives him a thumbs-up, then points off in the distance and says, "It's up there." Grinning, she claps her hands a few times and starts walking. He steps to her side. A brisk wind cuts through the square, blowing discarded paper plates and soda cans across the pavement in front of them. She folds her arms, trying to stay warm against the passing chill. "How long have you had the bike?"

"Just a few months. Got it when I turned eighteen."

"Why'd you get one?"

He doesn't speak for a bit. "You ever see the movie *Easy Rider*? With Dennis Hopper and Peter Fonda."

"Jack Nicholson's in it too, right?" He nods. "Yup. Saw it."

"About four years ago I really got into that movie. Right around the time I moved here. Just something about them not being attached to anything. You know? Like having no baggage I guess. I thought it was cool. I always said to myself I'd get a bike when I turned eighteen. And I did."

"Why'd you move here anyway?" she asks, arms still crossed.

Avoiding the question, he motions toward an intersection and asks, "Which way?"

"Left." They walk another block, sun sinking above them in the late-November sky, everything around touched by an auburn glow. "There," she says, pointing at the Happy Dragon sign, bright red letters with a burnt-out "O." They approach the karaoke bar, a drycleaner to the left, a pawnshop to the right.

As she opens the door, he scopes the graphic in the front window, a green cartoon dragon in sunglasses drinking a martini and smoking a cigarette at a silver microphone. They enter, stepping on the stained purple carpet. He glances at the small circular stage, a middle-aged woman singing an off-key version of Blondie's "Atomic," ten people or so watching from little square tables. He turns to Natasha and says in a playful way, "You're not getting me up on that stage."

"We'll see about that." She winks.

"Yes, we will see about that." He spots the bar. "I'm grabbing a beer. Want one?"

"Sure."

As she sways to the Blondie song, he walks to the bar. Four Asian tourists, three men and a woman in their fifties, sit there on stools. He signals to the bartender, a sleepy-looking twenty-something with a crooked bow tie, and says, "Two Peronis." In a minute or so the bartender sets two bottles in front of him.

As Sean takes some bills from his wallet, Natasha strolls back to him with a skip in her step, still bobbing her head to the music. Glancing across the bar, she notices a Polaroid camera hanging around the neck of the Asian woman and says, "Cool camera."

"Thanks," the lady says. The men next to her lean over and ogle Natasha.

"My birthday," one of the guys says to her in slow English. "We're taking a lot of pictures. We came from Korea. To celebrate." He puts his hands on the woman's shoulders and pats twice. "My wife."

"You have a very beautiful wife," Natasha says. He bows his head in gratitude. "Happy birthday. You picked the right place."

"My brothers," he says, pointing at the two men next to him, one in a blue suit, the other a gray one. They wave, goofy smiles on both of them, their faces a tad sweaty from all the booze they've been drinking.

"I'm Natasha." She points at Sean with her thumb. "That's James."

Handing Natasha a beer, Sean looks at them with a grin and says, "Hey."

Natasha takes a sip, then puts her hand on Sean's right shoulder. "He's never done karaoke before. Can you believe that?"

"Never?" the husband asks. Peroni to his lips, Sean shakes his head. The man nods at the beer bottle. "Just have plenty of those. You'll love it."

"With the kind of voice I got, everyone in here needs to have just as many to be able to bear it."

The tourists chuckle. The husband leans to his wife and says something to her in Korean. She nods. He turns to Sean and Natasha and says, "We reserved a private singing room for my birthday. Upstairs. Will be ready in a few minutes. You two should come."

Looking at Sean, Natasha smirks, a this-can-be-fun expression on her. He shrugs. "Sure," she says to the man, eager.

About fifteen minutes later the sleepy-looking bartender escorts the six of them into a small room with metal walls, a disco ball rotating on the ceiling, purple and blue light spots all over. "This is so cool," Natasha says, squeezing Sean's forearm.

The brother in the blue suit beelines to a shiny table in the center, grabbing a white binder labeled "Songs." He opens it and flips through. "Not bad," he says, pointing at a couple songs on the page, getting motivated. "Oh yeah."

"All right," the bartender says in English, a strong Italian accent making it hard to understand him. "It's all yours for two hours. Pick your songs in the binder." He motions toward a monitor on the wall, a digital dragon logo bouncing around on it. "Type in the song code on the pad next to the screen, the music starts and the lyrics show up. Pretty basic. I'll come check on you every now and then." Looking at his reflection in the screen, he adjusts his bow tie. "Another round of beers before I go down?"

"And a round of shots," the brother in gray says with zeal. "We've got a birthday to celebrate." He bangs his hands together and circles his index finger above his head. "Vodka for the room."

"Got it," the bartender says, still perfecting his bow tie. "I'll be back up in a bit." He walks out, closing the door behind him, sealing the room from any outside noise.

Ten minutes or so later the brother in blue is standing next to the monitor singing, microphone in hand, tie off, Bruce Springsteen's "Rosalita" blasting from the speakers. Everyone else, in a booth across, claps along to the music, six empty shot glasses scattered on the table. "And my tires were slashed and I almost crashed, but the Lord had mercy," he sings. "And my machine she's a dud, all stuck in the mud, somewhere in the swamps of Jersey. Hold on tight, stay up all night, 'cause Rosie I'm comin' on strong."

A few minutes later the other brother has the microphone, belting out "Honky Cat" by Elton John. "It's like trying to find gold in a silver mine," he sings. He drops to a knee. "It's like trying to drink whisky, ohhhhhhh, from a bottle of wiiiine."

Sean glances at Natasha three cushions down in the booth, a big smile on her, the husband and wife listening to her tell a story, the disco-ball lights running across her face. He's never seen anyone with such a magnetic appeal, all the tourists gravitating toward her, Natasha not even trying to impress them.

In a couple minutes the bartender walks through the door balancing a tray of six more vodka shots. Everyone cheers as he sets them on the table. "To new friends," the husband says, grabbing and raising his drink. They all touch glasses and put back the shots. Leaning over the table, Natasha grabs the Polaroid camera, resting on the booth. Cradling it in her arms like a baby, she jumps on Sean's lap.

Catching her, he laughs and asks, "What the hell are you doing?"

"Picture time." She spins the camera and points it at them, her legs draped over his. He makes a funny face. So does she. She hits the button, a flash lighting up the room, a picture dispensing. She pulls it out and shakes it with enthusiasm.

In a short while the husband and wife are standing in front of the room singing Ella Fitzgerald's duet "Dream a Little Dream of Me" with romantic eyes on each other. "Stars fading, but I linger on dear," he sings. "Still craving your kiss. I'm longing to linger till dawn dear. Just saying this." The other four are still and quiet watching the married couple share the warm moment, a grin on everyone's face.

A few minutes later Natasha is holding the microphone, her pink sunglasses on, her back to everybody in the room, her right leg pumping to the rhythm, "All These Things That I've Done" by The Killers starting. "When there's nowhere else to run, is there room for one more son," she sings. "One more son. If you can hold on. If you can hold on, hold on."

As the beat picks up she spins and starts stomping around the room like a rock star. Everyone shouts in appreciation of her little performance. "I want to stand up, I want to let go," she sings, faster pace now. "You know, you know. No you don't, you don't." Hopping around, she goes through the rest of the verse into the chorus. "Help me out. Yeah, you know you got to help me out. Yeah, oh don't you put me on the back burner. You know you got to help me out." She sings another verse and chorus.

As the instrumental part plays she climbs on the table, her feet between all the empty shot glasses. She sways her hips for a bit, then sings, "I got soul, but I'm not a soldier. I got soul, but I'm not a soldier. I got soul, but I'm not a soldier. I got soul, but I'm not a soldier. I got soul, but I'm not a soldier. I got soul, but I'm not a soldier. I got soul, but I'm not a soldier. I got soul, but I'm not a soldier. I got soul, but I'm not a sol-dier. I got soul, but I'm not a soldier." She jumps off the table, landing in front of the glow of the monitor, going into another chorus. The two brothers shoot up from their seats clapping.

She tilts back her head, the bottom of the microphone pointed up, and sings, "Over and again, last call for sin. While everyone's lost, the battle is won. With all these things that I've done. If you can hold on. If you can hold on." As the music ends she holds out the sides of a pretend dress and curtseys, wild applause in the room.

In a bit "People are Strange" by The Doors runs through the speakers, Sean at the front of the room, beer in one hand, microphone the other, no eye contact with anyone. "When you're strange, faces come out of the rain," he sings, trying to mimic Jim Morrison's deep voice. "When you're strange, no one remembers your name. When you're strange, when you're strange, when you're strange. All right, yeah." Sipping his beer, he moves his head to the sound of the keyboard, Natasha cheering him on, his cheeks red with embarrassment.

"When you're strange, faces come out of the rain. When you're strange, no one remembers your name. When you're strange, when you're strange, when you're straaaaaange." As the music ends, the brother in gray gives him a big slap on the back. Sean waves at everyone with his head down while they clap, still blushing.

He takes a last sip of his drink, sets the empty glass on the table, and sits next to Natasha in the booth. He glances at her for a moment, then grins and turns away. "Told you I'd get you to sing," she says, poking his ribs. He gives her a playful dirty look.

That night Sean rides his bike through Natasha's ritzy neighborhood with her wrapped around him on back, her grip much more natural than it was before. He turns on her street, pulling up to her house. Motor idling, he helps her down. She slides off the helmet, brushing some hair out of her face, then hands it to him. "You want to go say hi to the neighbor?" she asks with sarcasm.

He laughs. "Yeah. I'll autograph his wall for him."

A few moments pass. "I can't believe I just went on a date with the guy in the bandana who punched my last date in the face." She curls her right wrist under her chin.

"He deserved it."

"Is that right?" she asks, stepping closer to him.

"It is." He rocks the bike back and forth under him. "Was my first date better than his first date?"

She smirks. "No. I had a terrible time today."

"Yeah?"

"Excruciating."

"I had a terrible time too."

"Well at least we have something in common." She laughs, looks back at her house in the shadows, then at him. "It's getting a little late. My dad's gonna get mad if I don't go inside soon."

He notices her shoulders tense when she brings up her dad. "Understood."

"Even though I had a terrible time, if I get really bored one night it might cross my mind to hang with you again." She goes up on her tippy toes, then comes back down. The tension in her shoulders goes away. "And I'd prefer not to communicate through your friend's art website."

"Neither would I." He pulls his phone out and hands it to her. "Type it in."

She clicks around a bit, then passes it back. "Vonlanden with a V."

"Got it."

A couple moments go by. "Good night," she says, lingering on him with her eyes. They look into each other's face for a while. She grins. So does he. Leaning in, he kisses her. After a few seconds they part. She grins again. So does he.

"Night," he says as she glides away toward her house's iron gate, his heart thumping. She stops about a dozen feet up, turns, and waves, then continues ahead. He wiggles the helmet on and drives off, a nervous thrill in his chest.

Firsts and Seconds

A few weeks later Sean rides along the highway on his motorcycle, Rome's skyline shrinking behind him against a bluish-orange backdrop. Arms around his chest, Natasha sits on the rear in a pink coat with big black buttons, a 1960's aura to it. They've seen each other almost every day since their first date.

They travel for about three hours, the congested atmosphere of the city replaced by rolling green hills as they pass into Tuscany. She gazes at the countryside, large plots of land accented by tall cypress trees, stone manors off in the distance.

He crosses an arched bridge. The stylish residences give an immediate impression of wealth, but the neighborhood still maintains a quaint, welcoming ambience, far from pretentious.

He turns into a driveway, dozens of uniform rows of wooden posts on each side, bare grapevines curling around them. She marvels at the private vineyard, the organization of it as much as its scenic beauty. He pulls up to a two-story villa on the property, shutting off the bike. He helps her down and they hang their helmets. As he disconnects a duffle bag from the back she wanders to the posts, running her curious fingers against the grape-less, winter-season vines.

"Ready babe?" he asks, slinging the overnight bag over his shoulder. She skips to him, grabbing his hand.

"They make their own wine? You didn't tell me that."

"Yeah." He takes a deep breath, air much crisper out here.

"So cool. This is like a serious setup, not something you'd expect at a house." They walk up a short flight of stairs to the entrance. He knocks a couple times.

The door opens, Aunt Mary standing in the hallway. Her hair is longer than it used to be, body fitter too. He walks in with a smile, Mary embracing him, a glimmering wedding band on her. "So glad you could make it," she says with a thrilled expression.

"Me too."

She studies him, a relaxation to his posture, something she doesn't remember he had two months ago, the last time she saw him. She turns to his guest for a moment, then back to him and says, "You told me she was pretty. But I wasn't expecting this." Natasha laughs, embarrassed and flattered. "Come in Natasha," she says in a warm tone as if she's known her for years. She takes two small steps inside, Mary closing the door behind her. They shake hands. "I'm Leanne. James's aunt."

"Nice to meet you," Natasha says in her slight-accented, sweet little way of speaking. She unhooks the black buttons on her pink coat. "Thanks for having me. Your home is beautiful. I can't believe you make your own wine here."

"It's a lot of work to keep up, but we enjoy it. Gives us something to do."

"James," an excited, booming voice says from another room.

"Marco," Sean says, matching the intensity.

Shifting to her nephew, Mary rolls her eyes. "He's been picking at the antipasto for about two hours. I begged him to wait for you. Go in there and distract him before he eats the rest."

Sean crosses the foyer, passing a Christmas tree, and veers into the kitchen among its panoramic view of the Tuscan landscape. Marco, wearing an untucked button down shirt, chops tomatoes on a cutting board. "There he is," Marco says, slicing one last piece, setting the knife down. He wipes his hands on his jeans and steps to Sean with a jolly grin, a few wines already in him, light from the window shining on his olive skin and salt-and-pepper hair. "You look great man."

"I heard you've been pounding all the snacks you slob," Sean says as they hug.

"You heard wrong pal."

"You got marinara sauce all over your chin," he says with a snicker.

Marco dabs it. "You're seeing things. Those motorcycle rides of yours are blowing too much wind into your eyeballs." Sean gives him a subtle push on the shoulder. Marco matches it with one on him. They start wrestling, playful but energetic.

"Can your geriatric knees handle all this activity?" Sean asks, getting him in a full nelson.

"They'll handle you right into a scissor lock," he says, flopping around. "Lights out." Chuckling, Sean lets him go.

As they catch their breath, Marco gestures at the duffle bag strapped on Sean's back. "Put that down. I got it."

"Just leave it here?"

"Yeah. There's fine. I'll grab it later and take it up to the room." As Sean unfastens it Marco saunters to the appetizers on the counter, assorted in pristine white trays and bowls. "So you got some cheeses in the middle," he says, still winded. "Grana Padano. Pecorino. Parmigiano Reggiano. Taleggio. A little meat over here. Vegetables and shit down there." He points at three bottles of wine. "I brought a few Chiantis up from the cellar. All of them we made on the property."

"Yeah?" he asks, rubbing his thumb against the texture of a label.

"Try them out. If you think they suck just tell me. I'll bring up some of the store-bought stuff."

"Crack one of yours," Sean says with a confident nod. With a nod back Marco grips the middle one and an opener and starts digging into the cork.

Natasha and Mary stroll in, mid-conversation with each other, something about Sean never closing the drawers of his dresser after he takes out his clothes. He can hear them but doesn't interrupt to defend himself, girls bonding over something at least.

"Perfect timing ladies," Marco says, yanking out the cork. He wipes the top of the bottle with a towel, sets it on the granite countertop, and walks to Natasha with an extended hand and a smile. "Marco Dellenti."

She shakes it. "Natasha. Thanks for letting me come along."

He lingers on her for a couple moments and says, "Let me give you some advice Natasha. You're too damn cute for him. Turn around and get out of here. Go find someone better."

She laughs. "He's not that bad."

"Oh, he's terrible. But we got good snacks. Hopefully they make up for him." Returning to the antipasto, he snatches a piece of Pecorino cheese and tosses it in his mouth. "You like food and wine?" he asks her, opening a cabinet. "That's pretty much all we do up here."

"Love both," she says, her voice dancing a little at the end.

"I'm a fan of hers already." He pulls four of his best glasses from the back of the cupboard, fills them with Chianti, and motions everyone over. "All right. Time for the first of many this weekend." They huddle around him, holding the stems. Sean glances at his girlfriend, checking if she seems comfortable around these new people. She does. "I would like to make a toast to lying, stealing, cheating, and drinking," Marco says, bouncing his eye contact to them one by one. "If you're going to lie, lie for a friend. If you're going to steal, steal a heart. If you're going to cheat, cheat death. If you're going to drink...drink with me."

"Amen," Mary says. They clink and sip.

Sean pretends to spit it out even though it tastes good. "Man Marco, are you fertilizing your grapes with jet fuel?" he asks with a groan.

"He's been busting on me ever since he walked in here, this kid," he says to the two girls with a lot of volume, an echo in the large den next door. They chuckle.

"It's delicious," Natasha says as if trying to soften her boyfriend's blow.

"Thank you Natasha. I've got a whole case of the stuff." He takes a swig. "Your asses better be ready to booze."

That night the four of them are at a wooden table on the back deck, a nice Chianti buzz on each, three empty bottles, porch lamps twinkling against the silhouettes of hills and cypress trees and faraway estates.

Marco dips a ladle into a bowl, scooping out red sauce, drizzling it on the pasta and rosemary chicken in his plate. He's in the middle of a story. Natasha asks with eagerness, "So…what happened after?"

He blots some sweat from his olive-skin brow, all the liquor and food giving it a thin film of perspiration, a slight sheen on it in the lights. "Me and the little guy with the curly red hair wind up back at my house. That kid Hook I was telling you about. I don't even remember why we called him that." He stops for a bit. "That's probably another good story. Anyway, my old man is upstairs sleeping on the couch like we figured. So me and Hook go into his stash in the basement and steal a bottle of wine for each of us."

Mary hangs her head in her hands, hearing the story no less than fifteen times since she met him. Smirking, he says to Natasha, "We didn't know any better. We've never been out drinking. We were thirteen. Christ, maybe twelve. We just thought it would be cool. Like what older kids did, right? So we go up to my room and it takes us frigging two hours to get the damn things pried with my old man's crappy corkscrew.

Neither of us used one before." He mimics a painstaking opening with make-believe objects. "We finally get the corks out, and we slam these things. I mean…slammed. We had no clue you were supposed to pace it out. We chugged them like juice. Gone in about three minutes."

"Three minutes?" Natasha asks, face leaning forward in surprise, a few blond locks bouncing. Her boyfriend's arm is around her, warmth from a nearby space heater radiating on them.

"Tops," Marco says, breaking a corner off a loaf of bread, dipping it in a pool of sauce on his dish. "It doesn't hit us at first. No big deal. Then a little later…it's like we were hallucinating. I don't remember much from the rest of the night except swearing to myself I was never touching wine again. Hook stumbled his way home. Who the hell knows how."

Sean forks some linguini from the bowl and slides it into her plate. "Here babe."

"Yum," she says, getting a whiff of the fresh basil in the brisk clean air. "Thanks."

He looks at her, contemplating how glad he is he found her. Yes, he realizes she's beautiful, but it's more than that. There's an effortless yet powerful energy in everything she does, the way she keeps eye contact with you while she's giggling, how she springs her shoulders up when she sits back next to you after being away, the dance her voice does at the end of a sentence when she says something she thinks you want to hear.

He moves his attention to Marco and asks, "How far away did this Hook dude live?"

"Far," he says, snickering. "Really far."

Sean laughs. "Picture seeing a kid walking up the road that drunk. People wouldn't expect someone as young as him to be hammered. They probably thought he was possessed."

"He had these buggy eyes man. Kind of look possessed when he was dead sober. I could only imagine the vibe he was throwing off on that walk home. I'm kind of shocked nobody got freaked out and mowed the bastard down in their car."

"You guys are awful," Mary says, doing a bad job pretending she doesn't think they're funny.

Marco gives his wife a loving nudge on the ribs, then looks at Natasha and says, "So I go to bed. Wasted. Keep in mind it's a Saturday. And I grew up in a strict Catholic family. You can guess what that means..."

"Oh no," she says in a drawn-out way. "Church in the morning."

"Not only the morning. Crack of dawn. My old man had a thing about going to the first mass of the day. The damn sky would still be black when you were driving over."

She smacks her forehead and says, "Bruuuuuuuutal."

"Really early, a hand latches onto me. It's my mom waking me up." He clenches his bicep and jiggles it a couple times. "Soon enough I'm on the bench in the chapel, just trying to come off like a normal human being. I got an arrow through my skull. My stomach is rumbling. Any sudden movement and I'm positive I'm puking. Few songs. Listen to the priest talk. I battle through it." He pauses, waving his index finger.

"But...my old man could tell something was up. He wasn't certain what though. He kept scoping me. You know, like this..." He looks forward, then drags a suspicious glance to the side on Natasha. She chuckles. "Some time goes by, I'm still holding it together. Then all of a sudden I see on the altar they're getting ready for communion. With the bread." Inching forward, he widens his eyes. "And the wine."

"It never gets old," Mary says, shaking her head.

"I got my mom pinching me, like, get up, let's go. I hobble to the back of the line. All I'm thinking is, how can I take a sip of this and not swallow it somehow? Not that I had an actual plan." Shrugging, he bites his chicken. "So I'm getting closer. And closer. Finally, after about a week, it's my turn. I step up to the priest. The smell hits me. That was it. I'm done. Didn't even need to taste it. I do a one eighty and start booking for the back of the church."

"Come on," Natasha says, left palm on her cheek.

"I'm about halfway down the aisle. Everyone is staring at me in their Sunday best. In front of all of them I start yacking in my mouth. I throw my hands over my lips to you know, keep it in. I make it outside. Into the street. Then just lost it. All over the pavement. About a minute later, and I didn't even hear him, I just sensed he was there. I peek over my shoulder and it's my pops. In his black fedora. With his big bushy eyebrows. He grabbed me by the neck, dragged me in the car, and laid one hell of a licking on me when we got home." Grasping a bottle of Chianti, he refills his glass. "I guess I kind of deserved it." He winks and has a gulp. "Never thought I'd be living on a damn wine vineyard thirty years after."

Natasha applauds, cracking up. "Great story. Wow." In ten seconds or so she quiets down, her expression going from hysterical to pensive. She observes the impressive property. "I got to say, for such a misfit, you didn't wind up doing that terrible for yourself."

"Boy, I was trouble. That's just one story." He scratches his head through his salt-and-pepper hair. "That's all you're getting tonight."

"You'd be surprised," Mary says, her fingers on Natasha's wrist. "For all his bad qualities, and there are many, he does have a few good ones. He ran his own fruit distribution business for twenty years before he sold it." She pokes his stomach. "How many employees did you have? About two hundred?" Swirling his drink, he hangs his attention on the tabletop without answering. She shakes his arm. "Tell them about it hon."

"They don't want to hear about my boring company. They're kids. They want to hear about me hurling in church."

"You can tell us," Natasha says.

He sips, gaze off in the distance, the part where it's tough to tell where the black hills meet the gray sky. "All I can say is this. You're young. Don't worry too much about things. Make some mistakes. I sure as hell did. You don't need to plan everything out. I had no idea I was going to be a damn produce hauler when I was your age. But hang out with good people. And don't do anything too dumb. And it somehow all sort of works out."

Natasha takes a moment to absorb his mini speech, then says, "Cheers to that." Bending across, she touches her glass with his. She drinks, then grins at Sean and rubs his thigh. He kisses her cheek. From the things she's told him about her overbearing parents, he doesn't feel an adult's assured her it all ends up working out in a while, if ever. He thinks about how content and snug she appears in the red shine of the space heater, Marco's words nestled in her mind. She looks irresistible to him, confident yet delicate. He wants to hold her and kiss her a thousand times.

Cutting his chicken, he overhears the others jabbering about a new topic, something in the paper about the Pope. But his head drifts. He reflects on the four of them together around this table, and for the first time since he can recall, he's happy. For a while he didn't think he'd have moments like this again.

Pondering why it took so long, he decides he'd been trying to force joy on himself, viewing it from a logical angle similar to a math problem. He considers something the therapist warned him about in the hospital when he overdosed on OxyContin, how he'd never be happy if he deemed himself a victim. He'd been doing just that since his parents died, for over a decade. He'd imagined himself a victim of nature, born different than everyone else and forced to suffer the consequences. He'd always hoped he'd uncover some formula that could snap him out of it. But he never did. He realizes it's because it doesn't exist.

The feeling he has now is far from formulaic, brought about in a natural way when his path merged with Natasha's. Though he still knows he's different than everyone else, he doesn't feel like a victim anymore. The world is easy again, how it was that day in the Poconos when he took the photo with his mom and dad.

"Who wants dessert?" Mary asks, conversation about the Pope tapering off. "I have a chocolate cake in the fridge. Fresh strawberries."

"Definitely for me and Natasha," Sean says.

Marco pats his stomach over his button down shirt. "Screw it. Bring me a slice. I'll work out tomorrow."

"You made the same vow last night after the giant sundae at the restaurant," his wife says with a smirk. "And your dumbbells look like they're still in the same spot in the garage…" He squeezes her thigh just above the knee to tickle her. With a giggle she pushes him away and sweeps some of her long brown hair from her eyes. "I'll bring you a half." As she saunters toward the house Marco changes the subject and chats with the two teenagers.

A few hours later Sean and Natasha lie in bed in just underwear, the moonlit countryside out the window, the heavy down comforter pulled up, the sheets toasty on their half-naked bodies. Hands behind his head, he's looking at a painting of a wine barrel on the wall, bottom-right corner signed "Leanne." He pictures his aunt scribbling this new name on everything, checks, order forms, receipts, Marco not even aware of her secret. He recollects the time people used to call her Mary, an era that seems an eternity ago. Then he considers Natasha, right next to him, oblivious to that whole part of his life too. *Jeopardy!*, SoCal Tech, the Traveling Salesman Problem, his extreme intelligence, everything.

"They're amazing," she says, her index finger making little circles on his chest, voice soft.

"Yeah, they're pretty great. They think you are too."

"Aww really?"

"Yeah. She was telling me in the kitchen. When I brought in the empty bottles."

"It's like they're the only two people I ever met that I don't know, figured it out. Well, whatever that means. They're up here, away from everything. And they do so much together. Grow grapes. And cook. And go for walks and stuff. And that's it. They don't need anything else. They make it look so simple, you know?"

"Yeah. I guess they do." He grins. "Babe, are you hungry? I think I'm gonna go downstairs and grab seconds on that chocolate cake."

"I'm gonna just eat you." She bites his shoulder, then makes the noise of a lion, or a tiger, or something like that.

Flinching, he laughs. "You got to stop doing that. It kind of hurts. I'm not kidding."

She snickers. "You know what I feel James?"

"What do you feel?"

"We can make our own wine. Not as much as them or anything. But we could do it. Like maybe once a month. We can go to a place like this and get away from the city. And it could be our thing."

"You don't know how to make wine silly."

"I'll learn," she says, slapping his leg over the covers. "And you can too. With me."

He rolls on his side to face her and adjusts the pillow under him. "What would it be called?"

Her eyes sway as she mulls it over. "How about Two Stones?"

"Two Stones?"

"I always liked that saying, 'a rolling stone gathers no moss.' You know it?" He nods. "Well, that'll be us. Rolling away every now and then, up here, and then going back. Always kind of moving. That can be the label. Two stones next to each other going down a big green hill. Not too fast. Just fast enough. With trees and flowers and stuff behind." She pats his arm. "You can paint it."

He wraps his hand just over her hip, his left leg entwined with hers. "Two Stones. I dig it."

"Deal? You'll learn with me?"

He kisses her forehead. "Deal."

She lingers on him for a second, then shifts to the ceiling, her lighthearted demeanor fading. "I don't want to go on this stupid holiday safari with my family. I'm gonna miss you."

"You'll only be gone for a week and a half. It'll be hard, but we'll talk every day."

"What does my dad expect? By putting me, him, my mom, and my brother in a jungle in Africa it's gonna magically make us forget he's an asshole?"

He puts his palm on her cheek. "Don't think about all that now. You'll be back in time for us to spend Christmas together. We're with each other in Tuscany now. Let's enjoy this." A pause. "I'm really glad you came up here with me."

She takes a deep breath, cheery expression returning, and says in a sweet little voice, "I'm really glad you invited me."

"I've never done anything like this with anyone else. Go on a trip."

"Me neither." She smiles, moonlight pouring over the top half of her face from an opening in the curtains.

About half a minute goes by. "I love you," he says, his heart fluttering as he hears the words come out of his mouth.

A couple moments pass. "I love you too."

"That's the first time I ever said that to anyone."

"Me too."

The Next Step

On Christmas morning two weeks later Sean shuffles a few slabs of bacon in a skillet, delicious aroma filling his apartment, holiday music playing from a portable speaker plugged into his phone, a gush of sun shining through the balcony's glass door. Setting the pan back on the stove, he grips his coffee and sips.

The sound of slippers at his side, he spots Natasha strolling toward him, fresh from bed in reindeer pajamas, a bit sleepy still. She follows the smell and says with delight, "Babe I didn't know you cooked."

"I figured I'd give it a shot. Little Christmas surprise for you. I experimented on Fabrizio the other day..." He chuckles. "Didn't turn out too well." He picks up a spatula and fiddles with the scrambled eggs, cooking in another pan. "I got the kinks worked out on him." He sprinkles in some pepper. "Well, I hope."

She kisses his cheek. "That's so sweet. You're the best. Merry Christmas. Mmm. Smells sooooo good." She rubs her eyes and stretches her arms, her expression waking up some.

He flashes her a smile, then flips the bacon. "I'm getting there. About five more minutes."

"Well in that case…present time," she says with excitement. "Wait right here mister." She claps a couple times, then skips across the living room.

He hears her go through her overnight bag, some makeup cases clunking. She returns with a small box wrapped in blue paper, a red ribbon around it in a bow. She rests it by his mug and says in a slow voice, "Whenever you're ready."

Glancing at it, he lays the spatula on the tile counter. He wipes his hands on the front of his flannel pajama pants, lifts it, and rattles. "Let me guess. A stapler?" Grinning, she shakes her head. Another jiggle. "A screwdriver?" She slaps his chest. He peels the paper, a cardboard box underneath. Pulling back the lid, he makes out a pair of gold-framed sunglasses with amber lenses.

"They're the Peter Fonda ones from *Easy Rider*," she says. "The ones you said you thought were cool when we watched the movie. No knockoffs either. Vintage originals." He removes them with care. "Ray Ban Olympian One Deluxe," she says with familiarity, accustomed to the jargon after hunting for them online during her safari in Africa whenever she had internet access. "Never been worn before."

He studies them under the bulb above, a shimmer on them. "I've wanted these for about four years. You've got to be kidding me. Where the hell did you find them?"

She sweeps her thumb and index finger across her lips, pretending to zip them. "Put them on. Let me see." He does. She folds her arms, checking him out. "Boss as hell."

"One sec." He dashes across the hardwood into the bathroom and scopes his reflection in the mirror, pupils somewhat visible under the partial tints, just like in the film. Spinning to his right, he inspects the profile view.

In a bit he struts back to the kitchen and says, "Babe you killed it. Great gift. Thank you so much." He kisses her forehead.

She bops his nose with her finger. "Now stop admiring yourself and get back to those eggs before you burn them."

About an hour later they're finishing breakfast, his shades still on, a Christmas oldie by Bing Crosby chiming from the speaker. He chews his last bite and says, "Time for yours."

"My oh my, what a lucky girl am I," she says in a Southern-belle accent, hand over her heart.

He gets up and veers toward the bedroom. He emerges with something flat and square-shaped, about three by three feet, under yellow gift paper with little red dots. "I suck at wrapping. Don't make fun of me." He leans it against the table. "But...I think you won't hate what's inside."

"What is it?"

"Open it silly." She puts down her fork, grasps the present, and places the bottom on her thighs. Ripping the corner of the wrapping, she notices an art canvas below. She keeps tearing to reveal a graffiti painting of the Hotel Vanessa rooftop he made himself. Over her shoulder he says, "Our first date."

"Whoa," she says, admiring his abstract rendition of the place.

He rubs the back of her arm. "Well?"

"Love it babe." She touches his hand with warmth and catches his eyes. "Love you."

"Love you too. Merry Christmas."

A couple hours later he's riding his motorcycle in town, sunglasses still on, Natasha hugging him behind. She's wearing fashionable, tribal-inspired earrings she got on her safari.

He coasts to a stop at the base of the Basilica of St. Mary of the Altar of Heaven, a big Gothic church on a high hill, a one-hundred-twenty-four-step staircase rising to the entrance, bottom half covered in sun, top half shadows.

She slides off her white helmet with pink racing stripes. He takes it from her and helps her down. She opens the cargo case, collects two boxes wrapped in the same blue gift paper his was, and says, "I'll be just a couple minutes."

"You sure your parents are here?"

"Yeah. My mom texted me." Reaching into her purse, she checks the time on her phone. "They should be getting out of mass in a little. I'm gonna give my presents to them quick and come back down with both of them. They want to meet you." She tucks one of the gifts under her left arm and holds the second in her hands. "My dad is kind of an asshole. Be ready. Just warning you."

"Oh, you've told me before." He smiles, bike rocking under him. "I'll survive. I've had to deal with a handful of assholes in my eighteen years." He removes his helmet. "I'll be hanging here."

She leans in and kisses him. "Be right back." He watches her climb the massive flight, her blond head getting smaller and smaller as she gets closer to the church.

He looks around, families scattered here and there in suits and dresses, holiday greetings circulating in Italian. He can hear the choir inside, faint but clear. He recognizes the song, "Exultate Deo," from a chapel in Shipville Mary used to bring him every Christmas and Easter. Listening to the many nuances, he figures the chorus must be large, thirty singers at least. It sounds different than the five-person crew in Pennsylvania, more complex, but the underlying heart of it is the same.

A high-pitched scream rings through the air, drowning out the music. He darts his eyes around, attempting to identify it. He spots a middle-aged man and woman standing on their toes, examining the area above the staircase. He makes out a small blue box dropping from step to step.

Jumping off the motorcycle, he hears another shriek, louder than the last. Glancing upward, he notices about fifteen people huddled by the church's main doorway, a short old woman in a brown veil wailing among them.

He bolts up the stairs, covering two with each stride. His legs start tingling. He crosses the lower bright end of the flight into the dark top. By the time he's done going up, both his thighs are scorching. He shoves his way through the crowd. As the bodies split, and he gets a clear view, he freezes. Natasha is flailing on the ground in a full seizure, eyes rolled back, skin drenched in sweat.

A shouting policeman sprints over from inside the church, dropping to a knee by her. "Ambulance," he says to the onlookers in Italian. "We need an ambulance." He wedges his hands under her arms and peels her convulsing torso off the surface. Another officer breaks through the group, clenching her ankles and hoisting her legs up. Her body suspended between them, they advance onto the steps, those blond locks of hers jerking in the air.

Sean tails them. "Baby," he says, his face close to hers, his feet pacing the cops as they lug her. "Natasha." Quiet. Nothing.

"Move away sir," the first policeman that arrived says.

He doesn't. "Sweetie?" He lingers on her expression, waiting for it to do something to acknowledge him. Anything. It doesn't, the blues of her eyes hidden in her skull. The sight makes the hairs on the back of his neck stand.

Siren blasting, an ambulance screeches to a halt by the base of the premises, red and white lights flashing. Two paramedics storm out with a calculated rhythm, one opening the backdoors, the other heaving out a stretcher. The officers lay her on its thin tan cushion, her shaking right leg hanging off. A concerned audience of about twenty gapes at the scene from the street.

Sean lunges for her, but the cops block him, clasping his forearms. "Let go of me," he says with hostility, his boot heels scraping against the cobblestones as he tries to escape. In their clutch he observes the first EMT slide his girlfriend's head through a yellow neck support and lay an oxygen mask over her face. The second clamps her quivering shins, runs a thick black strap across them, and yanks it secure. He does the same with another over her stomach. As she trembles within the restraints, the metal frame beneath her squeaks and clacks.

They shove the stretcher into the vehicle, wheels ratcheting up. They slam shut the doors and climb inside. Sean watches the ambulance race off with its lights whirling, his heart banging into his ribs.

In the Caves All Cats Are Grey

An ant climbs across the couch cushion in the dim hospital wait-ing room that night, Sean watching it roam the vinyl, a lopsided Christmas wreath on the wall above him. It's silent other than two older women here for another patient, one on the verge of tears, the other trying to comfort her by whispering something.

He gets up and walks to the receptionist, putting his hands on her cold metal desk, leaning forward. "Please," he says in the native language. "I am begging you."

In a few moments she looks up from her paperwork, the mole by her top lip springing into sight, and says in Italian, "Sir, family only. I've told you about a hundred times."

"I. Am. Begging. You."

"Sir." She leers at him for a while, then drops her attention to her forms, checking some boxes, ignoring him.

He stomps to the sofa and sits, pressing the tips of his fingers into his forehead. He slides them down, his temples, his cheeks, his chin. Rocking back and forth, he peers at the blackness through the window. One of the elderly ladies starts weeping, coarse guttural moans, the other patting her thigh and murmuring something he can't make out.

In ten minutes or so the door cracks, a late-twenties nurse in the opening, a foot on the gray rug, another on the linoleum hospital hallway. She scans the room, stopping on him. "James?" He pops up. "I've been part of the team...caring for Ms. Vonlanden," she says in Italian.

He examines her face for a clue. An indication of anything. "What did you find out?" he asks in the same language, voice jumpy.

"The convulsing died down."

"That's amazing," he says with a grin, his posture loosening.

She doesn't smile back, her stare dipping down. "But... that's not an indication she's...in the clear."

"In the clear from what? What caused it?"

She peeks over her shoulder, then back at him, her hazel eyes narrowing. "We have reason to believe she picked something up in Africa. When she was on the safari. Although she's the only one from the trip showing symptoms, all four of the Vonlandens are...being brought to an area where we can be certain nothing in them...spreads. A precaution."

He processes this for a few seconds, his brow creasing. "They're being quarantined?"

She doesn't talk for a while, her fingers tapping the edge of the wooden door. "They're all being driven to a clinic in Zurich, where the family is from. They're on their way right now. More answers will—"

"What kind of clinic?" he asks, stepping closer. "What's wrong with her?"

"We don't know...what exactly it is yet. The safety measures can very well be unnecessary. But we just aren't positive now." She reaches into the pocket of her light-blue scrubs, pulls out a piece of hospital stationery, and hands it to him. "But the specialists in Switzerland will have a full break-down. This is the place. It's the best in the world with…making sense of these situations. She'll be in good hands." She tilts her chin to the left. "Do you think you can make it there?"

He glances at the paper, a Swiss address scribbled in blotchy black ink. "Of course. Are you kidding?"

She shifts her attention from him to the darkness outside. "You mean a lot to her. We were chatting just before. She knew you'd be here." She offers him two quick, jerky nods. "You should try to get to Zurich, as soon as you can. They'll be arriving by car early tomorrow morning." She gives him a limp wave and retreats into the corridor.

A while later he's on his motorcycle with his new sunglasses on, zipping about ninety miles per hour down the highway, no destination in mind, air crackling in his ears. He weaves through cars, a burst of honks behind him, one person even hanging out the window cursing. He figured the physical rush of a reckless ride would help distract him from the conversation he had in the waiting room. It's not working.

Around eleven o'clock he's on a stool at the corner of an almost-empty bar, a fortyish husband and wife eating turkey sandwiches at the other end, fake Christmas tree by the entrance, heating vents emanating hot air in an unpredictable rhythm of spurts and lulls.

He stares into a glass of straight vodka, skin on his cheeks a bit chapped from the cold wind when he was on the bike. He sips, the familiar beverage not tasting like he's used to. The popular holiday jingle playing on the radio doesn't sound like he remembers either. He recalls this feeling, when he was fourteen, the time he was battling with the guilt of Operation Golden Bear. Things he once thought were immutable, like the voices of the characters on his favorite TV show, changed as depression tightened its grip over everything, sucking out all its flavor.

He chugs the rest of his drink and sets it down. Hearing the hollow chime of the cup, the bartender puts aside his newspaper, saunters to him, and asks in Italian, "How we doing pal?"

"One more," Sean says in the same language, a mild slur to his speech.

"That would take us to eight. I can't do that." He points at a blackboard behind him, names of the daily food specials jotted in red-and-green chalk. "How about something to eat?"

"I'm fine. Bring me another."

"Sir, I'm afraid I can't. House policy."

"It's Christmas man," he says with a hiccup.

"I'm aware it's Christmas. The roads are dangerous enough. I can't have another person driving around with the potential to hurt someone."

Sean stands, his chair thrusting back. Glaring at the stocky employee, he hiccups again. "You don't know what I'm gonna do when I leave here. You don't know me." He pauses. "You don't know anything about me."

"I do know you've had seven pure vodkas in about two hours."

"Yeah and I want another." Sean tries to grab the glass, knocking it over by accident. It rolls off the bar, shattering on the floor.

"That's it. You're out of here idiot." The bartender crouches under the counter and marches toward him.

"What are you gonna do about it huh?" Sean asks, throwing his arms in the air. The couple eating dinner gawks at him.

The bartender, bigger than him by about fifty pounds, latches onto his wrist and tugs him to the exit, Sean's intoxicated body not putting up much of a fight. The man kicks the door open, tosses the drunk on the rough cobblestones, and says, "Merry Christmas."

"Asshole." In a moment or so Sean pushes himself to his feet. Hands on the knees of his dusty jeans, he catches his breath. He lifts his head, streetlights rushing into view, hazy blurs in his discombobulated state. Straightening out his leather jacket, he wanders down the sidewalk, most of the businesses around closed, only a few pedestrians out this late on a holiday. He hums "Here Comes Santa Claus," meandering nowhere in particular.

A half hour later he's passed out facedown at the Roman Pantheon temple, back puffing up and down. Most people going by don't notice him, others dismissing him as a hobo.

"Hey," a faint voice says. Sean's eyelids quiver, then open. A slender old man in a wrinkle-free, tailored suit hovers above him. Looking down at the boy with a comforting expression, he says, "You need to get up." He speaks English with no foreign accent, an American pronunciation to his words.

Sean blinks for a bit, then sits against one of the columns. Rubbing his forehead, he asks, "Are you a security guard?"

He lets out a soft chuckle. "No."

Sean stretches his legs in front of him with a groan. His chin is numb from being on the cold surface. "How long was I out?"

"You didn't suspect I was watching you this whole time, did you?"

"I guess not." Sean glances up at him. "What are you doing here so late?"

"I was about to ask you the same thing."

Sean takes in the Pantheon, the pillars, the roof, the cavernous inside. "I like it here." He pats the dusty floor. "Right in this spot."

"I like it here too."

"I'm not sure why. But I always come when I'm…you know…"

"Having a bad day?"

"Something like that." Neither of them talks for a while, the soft drone of other conversations in the distance.

Resting his palm on the rotunda, Sean recollects the hooded crow he saw last month, less than a foot from where he is now. He remembers his envy for it, how the creature wasn't able to understand the pain in the world. Like the kind he's feeling now. The elderly fellow's easy demeanor urges Sean to open up about it. "You ever want to be something else?" he asks. "You know, something simple. Like an animal."

He snickers. "Now why would I want a thing like that?"

He swivels his left foot back and forth. "I realize it sounds weird. But sometimes I think about it. Easier that way. Have to deal with less."

The old man folds his arms. "What type of animal would you be?"

"I don't know. Bird I guess."

"A bird. I see." He nods. "You think a bird doesn't feel anything negative?"

A few moments pass. "It does. But not…the same as us."

"It has many rules it lives by to avoid negative things. Just like us. For instance, if there was a fire in a room, I guarantee neither you nor the bird would willfully go into it."

Sean pushes a hand through his hair. "Yeah. Okay. But that's just a basic need to survive. Instinct. I'm talking…" He points at the side of his head. "More advanced thinking. Where human intelligence comes into play."

"Ah," he says with a smirk. "Advanced thinking. Well, I wouldn't rush to any conclusions. I believe you're underestimating our friend the bird. Nature has given it some impressive abilities. Quite impressive in many cases I would say." He sways back and forth in his shiny wingtip shoes a couple times. "Have you ever heard of the breed Manx Shearwaters?"

"Once or twice."

"Well, do me a favor. I want you to read about an experiment conducted with them involving Venice. The one here in Italy, not California. Can you do that for me?"

"Yeah," Sean says without paying it much attention, dragging himself to his feet. "I can do that." Now standing, he recognizes how much his hip was hurt from the toss to the cobblestones, whole side of his body throbbing.

"You have somewhere to be, don't you?"

"Why would you say that?"

"Just a guess. It is Christmas after all."

Sean studies his face for a few moments, a grin still on it. "I'm gonna get going now." He waves at the old man, receiving a nod in return, and veers toward the glow of the main road, hands in his jacket pockets, mind on Switzerland. Stopping a few dozen feet ahead, he turns, gazing back at the Pantheon, wanting to thank him for waking him up. But he's gone, nowhere to be seen in any direction.

True North

The next morning the seatbelt buckle on Sean's lap rattles as his plane hits a patch of turbulence. Head bobbing, he stares out the window at grayness, yesterday's outfit still on, sunglasses Natasha gave him wobbling on his collar, hangover pounding.

"Sir," a pleasant female voice says. "Sir?" Turning left, he notices a stewardess, early twenties, hands clutching the shaky drink cart. "Would you care for a beverage?" she asks in Swiss-influenced English similar to his girlfriend's. He fixates on a stack of plastic cups in front of her, near toppling with the jerky movements of the aircraft. "Sir. A beverage?" He shakes his head.

The conversation he had with the hazel-eyed nurse in Rome is playing over and over in his mind. He hangs on the words, trying to spin them into the most positive light possible. But deep down he realizes he's just lying to himself. He couldn't sleep last night, recalling Natasha's face in spasms descending the church stairs. As much as he tries to convince himself otherwise, he expects she's dealing with something serious.

He overhears the middle-aged man next to him yapping with the perky attendant, his tone pathetic as he attempts to impress her with some fake-sounding story about a famous chef in Switzerland naming a menu item after him. Sean drowns him out, reflecting on his parents. Every time he's on a plane he can't help but think of them. He pictures his mom cleaning out their closet in Shipville, boots on the floor, a pile of scarves, a cardboard box labeled "Jenny – Winter." He visualizes his dad watching the Pittsburgh Steelers, black team sweatshirt, a Miller Lite, a yell at the TV each bad call.

Around an hour later the plane touches down, wind roaring as it barrels along the landing strip, Sean's stare on the snowy Zurich sky, first time ever here. He gets up in a bit, leaving in the seat pouch a thick book he bought in the airport called *Learning German*. Knowing it's the primary language in this city, he figured he should teach himself on the flight. He did. The whole thing.

In a short while he funnels out of the terminal with a mass of others. About thirty degrees outside, he folds his arms and presses them against his chest, weather a piercing cold, the chill working its way under his clothing. He decides to put on a heavier coat, but remembers he didn't pack anything other than his passport last night in the preoccupied condition he was in.

Spotting a taxi sign, he trots to the back of a nearby line. Loud noises circle him, car horns, an argument between a husband and wife, a 747 taking off. When the wind gusts it picks up specks of ice from the ground and thrusts them through the air, the little crystals striking his cheek as he waits for a ride.

In about fifteen minutes he's the next up, watching a blue-and-white van cab lurch forward. Teeth chattering, he tugs the heavy sliding door and lunges in. The driver twists to him and asks in German, "Where to?"

Blowing in his left hand, Sean digs his right in the pocket of his leather jacket, pulling out the paper with the address. "It's on here," he says in the local language, fluent as of the last hour. Glancing at the sheet, the cabbie nods and flips on the meter. He veers onto a main road. Reaching to his console, he pokes some buttons on his stereo, "Barbara Ann" by the Beach Boys erupting from the speakers. Sean's head is slumped to the right, Zurich's skyline lopsided to him through the icy window as the song booms.

His focus on the buildings whizzing by, he contemplates Natasha's life here before time brought her to him in Italy. He imagines her as a little girl, doing things in all these places while he was a little boy in Pennsylvania a world away.

They advance for about forty-five minutes, the Beach Boys' greatest-hits album the only sound in the vehicle. They park in front of a five-story black building with bronze trim. Sean peels some cash from his wallet and holds it up. "Thanks," the driver says, snagging it. "Enjoy Zurich, yeah?" Sean exits without responding and heaves the bulky door shut.

Viewing the renowned Luffen Medical Clinic, he endures the harsher wind cutting into him off Lake Zurich, only a few blocks away. Angling his face down, he crosses the sludgy sidewalk to the entrance. He steps into the lobby, the trickle of water the only noise, a glass fountain in the center spilling into a basin of black and gray pebbles. A few feet away an old lady in a hospital gown sleeps straight up on a white couch, no other patients around.

He walks to the reception desk. A light-complexioned woman glances up and says, *"Guten Tag."*

"I'm looking for a patient," he says in German.

Tapping her keys, she asks in the same language, "Their name?"

"Vonlanden. Natasha Vonlanden."

"Is that V-O-N-L-A-N-T-E-N?"

"D. Instead of T."

More typing, her fast clicks contrast the slow hum of the cascading water. "Eighteen years old, female?"

"Yeah."

She scrolls, then peeks up at him with a different expression than she had before, pity mixed with urgency. "And you are sir?"

"James. Crates."

"Yes. They submitted you. Wait right here sir." She gets up, disappearing through a doorway. His palms patting the desk, he wonders what she just saw. He's alone with the murmur of the fountain for a while, his mind again replaying the talk he had with the nurse in Italy.

In about five minutes she returns with a white-and-yellow badge saying "Special Visitor – Zone R" in five different languages. "Take the elevator up to four and show them this. They'll let you know what to do from there."

It's the thickest guest badge he's ever seen. "Thanks." He grasps the rectangular piece of plastic and clips it on his jeans.

"Do you need anything else?"

"No."

"I'll be down here if you do." He keeps his eyes on her for a few moments, then wanders toward the elevator. He hits the button and goes in the empty cart, floor-to-ceiling mirrors on the walls, one flat light slab overhead as wide as the space. He hits level four and begins lifting, gears in the shaft grating. He takes in his reflection, chafed skin on his cheek from lying on the Pantheon, puffy bags under his eyes, thicker beard stubble than usual.

The elevator stops, doors separating, a shine pouring in, Sean squinting. Once his foot hits the polished white tiles, he freezes, anxiety holding him back, fear of the truth. He retreats inside, his image streaking across the glass, his heart bouncing. He takes a bunch of deep breaths. His flesh turns hot, producing an odd prickly sensation mixed with the hint of frost from outside still lingering on his skin. Crouching in the corner, he presses two fingers into the side of his throat, checking his pulse. It's fast, more than two beats a second. He doesn't move for about a minute, trying to talk himself out of this state.

Climbing to his feet, he shakes his arms and forces himself to confront reality. He exits, the smell of cleaning chemicals in the atmosphere. He notices an enclosed bridge stretching to a separate building about a hundred feet away, a steel door at the end closing off access, "Zone R" on it in block letters. A thirty-something man, suit, blond buzz cut, sits on a leather-and-chrome stool in front of the entrance.

Sean crosses the connecting path, snowflakes dotting the cylindrical glass tunnel around him, Lake Zurich to his left, green hills to his right. "They told me in the lobby to come up here," Sean says in German, inching his badge up.

The worker glimpses it and asks in the same language, "Visiting a patient?"

"Yeah. Vonlanden. Natasha."

He nods. "Her parents and brother were just cleared. Dr. Obrecht will be speaking with them…" He checks his watch. "In around two hours. His office is a floor up. I suggest you meet with the rest of them then."

Sean peeks through a thin pane on the door, trying to make out what's on the other side. No visibility, just shadows. "Is she back there?"

"Dr. Obrecht isn't permitting Ms. Vonlanden anyone back yet. Until he has a chance to talk with the family. I'm sorry. Again, you're free to join them for the discussion shortly."

He steps toward the entrance anyway, reaching for the big red button that opens it. "I want to see her now."

The employee springs from his seat and restrains him. "No visitors sir." Sean gropes again, missing by an inch or so. "Security," the guy says with alarm into a walkie-talkie.

"Just let me see her for a second, all right?" Sean shoves him. The man regains his footing, then slugs him in the face, the thump of bone hitting bone echoing.

Bending, Sean dabs his lips with his fingers, red all over them, his head pulsating. A couple brawny security guards rush over in white collared shirts with the Swiss flag on the shoulder. "Everything okay?" one of them asks his fellow employee in German.

"Fine," he says, shaking his punching fist.

Wiping his bloody chin with the arm of his leather jacket, Sean staggers off, the three hospital staffers scowling at him in front of the sealed passageway.

Full Circle

A couple hours later Sean is on a low black couch against the rear wall of an office on the fifth floor. Their backs to him, the three other members of Natasha's family are sitting a few feet in front in chairs, twenty-one-year-old brother, mother, and father. Facing them all is Dr. Obrecht, a sixtyish man in a white lab coat, mane of silver hair, square jaw. He's seated at a large oak desk, window to his right overlooking the snow-dusted city, bookcase behind him packed with about a hundred medical texts, pen spinning between his fingers in slow half-turns.

He tries not to make eye contact with any of the three Vonlandens. The mom, in between the two men, wails, the makeup she wore to Christmas Mass yesterday streaking across her skin in blue and black clumps, tip of her right shoe grinding into the hardwood. Every ten seconds or so she yells at the ceiling. This goes on for a while.

The dad catches his son's attention and motions toward his sobbing wife, then the door. Grabbing her hand, the kid rises and says in German, "Come on mom." He gives her a light tug on her arm. She doesn't seem to even notice him, lost in her own mind. "Let's get you some water." He grips her shoulder and side and starts lifting. She goes along with it, not even checking to see who's moving her.

As he walks her toward the exit, her knees go weak, the crying possessing her whole body, the young man straining to stabilize her. Sean watches him escort her past him, then out into the hall.

Room now dead silent, Dr. Obrecht continues rotating his pen, Natasha's father upright and stiff in his chair across, Sean about ten feet back on the sofa with a bruised chin and spots of blood on his shirt from the tussle before. Elbow on the armrest, he leans his head against his right knuckles, his gaze on the blue area rug, pattern composed of thousands of little interlocking white circles jumbled about.

"How can you be positive it's something as drastic as Ebola?" the father asks the physician in the local language, breaking the room's hush.

"Filoviruses such as Ebola are rather straightforward to detect," Dr. Obrecht says back in German. "After analyzing the blood samples from all four of you with our electron microscope, the reason we're so confident she has it is the same reason we're so confident the rest of you don't. The virions we evaluated in Natasha's sample had a characteristic shape." He holds up his index finger and curls the top. "A hook, which indicates Ebola with certainty. We found nothing of the sort in the submissions from you, your wife, or son."

The father takes some time to process this, then stands and steps to the window. Running a hand through his thinning sandy-blond hair, he stares at the snowy landscape, his own reflection blurry and partial in the glass. "Assuming it is the case, what can we expect? Don't sugarcoat it. Be honest with me."

"We've already observed fever and muscle aches in her. And the onset of internal bleeding. In addition to the sporadic seizures." He adjusts his glasses. "But that's just the beginning. Next is typically breathing trouble, then…failure of bodily functions. Finally, blood will stop clotting. Once this happens, the organs essentially liquefy. And then after that… well. I'm sure you can imagine there's not much that can be done then."

A long pause. "How long? Until…that stage."

Arms folded, Dr. Obrecht leans back, a pensive, almost scholarly, air to him. "As for timing the major factor to consider would be potential blood loss. Since she just started showing signs, it would be difficult to pinpoint—"

"Just tell me how long dammit."

A few moments pass. "Two weeks. If she's fortunate. Very fortunate."

He's still for a while. "I know people recover from this. What can we give her? There must be something."

"The survival rate with the strain she has…the Zaire variety…is the lowest of the Ebola types. Ten percent at best. We'll provide anticoagulants and continue to hawk over her fluid levels and electrolytes twenty-four hours a day, but…as for a curing serum…it…it doesn't exist. In rare circumstances the body can fight it off, but the vast majority of the time it just can't."

About a half-minute of silence goes by, then he asks, "What about an experimental treatment for Christ's sake?" His expression is frenzied now. He bangs his fist on the desk, shaking it, knocking a framed photograph of the physician, his wife, and two sons on its side. "There has to be something we can try," the parent says, drops of saliva spurting from his mouth onto the leather desk mat, bottom lip quivering.

Dr. Obrecht picks up the toppled picture and puts it in place. "There are people out there charging ahead on theories every day. In hospitals, labs, universities. All over the world. But they're works in progress. At best." He slips into that pensive look again for a moment or so. "I was at a conference in Paris about six months ago. There were some gentlemen there from a firm in the States working on a solution aimed at altering the way viruses, like Ebola, replicate their genetic material. Very experimental. Extremely. Colzyne Systems, I'm assuming you've heard of them. The vision was fascinating. But it was only that. Fascinating. Not a reality. They weren't able to figure out how to actually implement it."

"Why don't I fly to the States tonight and write the CEO of Colzyne a check for ten million dollars. He can fill a room with the best engineers on the planet until it gets done."

"I wish it were only that easy," Dr. Obrecht says with a reflexive chuckle, one he regrets right away. To compensate for the brief moment of lightheartedness, he takes on a mechanical pace with his speech and says, "A company like Colzyne probably does close to thirty billion dollars annually in revenue. Billion with a B. They have plenty of resources. Not to mention, each year worldwide the amount of funds raised for disease research is in the hundreds of billions. Money isn't the issue."

"I thought you were the best?" he asks, animosity building for this silver-haired man across from him with all these textbooks and no answers. "Nothing you can do but let her die?"

"With many infections there are things that can be done. But with ones like Ebola…unfortunately…there just aren't."

"Is that what you want me to tell my wife?" He points at the door. "And her brother? That there's nothing that can be done? As simple as that?"

Atmosphere tensing, Dr. Obrecht cuts eye contact, shifting to a remote control on his mat used to change the office's temperature. "I regret I don't have a different outlook. But the nature of the virus is…well. It stands out from others. It's quite frankly the deadliest known to man. The manner it builds and spreads inside the body is highly erratic. As a medical community we've made tremendous strides with research. But finding a methodology to isolate and eliminate it…we're not there. Not even close in fact." He raises his focus back to the father. "Tapping the underlying root of the disease, it's…it's just too complex. It's impossible to wrap the mind around all the facets of its behavior."

It's quiet for a while. Sean is still looking at the area rug, following the thousands of little white circles as they spill into each other. His body is frozen, but his eyes are alive.

"You're going to have to tell me something," the father says to the doctor, coming to the realization his daughter is going to die, hoping the physician utters any hint at an alternative.

"Mr. Vonlanden, if I may," he says, observing the calmness of the Lake Zurich water out the window. "You strike me as the type of man who likes being in control of his surroundings. Who seizes solutions to his problems. That instinct has likely played a major role in your professional success. I too regard myself as a man inclined to proactively resolve his problems. However, in a situation such as this...I would recommend you spend this time not thinking about ways to fix things." A pause. "Instead, spend it enjoying each and every one of its moments with your daughter."

The father holds his attention on the bookcase for a few seconds, the raw truth settling in. He gazes around with his icy blue irises, a plant in the corner, the crown molding on the ceiling, a black-and-white photo on the wall of a violin. He notices Sean in the back. He decides to take everything out on this kid he's heard has been dating his daughter. Consumed with rage, he asks him in Swiss-accented English, "What are you still even doing here?"

Sean straightens up on the couch, surprised he's being addressed, and says with a stutter, "I was just sitting."

"This is for family. You're not family. You're not anyone. You're a low-class nobody. Nothing like us. Nothing like my daughter. We want to be alone. So leave us alone dammit." He storms out, slamming the door.

Sean looks at the leather armrest for a while, then Dr. Obrecht. They survey each other's faces for a moment, the physician contemplating to engage him in conversation and field his medical questions. He reasons however, by the kid's youth and lack of manners with the hospital staff earlier, that he's not the type who would desire or grasp a scientific explanation anyway, so he decides against it. He pivots his stare from the boy to the window, Sean returning his to the little white circles on the floor.

Impossible Things

Around six o'clock that night Sean sits on the edge of a stone bridge, feet dangling over Lake Zurich as snowflakes fall, streetlamps glimmering across the shadowy water, sun just set. The rumble of passing cars behind him, he sticks his hand in a bag of airline pretzels he had in his jacket, pulls one out, and flings it. His eyes follow it in the shine for a bit, but the wind carries it into the darkness, out of sight.

He gazes at the lake for a half-minute or so, then up at the stars. Some are so old he figures the light he's seeing now was traveling for billions of years before reaching him. He ponders how some of the atoms in the world from the beginning of time got recycled generation after generation and came together eighteen years ago to create him. He thinks about all he is and all he isn't for a while. Checking his watch, he realizes he's allowed to see her in just over forty minutes.

In a bit he's in the hospital elevator viewing himself in the mirrored walls as the gears crank. He checks out his bruised chin, then the rest of his face. Living in Rome and Southern California for the better part of a decade, he hasn't been in snow for a while. He recalls his reflection as a young boy in Pennsylvania after a day of playing in the snow with the other kids on the block. Red blotches, dry skin, colorless lips.

Sean Malone feels he looks like that now, how he did on those days as a boy.

The cart stops and he walks onto the fourth floor, quiet except the thump of his boots. He crosses the enclosed bridge, Zurich's city lights twinkling outside the tunnel, and comes to a man in front of the steel door, different than the one who punched him. "Name of the patient you're seeing?" the employee asks in German.

"Vonlanden. Natasha."

"Badge?" He shows him the plastic card on his waist. "Pod two." The staffer hits the red button and the heavy metal slab rushes to the right without a noise. Sean steps through the opening. It closes right away behind him, soft shimmer of the glass tunnel vanishing. He notices a long, dark staircase and goes down it to a ground-level hallway, spotting an arrowed sign engraved with "1-4" and another "5-8." He follows the first toward pod two.

As he veers down the dead-silent corridor, the tile surface changes to cement, dome-shaped overhead bulbs in aluminum cages lighting the way. Once he reaches an alley marked "2," he makes out a door labeled "Observation." Beside it is a second called "Interaction," a yellow-and-black biomedical-hazard imprint on it. The sight of this universal symbol for contamination nauseates him, the thought someone as good and pure as his girlfriend now associated with it.

He opens the one without the warning, "Observation," and enters a dim area about eight feet by five with nothing in it but two metal folding chairs. At the front is a six-inch-thick sheet of glass, behind it a bright hospital room that looks just like any other, a bed, machines, equipment cabinet, among related things.

Closing the door, he notices Natasha through the window. She's on the foot of the mattress staring up at a small skylight on the ceiling. He knocks on the bulky glass, trying to get her attention. She doesn't turn to him.

He spots an intercom at waist level and says into it, "Hey." He waits for her to acknowledge him, but she doesn't, her gaze still on the square skylight above her, the three-quarter moon over Zurich framed inside.

"When I was a little girl I went to school not far from here, maybe five blocks," she says, her words grainy but audible through the speaker. "We had a guest come to science class one day. He was from the SSO. Swiss Space Office. He wore this pin on his shirt of a red-and-white rocket. He told us a whole bunch of facts. About the ships. And how the astronauts train. Stuff like that. I forgot most of it." Her voice gets soft, a notch above a whisper, and she says, "But he said this one thing I always remembered."

She twirls some hospital-gown material around her index finger and says, "He told us scientists were planning to create these colonies on the moon where people would be able to visit. Like a vacation. I thought that was just about the coolest thing ever. To go on a trip to the moon. He was about fifty then. He doubted in his lifetime the colonies would be ready. But all us girls were six or seven. And he said he was certain within our lives it would be a common thing. Vacations on the moon. For regular people."

She unravels the gown fabric on her finger and says, "I couldn't get it out of my head. I thought about it the whole rest of the day. The rest of the week. I just felt it was wild that this was gonna be possible. For me." A sadness consumes her. For the first time since he's been down here she doesn't seem herself. The energy in her face is gone, replaced by something empty and sterile. "It's not around yet, but I figured it would be in the next twenty years or so. I wouldn't even be forty then."

She's still for a while. He thinks about saying something, but before he can, she throws herself onto the bed and says with panic, "I'm scared. I'm scared. I'm so scared." She screams. She screams again. He has an urge to break through the barrier and hold her, but knows he couldn't if he tried. "Baby. Baby." She cries for a while, the curves of her little body expanding and contracting among the ruffled sheets.

She appears so helpless, alone in the small room behind the thick glass under the hot lights. Enraged, he punches the brick wall. His fist throbs, but he doesn't perceive the actual pain, the disturbing view has put his senses in a state of numbness.

Leaning over, he catches his breath while her gravelly whimpers flow through the speaker to his side. Around ten seconds pass, then he steps to the intercom and says, "Sweetheart, come over here." Her back to him, she doesn't pay attention, her bare calves and feet the only parts of her he can see. The toes of her right foot curl all the way down, then up, then down, then up. "Honey." He taps the window.

About a minute passes, then she rolls over and stands on the shiny floor. She goes to him with slow, weak steps. She tilts her head up, blond strands falling in front of her tear-soaked cheeks. Up close he notices her skin is red, a fever burning below he assumes. Her eyes too, a crimson hue surrounds her radiant blue centers. It's apparent something's in her.

He presses his left hand on the barrier. She touches her right on top of it. They look at each other for a while, then she starts crying again. He kisses the surface and says, "Shh. Shh."

"I can't do it baby," she says, voice quivering. "I can't."

"Shh. Shh." He doesn't make a noise for some time. With his attention on the floor he says, "I need you to do something for me."

She peers into his eyes through the wetness on hers. "What?"

He pats the glass twice. "Be strong for a few days. Maybe a little more."

"I don't know," she says with hopelessness. How she nuzzles toward him reminds him of the way she lies with him on his couch back in Rome. All the days and nights they held each other there, talking about this thing and that, having sex, then talking about this thing and that some more.

"Do it for me," he says. "I might…please just trust me."

"What's the point?"

"There isn't a lot of time." He kisses the window by her face. "I have to go."

"Go where?"

"I just…I have to go."

"No," she says with a high-pitched squeal, yanking her palm away.

"I have to go."

"No." She whacks the glass in anger, a rumble blaring through the entire area. "James. No."

Alarmed by the banging sound, a security guard wearing a white collared shirt with the Swiss flag on the shoulder barges inside. He scans the scene, stopping on the weeping girl. "What's going on here?" he asks Sean in the native language.

"Let us be," Sean says in German with defiance.

The guard clasps his leather jacket. "Let's go." He begins dragging him toward the exit.

"I love you," Sean says to her, legs kicking under him.

"No," she says, still pounding the window. The yelling overwhelms her weak respiratory system. Wheezing, she drops to a knee.

"Baby?"

"Come on," the clinic employee says, swinging the door open, shoving Sean into the hallway. He lunges for the entrance, but it slams shut. He rattles the handle. No budge. He's locked out, Natasha no longer visible, nothing around but the cement beneath him and aluminum cages above.

Come to Me Scared Princess

About twenty minutes later Sean is advancing through a popular city mall, hundreds of people bustling, voices young and old and in-between going back and forth in German, mellow jazz music spilling from speakers.

Glancing at an overhead sign, he veers right. LCD screens on both sides of the hall advertise products via soundless video, neon shine from the monitors dancing on the side of his face. He closes in on an electronics store, weaving through a group of kids his age toward the automatic glass entrance.

He steps inside, shelves sparse after the recent Christmas shopping blitz. Skimming the aisle names, he heads toward the laptops area. He clutches a MacBook Pro, then turns into the music section and picks out a set of headphones, large studio-grade ones that cover the ears.

He carries both items to the cashier. "How're you paying?" she asks in the local language, scanning them. He hands her a credit card. She studies it for a moment, then swipes it and passes it back, glimpsing his bloody shirt and bruised chin. "Thank you Mr. Crates."

A bit later he's outside climbing into a taxi with a light-blue plastic bag from the store. He situates it on the cloth seat next to him, closes the door, and blows in his hands. "Where to?"

the cabbie asks in English, spotting him in the rearview, gauging him as American.

"I need a hotel."

"I can take you to a lot of hotels. What kind?"

"Something with internet in the rooms. And a desk. Nothing too noisy either."

He's still for a moment, then nods as if he has a place. He pulls onto the road, tall streetlamps on both sides throwing cones of light through the air, snowflakes floating in the beams. He makes eye contact with his passenger in the mirror and asks, "You here on business?"

"No."

"Pleasure?"

"No."

They don't talk for a while, driver glancing at him every minute or so, an unwavering concentration on the kid's expression that intrigues him. Sean peers out the window at the rooftops whipping by, moonlight glimmering on about half, shadows blanketing the others.

In a bit they coast to a halt at the Hotel Merden, mounted on a hill next to a stone chapel. Sean hands him some cash and exits into the night with his new things, flecks of ice in the wind nipping his cheek. He scales the hill toward the entrance, church bells ringing above him.

In about fifteen minutes he's marching down the fifth-floor hall of the hotel, tables with orchid flowers in vases at each end, recessed lighting on the ceiling. He stops at a door labeled "5327," slips his Hotel Merden keycard in the slot, and opens it. He enters the dark room, snow from his clothes sprinkling onto the blue carpet. Flipping the light switch, he illuminates a bed with a striped comforter, white-lacquer desk, oil painting of a ship at sea.

He tosses his bag of electronics on the mattress, pillows toppling from its weight, and grasps the Apple laptop box, still chilly from outside. He sits at the desk and slides the computer out, then sets it down. Lifting the screen, he catches his reflection in the black glass. He thinks about how focused he is, hasn't had a look like this his whole life.

The MacBook hums as he plugs it in. A white glow radiates on his face. He enters the required setup data, then connects to the hotel Wi-Fi. With a push of his boot heel he rolls himself in the chair to the bed, shimmies his headphone package from the shopping bag, and opens it. He frees the product from its plastic casing, its black wire springing out and dangling to the rug. He inserts the jack into his phone. Opening its music player with one hand, he wraps the earpieces around his head with the other. He scrolls to the album *Siamese Dream* by The Smashing Pumpkins. He hits play.

The first song pumps. He lets it take over him, closing his eyes, bouncing his knee. The analytical mindset he's been suppressing the last few years starts resurfacing, a constant questioning of things, an inclination to dissect ideas down to their component parts, a need to solve.

He imagines the virus inside his girlfriend. He pictures it laughing at him, smug in the wake of the tens of thousands of doctors who tried and failed to defeat it in the past. The disease has won so far. But it hasn't come across him yet.

He taps his fingers on the Mac's black keys, deciding where to begin. He remembers Dr. Obrecht mentioning an experimental drug discussed at a Paris conference by a company called Colzyne Systems. He figures that's the best place to start.

Visiting Google, he searches for "Colzyne Systems Paris medical conference." The top result is a PDF of a transcript from something called the Legrand Medical Assembly. He selects the link and reads the entire forty-three-page document in a little over a minute and a half, every iota retained. He learns the firm is in fact working on a genetic-based anti-viral serum as part of something it calls Project Michelangelo.

The meeting record only contains an overview though. Craving more information, he goes to the source. He Googles "Colzyne Systems" and clicks to its homepage, on it an image of a pretty lady in a lab coat, graphic of a DNA strand in her palm, "Our Work Is Your Life" in bold letters above. Since the corporation would never post Project Michelangelo material on its public website, he realizes he needs to hack the site and break into its server.

He cracks his neck, then knuckles, envisioning the algorithm he created for the Traveling Salesman Problem. He downloads a hacking application and types in his formula. He runs it against the Colzyne firewall. In about ten minutes he busts through, gaining full access to the private network.

With a quick scan he locates everything related to the project. He opens and reads the first file, a summary of tests performed with the latest version of the drug. Then the second, an analysis of where the mixture fell short in the experiments. Then the third, a chemical diagram of the eight major ingredients used. Perusing all three documents in just a few minutes, he becomes aware the company has started something but is far from finishing it, the medication having major holes, no possibility even for human trials.

He opens a fourth file, containing solutions engineers have proposed to fix the problems. He reads all twenty-three and concludes none of them would ever work. The engineers were overlooking things, important things deep in the details that he can see. If he's going to do this he needs to think of something new, something the other minds haven't even considered.

He looks out the window, Lake Zurich stretching to the horizon, little dots of people circling it, moon casting its light on everything. He pores over the medical possibilities. For a while. An hour passing, then two, then five.

He gets up, walks to the bathroom, and turns on the sink. Bending, he gulps cold water, then splashes some on his forehead. He smacks his right cheek twice, grunting, trying to invigorate himself.

He leaves and begins pacing by the bed, corner of the striped comforter grazing his knees as he goes back and forth. He contemplates thousands of different compounds he might be able to combine with Colzyne's initial eight to finish the serum. He has to not only pinpoint the substances but the exact amounts, just as Herculean of a task.

His mind battles with a swarm of questions as he assesses how new chemicals and their portions would interact among themselves and the existing eight. Would any cancel out the others? Would they work but with bad side effects? Would they quiet the virus only for a patch of time, enabling it to regenerate in the future? He fights through these and dozens more like them.

He treads the carpet for about half an hour, palms tapping the sides of his thighs. Then he stops. A thrill bursts in his chest. He thinks he might have something. Rushing back to the desk, he yanks open the drawer and fishes out a hotel-stationery pad and pen.

He starts sketching a diagram of a genetic mutation, drawing dots, connecting them to each other with short lines. As soon as he's done he rips the sheet off, lets it fall, and begins on a second. His eyes are intense, his breath quick.

He writes for a while, his fingers sore, fifty or so pieces of paper scattered on the rug. His heart pounds. He's close. Scanning the sheets on the floor, he snatches one labeled "Path 3.2.3," then another "Path 4.9.5." He scurries to the corner, picks up one marked "MR37: Cascade," then carries all three to the mattress, laying them on the striped bedspread between the electronics bag and pillows.

He stares at them, the moon throwing ovals of light on him from the window. He has four new compounds, along with their amounts, he feels he can merge with the initial eight to complete the drug. He seals his eyelids and starts running the slew of possibilities through his head of the twelve substances combining, making sure nothing counterproductive can arise as their particles collide.

As his mind rips through the potential outcomes, it conjures up an old memory. When he was three his mother took him to a cognitive specialist in Philadelphia for an IQ test. After he broke the ceiling, the expert told them he never observed someone like the boy in his career or even came across documented proof of similar abilities. The results of the exam were the motivation for him getting sent to a special school. Sean descending from parents of average mental capacity, the analyst explained it was a random genetic mutation when his brain was developing in the womb that caused such a high level of intelligence.

He always wondered about that mutation. What caused it? Why him? The memory of that day in Philadelphia has haunted him his whole life, a constant reminder of how different he is, a constant reminder of why he had to go to special school, a constant reminder of why his parents are dead. For well over a decade he's associated every feature of the experience with torture, the colorful paintings of rabbits on the office wall, the nasally way the researcher spoke, the confused look on his mother's face when she was informed how unique he was. Each of these memories has evoked nothing but gut wrench in him.

However, as he finalizes the cure in the hotel room in Switzerland, his subconscious begins re-evaluating the event in Philadelphia. And the story surrounding that slice of space and time of his life morphs. The rabbits, the man's voice, his mom's expression, are all getting pulled out of their existing cave in his head and becoming reborn in a brighter nook. This is happening because he's convinced himself in the last couple minutes that maybe, just maybe, there was a reason those microscopic DNA fragments came together in the precise way they did in his fetus brain eighteen years ago. They did for this moment right now.

His eyes open. He solved it. The four new components work, their particles colliding and combining in just the right fashion. He's certain. Hunching over, he clamps the bed sheet. He feels drained of everything. His knees give out and his stomach drops to the floor, rug fibers pressing against his cheek. He lies there for about ten minutes, his mind focused on nothing but the rhythm of his breathing.

Once recovered from the initial shock of it all, he pushes himself to his feet. The answer in his head, he realizes he needs to make it a reality, a physical solution Natasha can consume. His attention darts around the room and stops at the computer, unauthorized information he hacked into all over it. He figures the first thing he needs to do is destroy the evidence. Any police interference can only slow him down.

He dashes to the desk, clasps the MacBook, and bolts into the bathroom, tugging the shower curtain to the side. He lifts the laptop high above him and spikes it in the fiberglass tub, screen severing from the base with a boom, a dozen or so dark keys shooting around the polished white surface. He flips on the shower, drenching the metal guts, eliminating any chance of someone repairing them.

The hum of the water behind him, he hustles out of the bathroom and starts scooping up his sketches, more evidence. He fills his arms with a heap of pages, dumps them on the bed, then reaches for the rest. He crams them in a pile, folds the striped comforter around it, and knots the top. Swinging the comforter over his shoulder, he snags a book of Hotel Merden matches with his free hand off the dresser. He clenches them between his teeth and exits.

Murmurs of two bellhops in the background, he advances up the fifth-story hallway. He enters a stair shaft, spirals his way to ground level, and bursts into the parking lot, three dozen or so cars around, snow plowed into tube-shaped stacks along the curb, darkness outside at around three thirty in the morning. Crossing the pavement, he approaches a dumpster, the weight of the bedspread digging into his collarbone.

The smell of garbage in the air, he stops at the metal bin, an open doorway a few feet to the side, sound of footsteps through it, a conversation in German about eggs, some laughter. He figures it's the room-service cooks. He heaves the comforter into the dumpster with a groan. He checks the entryway on the building, no movement, still just talk. Loosening his mouth, he frees the matches into his right hand. He breaks one off, strikes it, and watches the tip go hot. He tosses it in the bin, chemical diagrams engorging in fire.

A glow rising in front of him, heat hugs his face while the back of his neck stays cold against Zurich's winter air.

"What're you doing?" a voice asks in German. Sean turns to it, a man with an apron hanging out of the hotel, stare jumping with suspicion between him and the flames. Sean sprints away, the employee screaming something inside he can't make out.

Hooking around a corner, Sean races out of the lot toward the front of the property. He staggers down a hill, jacket bouncing. "Hold it," another voice behind says in German, angrier than the first. Sean twists his head to a chasing security guard, vein bulging on his muscular neck, nightstick bobbing on his belt. Sean cuts across the grass onto the road, the thump of the watchman's footsteps nearing, then zips through a muddy alley, spotting a strip of woods a little ways off, deciding to hide out in the brush.

He latches onto a chain-link fence with both hands, kicks the toes of his boots through two metal diamonds, and climbs. He flops one leg over the top, then the other, and plummets onto the dirt, losing his footing. He springs up, then ascends a hill into the woods. Hearing the heavy thud of rubber soles on asphalt, he makes out the guard in the alley with the nightstick in his clutch.

Wanting to elude his view, Sean plunges to the ground, then slides over the freezing, snowy earth, rocks scraping his chest. In a few minutes he's deep in the brush, out of sight. Assuming he's safe, he stands and catches his breath. He rolls up his damp shirt and inspects his sliced torso, a bit of blood, pain starting to settle in as the numbness from the frost wears off.

He removes his phone from his pants, looks up a US number online, then dials. It rings for a few moments. "Hi," he says, roaming among the icy trees, angling for better reception. "I need to be connected to a professor at the school. Merzberg. Computer Science."

He listens to the rustles of small animals while he waits. "Dr. Merzberg," he says into the phone with urgency, pressing it tight to his cheek. "It's...well. I suppose there's a lot I have to explain, but I'll do that later. I need your help. I'm coming to Los Angeles." He shuts his eyes, recognizing how non-believable what he's about to say will sound. "It's...Sean. Sean Malone." He rubs his forehead with his thumb and index finger, anticipating the reaction. Sure enough, the voice on the other end responds as he assumed. "It's not a prank dammit. Don't hang up. It's not a—" He glimpses the screen, call ended. "Shit." He kicks a rock jutting from the ground, then paces for a while, his boots leaving a hodgepodge of imprints in the virgin snow.

He dials again. "Hi, I was just on before with Dr. Merzberg," he says into the phone, his breath visible in the chill. "Would you mind connecting me again? Thank you." About a minute goes by. He hears a grumble on the other line and says in a rushed, desperate tone, "You have a picture on your desk of your wife and you on a boat in blue ponchos at Niagara Falls. When we were at the NSA together we ate pizza for lunch with hot peppers on my half and just cheese on yours." He nods as his old teacher says something back, a slight smile on him. "Yes," he says with relief. He pushes his fingers through his hair. "Yes."

Housemates

A silver Ford Explorer zooms out of an LAX Airport parking lot fifteen hours later, Sean behind the wheel in a fresh T-shirt, morning sun shining over Los Angeles. A receipt from the car rental company rests on the passenger's seat, "Merzberg" on it, the teenager too young to rent his own vehicle, the professor putting it in his name. He rides the freeway toward Pasadena, traffic not terrible the week between Christmas and New Year's with so many people on vacation, SUV doing a steady sixty-something miles per hour.

Being on American soil for the first time in four years is strange. He thinks about how modern the scenery is compared to Europe's, Renaissance-era buildings nowhere in sight, nothing but the glossy faces of malls and billboards for films he's never heard of. Even the way he's moving feels odd, a motorcycle familiar to him, a car something he's driven two, maybe three, times.

Being considered dead after the identity-change program, he was supposed to give the FBI a month's warning before he set foot in the US again, not done of course. But he doesn't care. He's part of something much bigger now, something much more important than any rule.

He cruises for forty minutes or so into the serene suburban pocket of Pasadena. He coasts through the center of town observing things he remembers when he lived here, street signs, bends in the road, patches of trees. He recognizes a deli he used to get lunch between classes at SoCal Tech, a shoe store Mary took him once, a curb he used to skateboard on with his childhood buddy Kyle. It all seems so long ago, much longer than four years.

He peeks at his phone in the cup holder, GPS instructing him to turn right on his old block, Penny Glenn Court. Leaning over the wheel, he peers at the places of his previous neighbors. A peach house with a swing in front a dentist and his wife lived in. A ranch with white shutters a single mother occupied with her two teenage daughters. A Victorian with a big front lawn a widowed man lived in.

He drinks in the sight of his former home at the end of the strip. It looks different, front door painted a new shade, basketball hoop now in the driveway, refurbished gutters. But it also looks the same, his bedroom window with its old blinds, Mary's too, unchanged square pattern on the garage door, old stoop, original-color wood everywhere. All the traces of the past are still there, even if among some modern changes.

About ten minutes later he pulls in front of a red house around a mile from the college, parks the rented Explorer just outside a fire-hydrant zone, and shuts off the engine. Taking a deep breath, he steps on the asphalt, air brisk but not close to as cold as Zurich's.

He passes a mailbox shaped like a bass fish with the address number eighty-six on the side, then strides down a stone path on the front yard toward the boxy home. He climbs a couple stairs to the porch and knocks on the door, a rattle to it. The professor's wife, a thin woman in her sixties with shoulder-length red hair, opens up. Gawking at him, she puts her right hand over her heart, left her mouth. "Hi Sean," she says in a faint voice, never having met him but having heard all about him. "Aliza."

"Hey," he says feeling awkward, the lady marveling at him as if he's risen from the dead.

He hears the rush of footsteps and notices the professor scampering across the foyer. Clutching the doorway rim with an anxious hand, he inspects his former student in amazement, then clamps his shoulders, brings him in for a hug, and says, "Oh Lord, oh Lord." Sean gives him a few pats on the back. The professor is still shocked he's alive, lingering in disbelief.

He's aged a bit around the neck and eyes but appears as Sean recalls for the most part, that bald head, that tire around his waist that never seems to go away no matter how many miles he claims to bike.

Hands in his front pockets, Sean rocks back and forth with a nervous demeanor, Natasha the only thing on his mind. The professor can sense his distress. Sean only gave him an overview of his dilemma on the phone, but he got the gist it's serious. He says to his wife, "Set up Josh's old room dear." Then he turns to the boy with a reassuring grin. "Sean will be staying with us as long as he needs."

That afternoon the three of them are sitting in the kitchen, pot on the stove with a ladle inside, aroma of chicken soup in the air, amber lamp above them from the 1970s casting a soft glow on their faces. Sean sips from a straw in his can of Coke, taste not the one he's used to, his world remaining flavorless with his girlfriend still sick.

Holding hands, the professor and Aliza are hunched over the table, processing the four-year life recap he just gave them. "I know every single ingredient I need," Sean says. "And I know exactly how to mix them." He inches forward. "I just need someone to get them for me." He glimpses the professor. "These are really powerful chemicals. Not over-the-counter stuff I could've gotten at a pharmacy in Switzerland. Most hospitals wouldn't even have them. A lot are unproven." He knocks the floral placemat with his knuckles. "But I'm positive it'll work. And I figured SoCal Tech should have them on hand as the number one research university in the country."

"It sounds like you really love this girl," Aliza says, head tilted to the left, her gold-heart earring dangling.

He nods. "Yeah. I do. I really do."

She spins to her husband, her red hair swaying for a second, then settling. "Honey there must be someone you have a relationship with in the Chemistry department that can get Sean what he needs."

"There is. I'll go over to his house today and run it by him. I don't see it being an issue."

"That's wonderful," she says with a smile. She keeps her stare on him, waiting for him to smile too, but his expression is serious and pensive.

He doesn't acknowledge her, instead, has all his focus stuck on Sean. He rubs his temples and says in a slow voice, "Sean." He inches the kid closer with two fingers.

He moves in. "Yeah. What?"

The professor clears his throat. "Sean." He chuckles, cheeks dimpling. "I've listened to every word of your story. And I am here to help you in any capacity I can. However, it was a lot of information you just unloaded on me. Between the FBI, then Italy, and your girlfriend. Natasha. And Switzerland. And Colzyne. The whole extent of it." He pushes his bowl of soup out of the way and situates his elbows on the table. "I may have misunderstood something. And please correct me if I'm wrong." He pauses. "Sometime between getting to Zurich and walking through my front door a couple hours ago, did you or did you not find a universal cure for all human viruses?"

Sean looks around the room for a while, magnets on the refrigerator with phone numbers of food-delivery places, purple sponge on the edge of the sink still moist and bubbly, pile of bills on the counter. "Well," he says in an even-keeled way, tilting back so just the rear legs of his chair remain on the floor. "I guess I did."

Scientific Reactions

Early the next morning Sean is crossing a SoCal Tech quad with the grown Merzberg son's old Little League baseball cap pulled low, shielding his identity. His eyes dart around under the brim, suspicious of anyone passing. Though he doesn't care if he gets in trouble for returning to the country without notice, he doesn't want any delays. If someone spotted him and word got around he's still alive, the FBI might overhear, come after him, and detain him.

The professor, a few steps ahead in a windbreaker and beanie, points at a dome-shaped building surrounded by palm trees. He marches to the entrance and opens it.

Sean peeks around, no people in the hallway, just a few bulletin boards and portraits of retired chemistry faculty. "It's holiday break," the professor says. "Just about everyone's gone. I doubt you'll run into anyone who knows you." Trying to be funny, he stands straight and stiff in an exaggerated pose, then lets out a big exhale. "Ease up." Sean doesn't find it amusing.

The professor veers right, his old pupil following, their footsteps echoing in the wide, hollow space. As they advance, Sean thinks about the challenge in front of him. Even if he gets access to the correct chemicals he still needs to mix them and bring them halfway across the globe without being detected by US officials, all before Natasha's unpredictable disease overcomes her. He starts getting anxious. "What does this guy know?" he asks.

"I kept everything a secret as you suggested. I told him last night you're a visiting student from Canada who needs some chemicals for an independent study you're doing with me."

"How the hell did you convince him I need exotic chemicals to work on a computer project?"

"I said you were writing an algorithm to predict the movement of particles when volatile substances combine."

"Okay, that works I guess," he says, stare on the floor. The kind of tile, glossy beige highlighted with small gray squares, is familiar to him, the design used throughout many university facilities.

He recalls the last time he saw it, in an administrative office the day he dropped out. He remembers how he felt then, overwhelmed by the world. He reflects on Italy and how much he'd grown after meeting Natasha, life having a natural ease to it, things starting to make sense. But that comfort is gone. All is chaotic now just like on the day he quit school.

They come to a stainless steel door at the end of the corridor, the professor pulling from his wallet an orange-and-white keycard with his photograph and the term "Staff" on it. He swipes it through a scanner, green light turning on, slab freeing from its thick frame. They enter a laboratory, fifteen-foot ceilings, brushed-nickel ventilation units, high-tech gizmos all over.

A man with a horseshoe hairline, about forty, is slouched on a folding chair in the corner, crumpled McDonald's bag at his side, Egg McMuffin in one hand, cup of Hi-C in the other. He's thin in places he should be thicker, like his shoulders, and thick in places he should be thinner, like his stomach. The lab fills with a slurping sound as he sucks the last of his fruit drink through his straw. "Ah, there you are," the professor says.

Cramming what's left of his breakfast in his mouth, the guy stands, then shakes his hand. "Howdy."

"I appreciate you meeting us."

Still chewing, he says, "The next time I need a really annoying favor I know who I'm calling. Hint. It's you." He swallows, then laughs at his own joke, the professor forcing a smile. Wiping the corner of his mouth, the man eyeballs Sean. "And this must be the bright student you were telling me about."

"Nice to meet you sir," Sean says, locking grips with him.

"Hank."

"I can't even begin to tell you how important this is to me. Thank you."

"So I understand you're looking for some chemicals." He smacks his left palm on his khakis, knocking the muffin crumbs off. "You came to the right guy."

The professor says to Sean, "Hank here is the top chemist at the university. He gets flown to conferences around the world. Consults for all sorts of biomedical firms. Guest lectures at prestigious societies—"

"If my wife talked about me like that I might get laid more than once every six months," he says, again chuckling at his own line. He lifts his paper cup in front of his face and shoots it at a metal garbage can five feet away. It clangs against the rim, ice cubes flying all over. "Don't let me forget to grab a janitor for that later." He strolls toward a set of cabinets on the wall as the other two glance at the mess. He unlocks the doors with a key, revealing hundreds of test tubes racked in symmetrical rows with colorful liquids at the bottoms. "Welcome to a drug addict's paradise."

Sean gapes at the glass receptacles, sun streaks from the window glinting on them, the cure right in front of him so palpable and real. "Kid, you got anything for me?" Hank asks. "Merzberg said you had a list or something."

Sean reaches into his jeans, slides out a piece of yellow notebook paper folded twice over, and passes it to him. "They're all on here."

He peels it open and lays it on a table. Scratching his neck, he reads it. He reads it again.

"What do you think?" the professor asks, discerning some apprehension in his expression.

He tucks the page in his chest pocket and says to the kid in a deadpan voice, "That's not your run-of-the-mill request."

"I realize," Sean says, agreeable. "But a place like this should have it all, right?"

He juts out his chin. "Tell me a little more about this project you're working on."

"It's an algorithm for predicting changes in the positions of particles."

A pause. "Particles, huh?"

He nods. "When chemicals combine. Ones that behave… impulsively."

Hank taps the pocket he put the list in. "You bet your ass this stuff behaves impulsively."

"I'm aware they're…potent. But I need them. And I'll take full responsibility."

The professor steps closer to Sean and says, "I vouch for him. I'll shoulder just as much responsibility for the handling of the substances as him. If anyone from the university has any doubts, send them to me."

Hank doesn't speak for a while, his demeanor distrustful as he watches Sean. "Give me some time. I'll get back to you tomorrow."

"Tomorrow?" Sean asks, hoping for a quicker turnaround.

"Is that a problem?"

A couple moments go by. "No. Tomorrow should be fine."

"Talk to you then," he says, closing the cabinets, masking all those rows of colorful glass.

Around one in the afternoon Hank is alone in a booth at a dive bar near campus, bang of pool balls in the background, voice of a basketball game announcer coming from a TV.

Sipping his beer, he sticks his hand in his shirt, wiggles out Sean's sheet of paper, and flattens it on the surface. He stares at it for about ten seconds, then pulls out his cell phone and dials a number. It rings for a while. "Mr. Phlace," he says into it, tone upbeat and energetic as if he was on a job interview. "Hank O'Mara…yes. I was at your lab in Redwood City…in March…with Ike Marrow from Stanford." He snags a few cashews from a bowl on his table. "Yup…well I came across a little something today that I thought could be of interest to you." He chucks the nuts in his mouth.

Chewing, he says, "I had a student a few hours ago asking me for a whole bunch of chemicals. Unusual kinds. Supposedly for a computer-science project." He listens for a bit. "I'll explain. Now, I always get kids at this school bugging me for chemicals. They all have some wacky idea for some experiment. I usually just give them what they want and send them on their way. This kid before asked me for twelve of them. Now here's the thing…eight were identical matches to the ones we were analyzing in your lab in March. Exactly. Michelangelo."

He swigs his beer and says, "He's not actually enrolled here…never even gave me a name. Visiting student from Canada apparently." He nods a couple times. "Sure…I can do that. I'll let you know what I find. Thanks Mr. Phlace. And if you ever have any more consulting contracts don't hesitate to give me a ring. It was a pleasure working with all you guys at Colzyne. You too. So long." He hangs up and opens the SoCal Tech website on his phone's browser.

Logged into the faculty area, he scrolls through the contacts and selects "Steven Merzberg." He types "independent study" in the search bar, clicks enter, and gets back a chart of every study the professor ever presided over, containing the research subject, name and photo of the student, final grade, and semester it was held. No topics on there are related to predicting particle movement.

He scoops another handful of cashews from the bowl. As he chomps, something catches his eye, an older project without a grade, one called "The Traveling Salesman Problem" with a student named Sean Malone, kid in the thumbnail picture looking similar to the person he met at the college earlier. He Googles "Sean Malone," images of the boy during *Jeopardy!* appearing. Fascinated, he inches closer to the screen. He taps the link to his Wikipedia profile, reading:

Sean Malone, originally from Shipville, Pennsylvania, was a child prodigy and Jeopardy! *champion who attended the Southern California Technology Institute for five and a half semesters, beginning at age twelve, until he dropped out. Shortly after leaving the university, at fourteen, he was killed in a motor vehicle accident in Arizona. He was speculated to have had an IQ of approximately 250.*

Hank closes the web browser and says to himself, "Jesus Christ." He hits redial.

Blown Safe

Three mornings later, New Year's Eve, a suited man in his early fifties, *Wall Street Journal* tucked under his right arm, marches toward a monolithic tinted-glass tower in Redwood City, California, lasers of sun reflecting off the walls. He passes a Japanese-inspired garden, massive sign in the center with "Colzyne Systems" etched in black, "Our Work Is Your Life" in smaller writing below.

As he approaches the building, a bunch of people with corporate badges on their waists clear out of his way. "Good morning Mr. Stone," the doorman says with a nod, pushing open the entrance.

"Hello," he says without looking at him. He scans his ID card on a sensor by the elevator. Stepping inside, he presses "17," the second-highest-numbered button.

"Can you believe this Goddamn bond market?" another suited man asks, sliding in before it closes.

"Our stock's already down a quarter percent this morning," Stone says to him, no eye contact.

"I don't see it stabilizing before the next earnings call."

"Thanks for bringing that up."

The man laughs and asks in a dry tone, "Happy New Year, huh?"

"Yeah," Stone says, even dryer.

"You and Elizabeth have any plans for tonight?"

"Just dinner. We have an early flight to San Tropez tomorrow."

"Yes, that's right," he says, clenching his fist as if he made a mistake forgetting about the trip. "You go every New Year." The doors open. "Have a good one."

"Yeah." Both stride onto the seventeenth floor, veering off in opposite directions. Stone heads down a hall buzzing with dozens of executives and their assistants, a few original Impressionist paintings hanging, view of Redwood City's seaport outside the floor-to-ceiling windows.

He opens a room labeled "Bruce Stone – Vice President of Global Sales," tosses his jacket on a leather couch, and sits behind his desk, unfolding his *Wall Street Journal*. He crosses his legs, leans back, and reads about the bond market with a sour expression. He hears a knock outside. "Ashley?" he asks, still focused on the article.

A woman in business attire, late twenties, peeks inside. "Good morning sir," she says with timidity.

"What is it?"

"I just got off with Mr. Phlace's office. He's calling an emergency meeting. Between all the vice presidents."

Lowering the newspaper, he glances at her. "Emergency meeting? Now?"

"Yes sir."

"Because of the bond market?"

"I'm not sure."

"It's your job to be sure," he says, irritated.

"They didn't give any details. All they said was they need-ed you there."

"Jesus. All right." Standing, he gazes into a mirror, ad-justing his silk tie, examining his profile. "Have my breakfast waiting for me in here when I come down."

"Yes sir. Anything else?"

"No." She slips away. He pats the sides of his wavy chestnut hair, then exits, walks up the hallway, and returns to the elevator, hitting "18." In a few moments he gets off, a large set of double doors in front of him, "Donald Phlace – CEO" emblazoned in thick chrome letters.

He turns the knob and enters, a tall, fit man in a tailored black suit at a desk, an eight-foot-high painting of two samu-rai behind him. "You're late," he says to Stone.

"I'm sorry Mr. Phlace. Ashley just told me."

"Sit with the rest of them." He joins five other men in de-signer suits at a cherry conference table, an air of worry to them. Phlace, Colzyne's CEO, holds a gold letter opener with his manicured hand, tip digging into his leather desk mat. Eyeing his six vice presidents, he spins it for a while, then lays it down and picks up a thick laminated report.

He pushes back his armchair, rises to his feet, and ap-proaches them with the document, each avoiding eye contact with him. As he circles them, the morning sun in the window stripes his clean-shaven face, his skin tight for a man in his late forties, not a wrinkle on it. He dangles the heap of paper in front of them for a couple moments, then lets go, the blue backside smacking the tabletop.

They glimpse the title, "Colzyne Systems: IT Breach." Hands clasped behind his back, Phlace asks, "What are you people worth?" He fixates on an attendee, and another, then one more. "On average you all make what, about seven hundred fifty thousand a year? That comes out to..." He looks up for a few seconds. "Three seventy-five an hour. So in a ten-hour day each of you costs me three thousand seven hundred fifty bucks." He loops around them in a slow, deliberate fashion. "Times six and that's twenty-two thousand five hundred dollars. The daily rate for the lot of you." He stops behind a man with a big forehead and double chin and grips the back of his seat. "Vern?"

"Yes sir."

"Do you know what's in that report? That one right there." Phlace points at the inch-thick document. "Right in front of you."

The employee fidgets for a moment, then clears his throat and says, "I can guess sir."

"Oh, you can guess," Phlace says with sarcasm. "He can guess." He applauds. "Three quarters of a million dollars a year and I get a guess in return." He gestures at the report again. "This tells me that our computer network was hacked a few days ago. Hacked so badly that our most tightly held project, my golden baby, was stolen from under me." He slams his fist on the cover, a shake to the table, a grimace from some of the men. "So my question. Why, when I was spending over twenty-two thousand dollars on the six of you on Friday, did I need to get a phone call from some ex-contractor in Los

Angeles telling me there was a problem?" The room is near hushed for a while, the faint click of a chair spring, the groan of a hungry stomach, a cough.

"Sir, if I may," one of them says, the oldest, horn-rimmed glasses, rosy cheeks. "I read the analysis this morning. Verbatim. As you're aware I've been working with corporate IT systems since the late seventies. I've seen every type of hack attempt and hack defense." He folds his hands. "I logged into the network earlier. I inspected our entire security spectrum, pre-breach, then post. What happened to us last week was…it was a system intrusion foreign to anything I've ever witnessed in my life."

"What the hell do you mean?"

"Well. Picture it this way. Let's say a bank robber needed to break into a safe. And it was one of the strongest in the world. He needed to blow up the entire thing to gain access. Heavy explosives. Are you following?"

"Keep going."

"Now let's assume he successfully destroyed it. He blew it to pieces, collected whatever it was he wanted inside, and ran off—"

"Get to the point Meyerson."

"In our case sir, our firewall was destroyed in the same manner a physical safe would be blown up. Our cyber-security environment essentially exploded." He gazes out the window at the seaport, a block of clouds about to overtake the sun. "But here's the strange part. Every single piece of our so-called safe was put back in place perfectly after the intrusion. Almost instantly." He looks Phlace in the eye. "To be honest, unless you got that phone call and we scrutinized downloads of the Michelangelo files, nobody here ever would've noticed any sort of violation. There was no trace." He pauses. "Mathematically I've been trying to understand how the hacker was able to do that, especially with a firewall as sophisticated as ours. And quite frankly, I'm dumbfounded."

Phlace doesn't talk for about a minute as he processes what he just heard, then wanders to his desk and descends into his Italian-leather seat. Clutching the gold letter opener, he pokes the corner of a single piece of paper and drags it close. Lifting it, he leers at a printout of Sean's Wikipedia profile and says to the room, "Well we know who he is. The question is how do we deal with him?"

"Wait, we know who did it?" Stone asks, doubt in his voice since he missed the beginning of the meeting. Phlace slides the sheet to the edge of the desk, Stone getting up and grabbing it. "He's the hacker?" he asks, eyeing eleven-year-old Sean standing behind a *Jeopardy!* podium with his head sloped to the side.

"Apparently."

He reads the boy's bio. "Says here he's dead?"

"The contractor in LA assured me it's bogus. He just saw the kid in person. He said his face is an older version of the one in the picture. No doubt in his mind."

"What's his end game? Does he want to sell our research?"

"I think he may have finished our research."

"What?" He stares at the printout a while longer, grasping the magnitude of this potential disaster for Colzyne, then sets it down. "Why do you think he finished it?"

"This Hank in Los Angeles, who's a very accomplished research scientist himself, had a pretty convincing argument if you look at the compounds he's considering adding to ours. I already ran them by our chief chemist and he agreed. He's... onto something."

"If we know the substances he's using, why don't we just copy them and round it out ourselves?"

"It's the proportions. We have no idea how he'll mix them. That's the most complicated piece of it. Our chemist looked at it all night. He can't comprehend how it would exactly work. This of course doesn't mean there's not an answer. It just means we don't have it. And as I'm sure you can guess, without the proportions in our design diagrams we wouldn't even be able to use patent protection if he tried to sell what we started. We'd have no claim on any of it." That block of clouds in the sky takes over the whole of the sun, Phlace's creaseless skin darkening, then the rest of the room.

"We'd at least be able to take legal action on him for stealing—"

"Even if we could prove it, which would be next to impossible since he didn't leave a digital footprint, what good does that do me? Him getting punished just puts him behind bars, it doesn't give me the formula inside his head. It doesn't put any money in my pocket. If he sold it on the black market, could you imagine the price he could get?"

"It would be obscene," Stone says sweeping a nervous hand through his chestnut hair.

"But it's not his money to make dammit. The formula is ours to have. Not his. Not this quiz-show freak." He glares at Sean's photo. "He wouldn't even know what to do with it. We're Colzyne Systems. We're an American institution. A pillar in health care for a hundred years. It belongs with us." Hearing this, the troops around the table nod and grunt in approval.

"If we're not going with a legal angle, how are we going to handle it?"

"That's the point of this meeting," Phlace says on the verge of patronizing. "To figure that out."

"Where is he? This Mulaney."

"Malone. Pasadena supposedly."

"If we know where he is, let's send someone..." Stone leans closer and says with a murmur, "To, you know. Get him."

"I run a multinational biotech firm here, not a street gang. We need to be subtle about this. We can't just sic some random ape from the security staff on him."

"I have a name," he says with confidence. Intrigued, two of the other men wheel their chairs over, then two more, then the last.

"Name of who?" Phlace asks.

"Someone who does these sorts of things."

The boss leans back. "Is that so?"

"It must have been eight, maybe nine years ago. I was doing business affairs for a medical device firm in the Valley. We found out one of the lower-level engineers was planning to sell a blueprint to a competitor in Tokyo. They were going to make him an executive in exchange, give him a bunch of cash too. Felt the spec was his property because he came up with the idea, even though it was in his contract that any industry concepts he had while employed by us were owned by the company. It would've sunk us if the other group went to market before us. The engineer found out we knew what he was up to, so he went off in hiding. Our president hired someone…to find him."

A few moments pass. "Did he kill him?" Phlace asks, surprised Stone has a story like this in his past.

"No. No he didn't kill him." He drifts into a ponderous state. "That's not to say he wouldn't have if we asked. The fellow that did the job, though I only spoke to him for fifteen minutes or so, was the type who would do just about anything if the price were right. No emotions involved. He couldn't have been politer… but there was a mechanical coldness to him. Robotic almost. I've never quite seen it in anyone else. Gave us a number and did what he promised. We didn't need this engineer dead. We just wanted him not to move forward with the sale. And he didn't, after this man Dante…engaged him."

"Dante? Is that his first name or last?"

"To tell you the truth, I'm not quite sure. I've only ever heard him called that."

"Dante?"

"Yes sir."

Phlace looks out at the shadowy seaport for a few seconds. "Well, get me Dante."

Listen

Just awake, Sean climbs off an air mattress Aliza had set up for him in her son's old bedroom. He's in the same wrinkled outfit he's had on since being in the States. Peeking at the morning sun in the window, he realizes another day has come and gone, New Year's Eve already, Natasha that much closer to dying.

His skin is pale, his eyes glazed over with shock. He pictures her alone in that horrible little room six thousand miles away, hidden from the world, worried, withering.

Two days ago Hank asked for more time to collect the chemicals. After he didn't get in touch yesterday, Sean and the professor did everything they could to reach him, phone, email, even visit. Nowhere to be found.

Sean's body is exhausted and restless at the same time, no more than a couple hours of sleep, nerves keeping him up through the night. Stepping into his boots, he notices a small hole in the wall left by a ripped-out picture hook. He imagines what was mounted there years ago. A baby portrait of the son? A shot of him camping with his dad? A photo from middle school graduation? He wonders if whatever was there is still intact somewhere today, maybe the mantel in the grown man's current home. Or if it's gone forever, lost in translation between one move or another, crushed into the earth at the bottom of some landfill God knows where.

His thoughts have been dark the last couple days. Random things he's been coming across, such as holes in the wall, have been provoking questions with ominous undertones. He doesn't like it but can't seem to help it.

He exits and walks along the second-floor hallway, then down the stairs, Aliza in the living room with a cup of chamomile tea. Blowing on the hot beverage, she spots him. She's been subjected to the tense atmosphere in the house the last forty-eight hours just as much as Sean and her husband. She's aware how hard this is for the boy. She nods and grins, trying to appear as comforting as she can. "Where did he go?" he asks.

"He still won't give up with Hank. He went over there about twenty minutes ago to see if he can finally...cross paths with him." She has a slow sip of her steamy tea, trying not to burn her lips.

"All right," he says in an unenthusiastic way, veering into the kitchen. He grabs a red Solo cup from a cabinet and begins filling it with faucet water. As the stream splashes inside, he spots his cell phone on the table, a blinking light on it indicating a voicemail. Hopeful it's from Hank, he puts the plastic cup on the counter and lunges to the phone. With excited fingers, he clicks a few buttons and holds it to his face.

To his surprise the voice on the other line doesn't belong to Hank, rather, a Swiss-accented woman speaking English. The recording says, "James, this is Mrs. Vonlanden at the hospital. I don't know where you went...or when you plan to come back. Or if you plan to come back. For what it's worth, I'm calling to tell you the latest...news. She's...she's taken a rough turn that..." The flash of optimism that's been in his expression fades. "She has good spells, but more bad. She's in and out of consciousness. It's...her lungs and kidneys...down...as of this morning. The original two-week timeline isn't accurate anymore according to the doctor. She has another forty-eight hours. Maybe. When she's up she...asks for you. She really...you should come see her. Before..." She doesn't say anything for a few seconds, just the sound of crying audible. "For what it's worth." The message ends. He keeps the phone pressed to his cheek even though no noise comes out, flowing sink the only thing he can hear.

About an hour later he's in the den, flicking the straw in an un-sipped glass of orange juice, watching the liquid bubble for a few moments, then flatten. A plate of waffles Aliza had made him remains untouched on the coffee table. The professor is on the couch next to him, a blotch of nervous sweat under each armpit. They've been talking the last five minutes, since the professor got back. "You promised me Hank would come through," Sean says with hostility. "You promised dammit." He twists in his seat, too anxious to stay still, then points at the window. "I would've been on the ground in Zurich right now with it in my hand if everything went like you said it would."

"I couldn't have predicted he would've dropped off the planet like this. It's...bizarre."

"Why did he?"

He sighs. "Nobody can be certain." He scratches an itch on his right thigh with his elbow. "When I went there this morning, to his house, and had a chance to speak to his wife, all she said is that he went on a fishing trip."

"A fishing trip?"

"It appears fabricated, I realize. I never heard him mention fishing once in the two years I've been a colleague of his. As if she was under...instructions from him to lie. Odd. The whole thing." He dips and shakes his bald head. "I just don't understand it."

Sean takes a deep breath, right leg pumping from stress. "Who else then at the school if not Hank?"

"He runs the department. Anyone would have to go through him. SoCal Tech won't be our best route." He offers him a reassuring nod. "I have contacts at other universities. I'll call every one of them."

Sean glances at the clock on the TV cable box. "Another place? That'll waste time. We're a couple blocks from SoCal Tech now. We're more or less positive he has the chemicals. How couldn't you convince him to just give them to me?" He bangs his fist on the coffee table, plate and glass shaking.

"Calm down." His hand on Sean's forearm, the professor gestures at the waffles, top one on its side from the vibration. "Have your breakfast. You haven't had a bite."

"I'm not hungry." He pulls his arm free. "I said it a million times." Silence for a while.

"This...the thing with Hank...it...it wasn't the news I was hoping to come back with—"

"That makes two of us," Sean says, right leg pumping again.

"You're not making it easy for me. Let's…let's think about how we're going to change course here and try—"

"I don't have time to change course dammit." He stands, jeans drooping a bit, his waist thinner from not eating much all week. "I need the stuff now," he says, jabbing his finger in the air at the professor.

"Sean. Calm down. This isn't helping anything. You're flustered after getting that voicemail. Please."

The kid stomps into the kitchen, clenches a gas-bill envelope from the counter and a pen. He returns to the living room, presses the envelope against the wall and starts scribbling on the back. "Here's the name of the hospital in Zurich," he says, still writing. "And her room number. Call her up. Ask her how she's doing. Listen to her voice. Listen to how scared she is." He smacks the paper on the table. "I heard it the other day. I know what it sounds like. Listen to it for just a word." He holds up his index finger. "And then look me in the eye and tell me I should calm down."

"Sean—"

"One word," he says, swinging his arm, knocking his juice glass and syrupy plate on the floor, staining the rug with a blend of orange and brown liquid. He storms toward the front door and rips it open.

Blowing in his hands, he crosses the lawn onto the blacktop, a fog hanging over Pasadena. He roams the streets for a while, going nowhere in particular, wrestling with his brain. The last two days his thoughts have taken on the sensation of physical weight, feeling to him almost like small metal coins clunking around his skull, trying to fit into slots.

A bit later he's on line in a coffee shop, craving some sort of stimulant, hoping it can help get his mind straight. "What would you like sir?" the girl at the counter asks.

"Large coffee. Black."

"Room for milk?"

"No. Black." He glares at her. "I just said that."

"I'm sorry, I missed it. One ninety-five." He hands her two singles and she sets a nickel down, but he doesn't even notice it. "We have a fresh pot brewing. It'll be just a few minutes."

He moves to the side and gazes out the window at the misty parking lot, a young mother yelling at her child on the way to their car, a van trying to squeeze into a compact spot, two elderly ladies getting out of a long Cadillac. "Sean?" a loud voice asks. He spins around, his old friend Kyle standing at the back of the line, eighteen now, UCLA sweatshirt on, shocked expression. "Sean Malone?" Splitting from the row of customers, Kyle approaches. "Is that you?"

Sean glances at him, then the floor, then him. Rubbing the back of his neck, he nods. "Yeah," he says, wishing they could've reunited at a better time, not wanting to chitchat now. "What's up man?"

"No. No way." Kyle wraps his arms around him. "Holy shit. I thought you were dead." People peek at them, word "dead" drawing some attention.

"No," Sean says in a spiritless tone. "Not dead."

"What the hell happened to you? I thought you got killed in a car crash?"

"It's a…long story." Sean surveys him. He looks different, face longer than it used to be, hair still black and pin-straight but much shorter. He soaks in this new appearance for a while, then darts his eyes around the coffeehouse with suspicion, calculating the probability anyone else inside recognizes him, then the probability of one of them talking about it, then the probability of the FBI coming across the information. He starts to regret leaving the house.

"I want to hear the whole story," Kyle says with eagerness. "Holy shit." He slaps his palm on his forehead. "I can't believe this is happening."

"Sir, your coffee," the attendant says to Sean, placing a paper cup on the counter, viewing him now with some intrigue after overhearing he was presumed dead.

He grabs it, has some, and wanting to avoid the public, says to his old buddy, "Let's go outside man. Come on." The coffee was too hot to drink. He needed a break from Kyle's intense stare, the beverage his only available distraction, a sip making sense just a moment ago. The roof of his mouth is burnt.

Running his tongue over the sore spot, he walks across the place and out the door. He sinks to a curb, Kyle joining a foot to his right. The fog has gotten thicker, clouding their view of each other even twelve inches apart. Kyle peers through it at the ghost, still amazed by all this, and says, "Dude you're blowing my mind."

Sean forces a chuckle, attempting to come off as empathetic to Kyle's astounded state, but his emotions are too numb for much of a conversation. He ponders Kyle's physical changes. He'd visualized him a bunch of times in Italy, wondered what he was up to back in the States. In all thoughts he'd appeared different than he does now, taller than he was at fourteen but with the same face shape and hair. Sean finds it strange to think he'd been envisioning something not real all those times, even if just small details.

He has some coffee, trying to shield his mouth burn with his tongue as he swallows, then says, "It's good to see you."

"It's great to see you too. You should've heard the rumors around town, dude. A few people thought the car-accident thing sounded fake. They said you were really abducted by aliens. You know, to harness your brainpower. A few kids even said they saw it happening. Light coming from the ship and beaming you up. I didn't buy it." He shrugs. "I didn't know what to think."

This would've bothered Sean in the past, wild rumors attached to his name. But it seems so insignificant now. He has bigger problems to deal with, real problems. "Sorry bro, but I've got some shit to do. I'll give you the whole story some other time." He stands. "I got to go now though."

"I hear you homie." Kyle gets up and hugs him. "Great to have you back."

A few moments pass. "I wouldn't really call it back."

"You're not here for good now?"

He's quiet for a while. "I don't know what I am right now."

Kyle can detect the distress on him. He remembers this look, the day he dropped the OxyContin off four years ago. "Well, hit me up when you can get together. I still have the same number."

"Yup. One more thing. Don't mention to anyone you saw me. Okay?"

Kyle can tell he's serious about this. "Yeah bro. Will do."

"We'll catch up. I promise." Sean turns and starts walking off.

"Wait," Kyle says with urgency. "You might as well have this now." He pulls something out of his wallet. "No need for it anymore." Curious, Sean returns to him. He hands him a creased old photo of the two of them in their baseball uniforms, both twelve years old. "After they said you were dead I kept it on me. You know, to remember you by." He lets out a soft laugh. "I also thought it would bring you back somehow. Kind of dumb, I realize a picture doesn't have the power to do things like that." He pauses. "Well, you're here now, so I guess I don't need it anymore. Figured you might as well have it."

Grasping the corner, Sean gazes through the fog at the slice of captured space and time, recollecting the exact moment. "Thanks man," he says, sliding the photo in his back pocket, appreciating the influence he must have had on Kyle's life for him to carry around his picture for that long. The guys wave to each other and go their separate ways.

Advancing into the haze, Sean starts thinking about Natasha and the influence he's had on her life. His insides get heavy when he realizes that pending a miracle he won't be able to do this next big thing for her and she may soon only exist as a photo in his wallet, just like he existed as one in Kyle's after getting smashed by a truck on his way to a camping trip in Arizona.

Outs and Ins

That night Dante, the man Stone recommended to the others at Colzyne Systems, drives a black Lincoln town car with tinted windows on the 101 Freeway toward Los Angeles. He's Native American by heritage but hasn't worn his hair long or dressed in tribal attire since leaving the reservation for the military over twenty years ago. He has a crew cut and athletic frame, maintaining the appearance of a combat soldier even in his early forties. The surfaces of his almond-shaped eyes are pure white, no little red veins or other imperfections, and his brown irises are so dark they almost look black.

In about an hour he enters Pasadena's Fresh Stop convenience store. Passing a display of New Year's hats and blowers, he walks to the magazine rack, plucking *Popular Mechanics*, *Hunting*, and *Muscle & Fitness*. He heads to the counter and places them down. As an attendant keys the prices on a register, Dante glances around, the backdoor, the window, the security camera in the far corner.

The employee jams the magazines in a small plastic bag and says, "Fourteen seventy-eight." He hands him a twenty and the man peels some singles from the drawer. "Thank you sir." Dante collects the change and bag and exits into the parking lot, glow of the store sign piercing the fog in thin rays.

He gets in the Lincoln, pulls out, and cruises a minute or so. He turns onto the professor's block, scanning the house numbers, slowing as they approach eighty-six. He coasts to a stop about a hundred feet outside the Merzberg home and shuts off the engine. He glimpses the time on his Rolex watch, then adjusts his fitted gray suit in the rearview. Reaching to the passenger's seat, he removes an In-N-Out cheeseburger from a to-go bag, unwraps it, then bites. Gaze on the front door, he waits.

Inside the residence, the professor flips through a heap of papers on his dining room table with his reading glasses on, each sheet filled with names and contact information of chemistry faculty in California universities, vase, decorative plates, and fruit bowl removed and stacked on the rug to make room.

He stops on a page and dials a number on his phone. "Hi," he says into it. "Marshall, this is Steven Merzberg from SoCal Tech…yes, the Lonheimer Conference. How are you? Excellent. I'm sorry to be a disturbance, but I'm in desperate need of a favor. I'm searching for some chemicals for a project. Tonight." He listens for a while, expression subduing. "I understand. Yes I realize it's New Year's Eve. All right. Enjoy the party. So long." With a sigh he hangs up and continues poring over the sheets.

Sean's body is stiff on the couch in the den one room over, live footage of Manhattan's Times Square on the TV, the New Year Ball in the background hours away from dropping, bubbly female announcer in earmuffs introducing a pop band about to perform. He can overhear the professor's frantic shuffling of paper above her voice.

Aliza enters, a cup of chamomile tea in each hand. She rests one in front of Sean and sits next to him with hers. "Have some of this," she says. "It'll help." She pats his knee. "Steven will find someone. Don't worry."

He observes the steam rising from the drink, how it curls and disappears reminding him of his breath in the cold weather the last night he saw Natasha in Zurich. He looks at Aliza sipping. The way the light from the screen hits her gives her red hair a kind of pink hue.

He starts fidgeting. "I'm gonna take a shower," he says, hoping it'll calm him down some.

"Okay darling. There's fresh towels in the linen closet."

He crosses the living room, carpet still stained from his spill earlier, then goes up the stairs, 1950's wood squeaking beneath him. He yanks a towel from a closet packed with over-the-counter medicine packages, brings it in the room he's been sleeping in, undresses, and wraps it around his waist.

Moonlight spills around the lawn's tree branches and through the window and onto the floorboards in diamonds. He walks across them with his bare feet into the hallway, where he overhears the professor on another call, tone of voice not promising. Sean goes in the son's old bathroom and turns on the lights, a bulb out, a shadow covering half the space. He peels back the Superman shower curtain and twists the handle, the plumbing groaning behind the walls.

He gets inside, water pressure low, a notch above a dribble. He watches the silver drain, a liquid stream winding around it, a gurgle below. Closing his eyes, he hums a song and sways back and forth, water trickling down his face. He thinks about death for a while, still not definite after all these years what becomes of people after they're gone from Earth. He pictures his sick girlfriend six thousand miles away without him, staring at the end. He feels connected to her at the deepest level, him a part of her and her a part of him. If she died, in a way, he'd die too.

"Sean," the professor says a level below, voice ringing with enthusiasm. Sean rips back the curtain and juts his upper body toward the door, moisture dripping from his hair onto the tiles. "Sean." He flips off the shower, ties his towel around himself, and bolts out the room. He trots down the stairs into the den, a trail of soggy footprints on the rug behind him. The professor, grinning with dimples, clasps his phone in his left hand, a piece of paper in his right. "I got one."

"You did?" Sean throws his arms around him, drenching the front of his shirt, and kisses his bald head.

"Quick, look up flight times. San Francisco International." He points at his laptop on the table with a trembling finger. "Get on the next one out. A colleague of mine, Victor Case, will pick you up from the airport, drive you to his lab at Benley University, and gather the chemicals for you. I'll give you all his contact info."

"Thank—"

"Thank me later dammit. Go. Find a flight."

About fifteen minutes later Sean comes down dressed, *Easy Rider* sunglasses hanging from his collar. He shakes the professor's hand and says, "I'll call you when I land."

"Good luck boy." He smacks Sean's shoulder, holding it for a couple moments before letting go.

Sean walks to Aliza, sipping her tea by the kitchen entrance. He hugs her. Balancing her cup with one hand, she pats his back with the other and says, "I want to meet her someday. Promise me."

He nods. "I promise." With a wave he strides to the door, pushes it open, and steps into the fog.

Left

Through the mist, Dante watches someone walk up the Merzbergs' stone lawn pathway, a match of his target's age, gender, and height. He lowers his *Popular Mechanics* magazine and spins his key in the ignition. As the kid climbs inside his Explorer, Dante creeps onto the street, headlamps slicing through the haze. Keeping some distance, he follows the Explorer as it coasts along the block, its red brake lights radiating in the darkness in front of him.

Sean puts on the radio, a classic rock station, "Crystal Ship" by The Doors playing. He leans forward to see better, fog impairing visibility. Chilly, he turns on the heat, vents blasting cold air for a while, then warm.

As he crawls toward the main road, Dante's Lincoln sedan appears in his rearview, only other vehicle around. Sean passes some businesses, all closed, pharmacy, cleaners, dentist. He turns right. So does the other car. He drives for about a minute, reaches a stop sign, then makes a left. So does the Lincoln. Studying it in the mirror, he attempts to identify the driver, wondering if someone's following him.

He glances at the clock on the console. 8:03 PM. He figures he can spare a few minutes to make sure he's not being tailed before going to the airport, next available flight not for almost three hours. He considers whether the FBI found out he was back in the country. Worse, Paul Pine.

He assumes if the vehicle trails him for two more lefts, three in a row, it'll be going in a circle with no purpose other than to stalk him. He approaches a traffic light, pulling into the left-turn lane. The sedan does the same. The signal flashes green, the car mimicking him as he makes his second consecutive left.

He ascends a hill, dozens of big houses tucked away off the street on tree-dense lawns, haze heavier up the slope. It's quiet in this part of town, his radio the only noise around, "Waterloo Sunset" by The Kinks now on. At the next stoplight, he noses into the left-turn lane, a suspicious eye on his mirror. The sedan doesn't stop behind to his surprise, instead to his right. Head straight, he twists his gaze to the side trying to see the driver, nothing in return except his own reflection in the tinted window.

The signal turns green, Sean hooking his third left. He glances back, the sedan idling. He distances from it, mulling over why it isn't moving. He advances for a while, then almost loses control of the Explorer as a white shine wraps it, the Lincoln's high beams on for the first time. He squints to battle the glare. Motor revving, the Lincoln speeds up. "Shit," Sean says to himself, a gust of nausea in his stomach. He pushes hard on the pedal, accelerating to sixty-something miles per hour.

He takes a sharp right onto a double-yellow-line road, brakes screeching, skid marks burning into the asphalt. The sedan makes the same turn. Listening to the roar of the chasing vehicle, he figures something other than a town-car engine must be under its hood.

They fly into a business district, sidewalks filled with drunk people barhopping for New Year's. Sean sees a yellow light ahead and decides to floor it to make it through. He cuts across the four-lane intersection at close to eighty miles per hour just in time, cars honking at him.

He spots the sedan in the mirror, stuck at the just-changed red light. "Ha," he says, banging his hand on the steering wheel in celebration. Swinging his attention back to the traffic, he notices a blurry octagon in his field of vision. He ran a stop sign while looking back, his SUV now barreling onto a crosswalk. He hears a girl scream, sees a young couple diving out of his way. He punches the brake before hitting anyone, the Explorer's rear whipping to the left, whole vehicle wobbling. It teeters along the street for a few moments, then topples, glass and sparks shooting as the driver's side grinds against the pavement.

It slides to a stop, smoke ascending, oil oozing from the bottom. Twelve spectators approach shocked. In ten seconds or so the passenger's door opens toward the sky. Sean squirms out battered, gravity slamming the metal slab back down, a wince as it strikes his collarbone. He lies on the side of the SUV for a few moments, gasping, still trying to comprehend what's going on. His heartbeat is so strong he can feel it vibrate against the steel shell under his back.

Groaning, he pushes himself to a knee, then stands. The onlookers gawk at him, busted *Easy Rider* sunglasses hanging from his shirt, specks of windshield in his hair. "Holy shit, dude," a Latino guy in a Dodgers cap says. "Are you all right?" Sean doesn't acknowledge him, scanning the road through the fog for the Lincoln. No sign.

He hops down, landing on a pile of glass and oil. The observers aren't sure what to do. He decides he needs to escape, get away from the driver of that black car. He jogs toward a strip-mall parking lot across the street as the volume of a police siren in the distance escalates.

Entering the lot, he notices the left hemline of his jeans is soaked, red all the way around. Stopping behind a closed GNC store, he bends and lifts the pant leg, ankle flesh torn in three directions. Almost to the bone. He leans against the cement wall, a yellow cage bolted above, a single bulb in it, the only light around. Head down, he thinks about his next move, the initial shock of the accident wearing off, his body no longer numb, pain from the wound rushing in.

He makes out a dumpster in the periphery of the light beam, a sign on it saying "Dumping for Grand Pasadena 16 Multiplex ONLY." He remembers going there when he was younger, on Thursday movie night with Mary sometimes. Wanting to avoid being in plain sight of his pursuer, he decides to hide out in the theater and call the professor for help. He spots a bunch of doors along the building, back exits for all the screening rooms, a number spray-painted on each. He limps to the first, ankle throbbing, and jiggles the handle. Locked. The second. Locked. He tries a few more, all sealed.

He sees the one labeled "12" isn't shut all the way, a crease between it and the doorway. He opens it, the dialogue of a romantic comedy spilling outside, something with Paul Rudd. He looks around for a while, confirming that nobody is watching him, then slips into the dark theater, closing the door behind him, assuring the lock catches so it can't be accessed again from the alley. Eyeing an empty seat toward the rear, he hobbles up the stairs, favoring his left leg.

Back on the street, police lights are flickering, an officer laying flares around the overturned Explorer, two others interviewing bystanders. The Lincoln creeps from the shadows of a side road onto the main one, parking along the curb about a block and a half from the scene. The engine quiets. The beams dim. The driver's door opens and Dante emerges, inspecting. The cops. The wreck. The audience. He walks up the blacktop and merges with the crowd, tapping a guy in his early twenties on the shoulder. "What happened here?" Dante asks him, voice rich and deep.

"Some dude was doing like a hundred miles an hour. Flipped his ride. Dumbass."

"Where is he now?"

"He took off that way." He points at the shopping center across. "Probably drunk. Sure he's long gone. With all these cops around. A lot of idiots out driving on New Year's. Let me tell you bro."

Peering over his shoulder, Dante examines the strip mall, everything appearing closed except the movie theater. He crosses into the parking lot and begins scrutinizing the cars for movement under or inside. Nothing. As he marches along the concrete ground something snags his interest. He crouches, a drop of liquid glistening on the gray surface in the glow of the theater sign. He inches closer. Blood.

He observes a second dab a short length away, then a third. He rises, noticing a trail wrapping around the building. Eyes following it, he turns the corner, heading toward the back of the theater. Standing in the shadows, he looks for motion. Zero.

Rolling up his jacket sleeves, he approaches the dumpster, then buries his arm inside and ferrets around. In a few seconds he pulls out a rusty piece of cracked cast iron pipe. He stares at it for a while, then throws it about fifteen feet in the air. It floats for a bit, then smashes on the asphalt, fragments shooting all over, echo ringing. He scans the alley for any activity provoked by the unexpected noise. None.

Peering through the dull rays of the single overhead bulb, he makes out blood in front of some back exits, the most at the base of one marked "12." Stepping over shards of shattered pipe with his leather loafers, he walks to it, then tugs the handle. Locked. He returns to the trash bin, sticks both arms inside, and clutches another chunk of broken pipe. Grunting, he hoists it on his shoulder and carries it to the door. He wedges the top under the handle, bottom into the pavement. He kicks the center, lodging the door in place so nobody can open it from inside.

Slapping the dust off his hands, he veers toward the front of the theater and passes the line of people waiting to buy tickets. He studies the black-and-red LCD screen behind the glass displaying movie names and times.

He enters and gestures to the attendant, a chubby teenager on a metal stool texting. "Hi," Dante says with a smile. The kid nods, attention still on his phone. "I'm sorry to trouble you. My daughter and I are seeing *The Adventures of Winona McGee*. She has asthma and left her inhaler in the car." He pats the front of his jacket. "I grabbed it, but unfortunately she has both ticket stubs on her. She's in there all by herself. Would you mind if I went back in without one?" The employee peeks at him, then points inside. "Thank you my friend."

Dante analyzes the scenery in the lobby, customers with tubs of popcorn, a five-machine arcade, promotional cardboard cutouts for upcoming films. He sees a hallway labeled "1-8," another "9-16." He progresses to "9-16," follows it as it winds, then stops by theater twelve. He watches an older woman, the only other person around, stroll to the bathroom. The moment she goes in he clasps a fire alarm and yanks, a shrill screech consuming the whole building as small lights on the ceiling flash.

He walks a few feet from the red handle, leaning on the wall, observing the mass shuffling out of theater twelve, searching for any young males that appear to have just been in a car accident. Dozens of people exit, toward the back a kid with a bad limp and a panicky expression. Dante licks his top teeth, then bottom, a pre-attack predatory calm to him. He blends into the horde of moviegoers about ten feet behind Sean.

Boos and obscenities in the atmosphere, the patrons funnel from the jammed lobby through the front door and into the parking lot. Sean hobbles outside, his vision jumping from car to car through the mist in search of the Lincoln. He runs his anxious fingers through his hair, windshield particles falling off. Contemplating his options, he feels a hand clamp his shoulder. He looks toward it, Dante at his side, face inches away, a slight smirk.

Dislodged

Watching the sun come up, Mary drinks coffee from her balcony in Tuscany, already New Year's Day in Italy. She looks at the cypress trees along the countryside for a while in the orangey-purple morning light, then the patio where she had dinner with Sean and Natasha a few weeks ago. A chill in the air, she squeezes her jacket over her pajamas, her arms inside but not through the sleeves. "Leanne," Marco says from the connected bedroom, staring at her goose-bumped ankles. "It's freezing. What're you doing?"

"Oh, nothing."

"Come back to bed."

"I will. In a bit."

He walks to her side. "What's up?"

She sips her coffee, lukewarm now from sitting in the mug so long. "Something. Happened."

"This morning?"

"A few days ago. James called me last night to tell me, when we were at the New Year's party. My phone was in my bag. I just listened to the voicemail an hour ago."

"What happened to him?"

"Well…Natasha. It's her."

He puts his right elbow on the railing, leaning his chin against his hand, assessing his wife's tight expression. "Is she okay?"

She shakes her head, then looks into his eyes and says with affection, "I love you."

"I love you too," he says in the same tone, kissing her cheek. "But I already knew that." He chuckles, hoping to ease the mood. She doesn't even grin. Grabbing her wrist, he asks, "What's going on?"

"Natasha isn't doing good." The breeze hits them, thin material of her pajama pants flapping for a few seconds.

"What's wrong with her?"

"She's sick." She gazes at the wine-country hills, focusing on the little dots of bodies of three field workers on another property way off in the distance. They remind her of how skiers appeared at a park in Pennsylvania she used to go to with her brother, when she was having hot chocolate at the peak's lodge looking down at the base.

"She's sick?" he asks. "Like sick sick?"

She nods. "Sick sick."

Rubbing his forehead, he sighs. "Jesus." He's silent for a few seconds. "What does she have?"

"Ebola," she says, voice crisp.

"Wow." He absorbs this, his knees getting a little weak. "How the hell did that happen?"

"Remember she was telling us about that safari her family was making her go on? She came in contact with it in Africa. They think she must've brushed against a dead...chimp or something in the jungle."

"My God." Grasping the banister, he leans forward, his shoulders stiff. "What did the doctors say? Anything they can do?"

"It's incurable." She can't tell him about Sean's plan, something he informed her of yesterday as part of the frantic message he left her. He swore her to secrecy. "James isn't taking it well. As I'm sure you can imagine."

"I can't even imagine."

"I haven't been able to get through to him. His phone's been going right to voicemail all morning."

"Lines get tied up all the time on New Year's."

"He always picks up. Even if he doesn't he calls me back right away. I must've tried him twenty times. It's unlike him."

"He's probably with her. I'm guessing he's not in the mood to talk. You can't take it personally."

"I don't think he's with her."

"Where is he?"

She doesn't speak for a bit. "I...don't know exactly, but I'm almost sure he's by himself. Wherever he is...I just hope he's okay."

"He's a strong kid. So is she."

"Sean doesn't do good with this sort of stuff. With death. He never has."

"Who?"

"What do you mean?"

"You said Sean."

"Sean? No I didn't." Nervous, she brushes some brunette strands from her eyes.

"Hon, you did."

She turns her attention to her coffee, a small chip on the handle, her thumb running over the roughness of it. "Sorry.

Maybe I did. I do know a Sean from back in the States. My head is…out of it.”

“Natasha was one of the sweetest girls I ever met. I still can’t even believe it.”

“Right? Just some freak thing.”

“Man,” he says, surveying the natural creations around them, the slopes and the trees and the clouds and the sun. “I don’t get it. Makes you think.”

She drags her finger back and forth over the nick on her mug. “There’s only so much we can control.”

“I guess,” he says in a deflated tone as if he agrees but doesn’t like what he’s agreeing to.

A pensive weight seeps into her expression. “He was looking for someone just like her. Since he was a little boy.” She starts tearing up. “I remember this drawing he did a long time ago. He was maybe eight. I’m pretty sure he never knew I saw it in his room. It was of some house at the top of a mountain. In it there was a dinner table and a bunch of kids around it. Maybe ten of them. And he drew himself as an adult at the end. Wrote ‘dad’ across his shirt. At the other end he put a girl with ‘mom’ across hers.” She wipes a dab of moisture from her cheek. “When I met Natasha all I could think about was the picture. She looked just like the girl in it. The eyes. Nose. Hair. Everything.”

He thinks about this for a while, his sinuses stinging as if he’s about to cry too. But he holds it back. “No use dwelling on it now.”

"Her personality too. She was perfect for him." She hugs him, her head against his chest.

"Come on," he says, rubbing her back. "Let's not talk like that."

"He'd never be the same." She lifts her palm to her mouth, her face cringing as she weeps.

"We'll be there for him."

"You've only been around him when he was in a good mood. You've never seen him when he was…down. He's…he's been through more than you'd guess. Let's just leave it at that. He doesn't need anything else on his plate."

"We'll do everything we can." Looking at the dust in the creases between the terrace tiles, she ponders how much Sean's demeanor has brightened in the short while since he met Natasha. He had a relaxation about him when he visited last that she hasn't witnessed in ages, if ever. Patting her arm, he asks, "Should we send something? To the family."

"I'm assuming her mother's not cooking. Maybe some food. Hopefully they'll appreciate that. To the extent they can appreciate anything right now."

"I'll take care of it. Do you have an address?"

She bites her lower lip. "They're in Zurich. I don't have the name of the hospital though. James does."

"I'm sure he'll call you back any minute."

Flushed

Sean is slumped in the backseat of the Lincoln, slivers of windshield glass glimmering in his hair, head bobbing over his right shoulder as this man he's never seen before tonight drives up the 101 Freeway. Sean looks at his dead cell phone in the cup holder, gutted of its battery, then the console clock. 10:21 PM. He imagines the line at the airport gate for the flight to San Francisco he was planning to take, boarding in progress now.

They're north of Los Angeles, no traces of big city in these parts, wooded areas on both sides of the highway, a few closed businesses, dead quiet other than the muted drone of scattered cars. A yellow Jeep Wrangler cruises on their right, four kids inside around his age, two boys, two girls, glossy New Year's hats and beads on. He stares at them. One of the girls laughs, the shape of her smile reminding him of Natasha's, lips plump even when curled. He thinks about the first time he had sex with her, the way she giggled when it took her three tries to unbutton her jeans in the dark.

They drive north for about a half hour, now among the mountains of Ventura County, less vehicles on the road than before. Peering into the rearview, Sean tries to catch Dante's attention. He contemplates where he could be bringing him. He can see his irises, dark pits among his dove-white eyeballs, but can't decipher anything from them, blankness, no gleam of humanity.

Dante exits, rides a bit, then turns onto a ramp shaped like a candy cane, rocky ridges towering over them on both sides, no signs of civilization, howls and whines of animals in the distance. Road bumpy, Sean feels the leather seat vibrate under him as the car winds along. They veer off the muddy path onto a patch of weedy grass and coast to a stop, head-lamps radiating on a foothill across, shadows of small crea-tures darting through the beams.

Dante opens his door, interior lights illuminating him, then gets out and locks up. Listening to his loafers scrape the gravel outside, Sean tugs the rear door handle in a panic, a failed escape attempt, no budge. "Shit," he says to himself. Biting his tongue, he yanks the opposite one, same result, then the pair up front, no difference. Out here in the middle of nowhere, seems to him this man's going to kill him. His breathing gets heavy, sweat building on his arms and neck, heart thrashing.

He spins to the back window, trying to spot him. In a few moments he hears a sprinkling sound to the left. He notices his abductor urinating, a gust of relief setting in. He rests against the leather surface, back of his neck sliding a bit with the new coat of sweat on it. The man zips his pants, gets back in the sedan, and slams the door, a metallic echo ringing through the mountain air. He pops the car in drive.

As he proceeds back toward the highway, Sean asks, "Who's paying you? The Defense Department? The FBI?"

He chuckles. "No, no. I haven't associated with the government since I got out of the military. Private work is where the money is." He adjusts his grip on the steering wheel. "Does it really matter to you at this point anyway? Who's paying me."

Sean looks out the window at the silhouette of a large bird against the gray backdrop, no other movement around. He's trapped and distancing farther and farther from society, nobody out here to help him, nobody even knowing where he is. He has no idea how to get out of this. All he can think to say, "There's a girl six thousand miles away who's sick. Very sick. She's dead unless you let me out of this car."

The Lincoln is hushed for about a half-minute. "All you people are the same. It's funny to me. You're principled in a way. Idealistic. I can't say I don't admire it on some level."

"What people?"

"Ones that find themselves in the backseat of my car." He meets Sean's stare in the mirror. "You're all very similar. You have been for the last fifteen years, since I've been...in this line of work. It's always a plea to be let go. Followed by some story that's supposed to appeal to my emotions."

"You think I'm making this up?" he asks with anger, leaning forward with his elbow on his knee. "You think it's a... Goddamn...story?"

"I wouldn't say you all are necessarily making anything up. It's more your general outlook, your nature. I don't feel you can control it. You tend to not...run with the pack, if you will. Nobody ever hires me to track down the normal guy with the normal life. There's always...a sense of deviation about you people."

"And there's no deviation about you? What are you, a professional kidnapper? Doesn't sound too normal to me."

"I'm more normal than you would believe. In fact, that's my business. To restore normalcy. I'm just an extension of some of the most established, recognized institutions in the country. They contract me to...reinstate order for them. When someone like you tries to knock it out of sync." He has a slight smirk on his face Sean notices in the glass, as if he's mocking him. Sean retreats to the rear, folding his arms, pondering this man's intentions.

They don't talk for an hour and a half maybe, sedan advancing north the whole time. Dante yawns, tired from driving all day. He shakes his head and says, "I need food and coffee. I'm stopping. You're coming with me."

In a few miles he exits in Suddsfield, a small pass-through town, and approaches a Denny's sign glowing above the hill line. He cruises down Suddsfield Avenue past a few gas stations, a shoddy motel, some droopy power lines, not much else. He pulls into the diner's lot, a semitruck and a few older-model cars parked there.

He kills the engine, climbs out, and unlocks the back-door, holding it open for his captive. Grimacing from his ankle wound, he ekes out, transferring as much weight to his right foot as he can.

Dante nods at the front of the restaurant, following Sean as he limps through the glass entrance. As the man walks to the greeter stand, Sean studies the people inside, a trucker drinking coffee at the counter, a tubby fellow reading a newspaper in a booth picking at a plate of bacon, a busboy in a dirty apron clearing dishes off a table in the center. He wonders if he can signal to someone for help without being obvious. Would be tough he assumes, nobody appearing to even acknowledge him.

He turns to a TV bolted on the wall playing live footage of Times Square, the same broadcast from the Merzberg living room earlier, everything on the street now covered in confetti, Ball dropped a little while back, that bubbly female announcer's mouth moving but no noise coming out with the volume off.

He fixates on the woman's big fuzzy green hat, something he remembers observing back in Pasadena, an odd, spiky design to it. He recollects all that's happened between the first time he saw it in the den and now, seems like a decade though a few hours. His arms start to go numb from worry, things in the place spinning, the logo on the window, the brass buttons on the trucker's overalls, the green fabric on the TV. He closes his eyes and takes a few deep breaths, trying to get a grip on himself.

"Happy New Year," a freckle-faced lady in a Denny's polo says stepping to the podium. "Anywhere you want." She hands Dante two menus.

He shifts to Sean and gestures at a booth in the far corner. Sean hobbles toward it, taking a while to cover ground with his torn ankle. Passing the overweight guy eating bacon, he bumps into a chair trying to catch his attention, but it remains on the local paper.

Once at the booth, Sean slides over the brown vinyl seat, resting his left leg on the cushion, getting the pressure off. Dante settles in opposite, dropping menus in front of both of them. "I'm not hungry," Sean says, pushing his away.

"You're eating. And having caffeine. They want you alert when I get you there."

"Get me where?" No answer, just the pulse of adult con-temporary music from a speaker above. Arms folded, Sean looks out the window at the rundown houses scattered in the hills, doors boarded on a few of them, broken-down backhoe in the front lawn of one, his own flushed reflection in the glass. He debates whether he'd be able to lose this guy if he made it outside into the dark woods and hid. But that's a major if. He has no clue how he'd do it. He takes a few more long breaths.

"You ever have the Lumberjack Slam?" Dante asks. "It's delicious." He snaps his fingers at him.

"I said I'm not hungry."

"I'd recommend getting something in you." He flashes that smirk again, subtle yet demeaning. "Trust me. You have a long night ahead of you." Sean glares at him, then twists his focus back outside.

In a few minutes the woman in the Denny's polo pops by, a notepad and pen in her hands, and asks with some pep, "Have we picked yet fellas?"

Dante collects both menus, bangs the bottoms on the table to square them, and passes them to her. "Two cups of coffee. Black. And two Lumberjack Slams. Grits. White toast."

"Done and done." With a smile on her freckled face she walks off.

"The Lumberjack Slam is exceptional," he says to Sean, the lamp over them casting a strong light on the side of Dante's head, specks of flesh visible under his tight crew cut. "I think you'll enjoy it."

They sit in silence other than the adult contemporary music, Sean's gaze turning to the heavyset man eating bacon. He envies this person, his freedom, ability to get up whenever he wants and go anywhere he wants, a luxury he always took for granted until now.

The waitress returns, setting a coffee mug in front of each of them with the Denny's logo on it. She notices Sean's mangled sunglasses, still hanging from his shirt, nods at them, and asks in all seriousness, "Is that like a fashion statement or something?"

Peeking at the shattered lenses, he says, "Nah. I just wasn't careful I guess."

She considers asking him what happened but can sense he's not in a chatty mood. "Let me know if you all need anything else." She scampers off with that same grin from before. Dante lifts his cup and has some, Sean not acknowledging his.

About ten minutes go by, no talking, just the soft music and the slurp of Dante's sips. Sean watches the chubby man with the bacon pay his bill, get up, and leave. He pictures the tingle of the brisk rural air about to be on his skin.

Listening to Dante raise his mug up and down, Sean realizes he needs to do something to get out of here. Anything. If Natasha died he might as well be dead too. Nothing to lose. Time for a risk. He envisions what Bruce Willis from his favorite movie *Die Hard* would do right now. He's seen the film so many times but never thought someone like him would need to reference it in a real-life situation. He can't try to run away, not with this ankle, has to be something else. He thinks, that brain of his weighing all its options. Sure enough he has an idea. "I'm taking a piss," he says.

Dante assesses the exit door, a few dozen feet away, and figures the kid would never be able to outrun him if he made a go at it, not with that ankle. He gets up and looks in the bathroom, checking if there are any windows. None. "Take a piss then," he says in a deadpan voice, walking back over.

Sean slides out and limps across the rug, Dante following him with his stare the whole time just in case he makes a move. He doesn't, pushing open the bathroom door and entering.

He limps past a black-tile counter, a urinal, and an "Employees Must Wash Their Hands" sign to the single stall. He steps in, closing it behind, fastening the silver lock. His heart rate accelerates, audacity of his idea a bit frightening, things like this foreign to him. He zeroes in on the toilet paper holder, two cylindrical brass bars about three inches long jutting from the wall. They're perfect, just what he imagined.

Clasping the stall door for support, he lifts his right foot and stretches it to the toilet handle. He presses down with his toe, then kicks one of the brass bars, noise muffled by the louder flushing sound. It breaks off and dings on the tile floor for a few moments, then settles. Two sharp screws protrude from the back, bits of drywall in the grooves.

He collects the rod from the dusty surface, a dull light glinting off it. His little weapon. He opens an interior jacket pocket, stashes it inside, and zips it up. Dragging his foot, he leaves the bathroom and returns to the booth.

The smell of grease in the air, he shimmies into his seat, his Lumberjack Slam waiting for him on the table. He glances at a plate overflowing with two slices of bacon, two sausage links, two eggs, a piece of ham, grits, and toast. A pair of pancakes sits in a smaller dish to its right. He looks at Dante carving away on his own meal, eggs and ham already gone.

Sean grabs a syrup pitcher, drizzling some on his pancakes. He stabs a piece with his fork and raises it to his mouth. Then another. "I knew you'd enjoy it," Dante says. He chews with a smug expression, taunting even.

"You're right. It's really good." Sean has another bite, then picks up a bacon slice and bites off half. He raises his coffee mug to his lips, movement of his arm tightening his jacket, weapon pressing against his ribs, feel of it exciting him.

He finishes with a few more gulps and downs the rest of the bacon, getting as much food and caffeine in him as he can for his upcoming escape attempt. Holding the dry cup, he signals across to the waitress. She gives him a thumbs-up, then strolls over with a pot and refills him. "Thanks," he says.

"No problem hon." She moves the spout to Dante's mug, topping him off too.

"Thank you ma'am." He watches Sean, content he's eating and drinking coffee as told.

"How you boys making out? Everything tasting good?"

"Phenomenal," Dante says. "You can bring us the check whenever you're ready."

"I gotcha right here." She wiggles her pad from a blue pouch on her waist, plucks off the first sheet, and rests it on the tabletop. "No rush guys." She walks off, same smile.

About ten minutes later their plates are empty, used cups, utensils, and napkins sprawled between them. Dante slaps down a twenty and a five and says, "After you." Sean slides out, a hot pain streaking up his leg muscles as his left foot meets the carpet. He limps toward the exit, presence of the brass bar against his chest delighting and terrifying him at the same time.

They step into the night, town of Suddsfield still and sleepy. Dante unlocks the Lincoln's backdoor, holding it while the captive crawls in. He shuts it, then gets in front, sticking the key in the ignition, bringing the souped-up sedan to life, engine, lights, dashboard.

He reverses, turns out the parking lot, and cruises up Suddsfield Avenue toward the freeway, passing that dinky motel, those gas stations, those saggy power lines.

Sean leans forward, elbows on his knees, and says, "The food helped, but if I'm supposed to stay awake for a while more I need a pick-me-up. You got some music or something? It'll keep me up."

Dante can in fact go for some too, still has a long ride ahead and needs to stay alert himself. He clicks a few buttons on the stereo, a CD loading, "Disc 5" blinking on the console screen. "Walk on Water" by Eddie Money courses through the speakers. "Are you a rock fan?" he asks above the guitar.

"I am. Yeah."

"I prefer the kind of the eighties and two thousands. I never quite could get into the stuff of the seventies and nineties. And I don't so much appreciate what's coming out today. It's as if I skip a decade." He enjoys this, toying with Sean, knowing he has all the power. "Have any favorite eras?"

"I kind of like it all," he says, pretending to be engaged, focusing on his next move. He needs to act before they get on the highway and start going seventy-plus. "Any rock is cool by me."

"There must be some specific point in time you prefer?"

"I dig Eddie Money, I'll tell you that. That era is cool." As the tune pumps, Sean lifts his right hand to his chest. Viewing Dante's eyes in the mirror, he slips his fingers under his jacket. He feels for the interior zipper, pinching the rubber grip. Once the booming chorus comes on he pulls down, the clack of unhinging metal teeth muffled by the stereo. The pocket is opened. He maneuvers his hand inside, clutching the brass bar. The coldness and realness of it on his fingers send a thrill through him.

They continue along Suddsfield Avenue for a bit, the freeway on-ramp only a few dozen feet away. Dante eases into the brake as the road bends toward the highway, the sedan slowing to about fifteen miles per hour. Now. Sean rips his hand from his jacket and whacks Dante's face with the sharp rod, slashing his skin, knocking him unconscious against the window. Nobody steering, the Lincoln flails along the asphalt and bashes into a curb, then the black-and-white "101 North" sign, the abrupt stop propelling Sean into the back of the driver's seat.

Sean's heart pounds, his body crumpled in the valley between the rear and front, bristly rug poking the skin of his neck. He gets up, examining Dante's expression, making sure he's out cold. He is, eyelids closed, mouth open, a stream of blood flowing from a hole in his temple.

Clamping the wheel as support, Sean hauls himself to the front, his legs dragging behind him. He reaches over the listless man's torso to the driver-side handle, opens the door, and slides out. Panting, he steps to the pavement. He can't believe it worked.

He needs a phone now. He spots his in the cup holder, useless without a battery though. He kneels on the asphalt. With a slow, steady hand he extracts Dante's from his suit-jacket pocket. But the screen is locked, password required. "Shit," he says to himself. He figures he might as well deprive his enemy of it. He spikes it on the blacktop, busting it to pieces. He considers taking the car and driving it up to San Francisco to meet the professor's colleague. But he'd have to get the larger man out first. Any jostling could wake him. No good.

Thinking, he lowers his hands to his knees and stares at the dim glow of the businesses on Suddsfield Avenue, his heart still thumping, "Walk on Water" still roaring from the stereo.

Window of Opportunity

A round-faced woman in her mid-thirties turns a page in her *Us Weekly* magazine behind the counter of Suddsfield's only motel, the California Gold Inn, walls lined with faded tourism posters of state parks, Yosemite, Joshua Tree, Sequoia, couple others. She's alone in the lobby, quiet other than her rhythmic chewing of gum, a click of her teeth every two seconds or so.

A bell on top of the door dings, snapping the lull. She glances up at a kid barging through the entrance with a panicky expression. "How can I help you?" she asks, lowering the magazine, looking at him funny.

"I need to use your phone," Sean says with alarm. "Right now."

She studies him for a few moments, then nods at an old cord telephone on the wall behind her. "Only for motel employees."

"It's an emergency. Please. I'll be a second. Please."

"Sorry sir. My hands are tied."

"It's an emergency dammit."

She lays her *Us Weekly* flat on the counter, keeping her place, and leans forward with a squint. "Sir, if you keep using that sort of language with me I'll pick up that phone myself and ring the sheriff," she says, pronouncing "sheriff" with a tone of familiarity as if it's someone she knows.

"Please, don't call the police. You can't do that." He shakes his head. "I'm sorry."

"What you can do is get a room." She kicks her chin toward five keys hanging from hooks on a pegboard strip on the wall. "They all got phones inside."

He digs his hand in his pocket, grabs his wallet, and smacks the James Crates credit card down. "Give me a room. Any one."

As she punches the computer keys he spins around, gazing through the glass front door into the parking lot. No movement, nobody following him. He watches her take her time handling a manual credit-card-imprint machine. His good foot taps with anxiety. He needs to get to a phone, fast. He looks outside again, a pickup truck passing through, its abrupt alteration of the static scenery making his heart flutter for a split second in fear of the Lincoln.

He shifts his attention to the round-faced woman, peeling the perforated edges off some motel-record document, chomping her gum slower than before. She opens a file cabinet, sorts the paper among a bunch of others, then shuts the drawer. Once done she unhooks a brass key from the pegboard and sets it on the counter, a red plastic circle labeled "8" attached to it with a Zip Tie. "Through the door on the left, down the hall," she says, pointing in the direction of her words. "Last one on the right." He snags the key. "Mr. Crates? Your card." He returns to her with two hops on his healthy foot, takes it, and begins hobbling away.

He drags himself out of the lobby and down a four-room hallway, two on each side, nature paintings on the walls from some local artist, a howling wolf, a sycamore tree, a stream with a fly fisherman in it knee-high. Stopping at the last room on the right, he opens up and steps in.

He flips on the lights and seals the door, fastening the knob lock, sliding the chain latch through its track. He yanks on the handle to make sure it's secure, doesn't budge. He limps to the comforter, sits, and grips the phone on a three-legged wooden stand. Resting his sore left ankle on the mattress, he dials a number.

It rings for a while, then he hears the professor's outgoing greeting, the sound of the recognizable voice comforting in a way right now he never imagined a message recording could be. "It's Sean," he says, jumpy. "I'm somewhere up in San Luis Obispo County. I missed my flight. Someone…kidnapped me. A professional guy. Don't know him. I got away. Don't call the cops. They'll just delay things. I need you to get in touch with your friend at Benley University and tell him I'll be in the Bay Area soon. I'm gonna try to hitch a ride out of here and take a bus up. Something. I'll figure it out."

He peers out the window between the ugly drapes, darkness, no headlights, no pursuer, then says, "If I'm gonna make it up there in one piece I need to know who's after me. Get to Hank dammit. I don't care how. Figure out who he talked to. Who else heard I'm doing this. It's not the government. The guy tonight mentioned that. It's someone different. It has to be a connection through Hank. Nobody even knows I'm back except…you, Mrs. Merzberg, my aunt, and my friend

Kyle. And I trust you all. Hank. Find him. No matter how. Or bribe it out of his wife. I'll pay her. Seems like she knows something. Then call me here. At the motel. I don't have my cell. Call the front desk and ask to be put through to room eight. Okay. Eight. The name is..." He thumbs the key from his pocket and peeks at the back of the red circle, the motel's faded logo on it. "The California Gold Inn. I don't have the phone number. Get it online. Room eight. California Gold Inn." He glances out the window again. "I don't want to stick around here with this guy in the area. If you don't call back in twenty minutes I'm gonna split and take my chances getting to San Francisco without knowing who else might come after me. I'd rather have a Goddamn clue though. Call me back. The second you get this." He hangs up, heart pounding.

Resting his hands on his knees, he tries to gather himself. The physical sensation his thoughts have been taking on has intensified in the last half hour or so, heavy now to him like metal marbles banging around his skull.

He drinks in the details of this strange room in this strange town, purple carpeting, cheap bedspread with rows of multi-colored triangles on it, matching drapes, TV from the 1990s. He reflects on the chain of events that happened today leading him here, everything so fast he hasn't been able to process much at any level higher than base instinct, Hank's backing out, the plane ticket to San Francisco, the car crash, the movie fire alarm, the drive up to the mountains, year changing to a new one somewhere along the road, the diner, the bathroom stall, the toilet paper holder, the attack on that man, slow hobble up the street to this place. He begins to realize just how close and just how far he is from saving Natasha.

His insides burst with guilt from his gut to his throat. He wonders how he let himself wind up all the way out here. He longs for the past, just twenty-four hours of it, the hope he'd do something different though unsure what. A heavy marble of thought whacks into his skull, an image of his girlfriend gasping her last breath through a machine behind that six-inch glass wall in pod two.

The concept of a future without her frightens him, this room and everywhere he'd go from here seeming part of someone else's life, not his, his life lost somewhere along to-day's sequence of events, things ahead part of some alien reality he couldn't imagine living in.

Outside an eighteen-wheel truck idles by the freeway on-ramp, the rumbling of its engine drowned out by Eddie Money's "I Wanna Go Back," a few songs down from "Walk on Water" on Dante's mix CD. A trucker, late fifties, flannel shirt, rubber boots, jumps from the vehicle to the pavement.

In the shine of his headlights he sees the Lincoln butted against the busted "101 North" sign, door swung open, sil-houette of a motionless body in the driver's seat. He leans in his truck, clutches his CB radio, and pulls it outside, a spi-raled black cord stretching tight from it. "Blue Dog here," he says in the handset. "Looks like someone banged himself up pretty all right by the on-ramp in Suddsfield. Probably need an ambulance. I'll check it out. Over." He plops the radio on the seat in his cabin and approaches the sedan with caution.

Stopping about a foot from the car, he bends and gazes inside. Studying the left of Dante's body, he doesn't spot any injuries. He walks around the vehicle, peeking through the passenger's window, noticing a hole about the size of a quarter on the driver's right temple. "Jesus," he says to himself. He returns to the other end, grabs Dante's arm, and shakes, his body flopping around, expression remaining devoid of life. Sticking his index and middle finger on the injured man's neck, he detects a pulse. "Hey partner." He shakes some more. "Fella."

Dante's eyelids spring open, consciousness setting back in. He catches his reflection in the rearview, angling his neck to examine the head wound. The ghastly sight of it doesn't bother him, but the fact he let himself get in this position does. The trucker tries to help him out of the car. "Come on now," he says, hands on his arm. "You gotta get a doctor to give that a look."

"Get off me."

The trucker backs away, startled by the dismissal of good-old-fashioned common courtesy. "I'm just trying to help." He holds both palms up.

Dante climbs out of the sedan and observes his surroundings, the lights of Suddsfield Avenue, the hills, the dark stretch of freeway on the other side of the ramp. Feeling something under his feet, he makes out the smashed fragments of his phone. He figures the kid wanted to make a call. Since he had a password in place he reasons Sean had no luck and went off searching for the closest available alternative.

He turns to the trucker and asks, "Are you from around here?"

He looks into Dante's eyes, coldness, black holes in milky white, no gratitude for the help. "No sir. Modoc County. Born and raised. Drive through here 'bout once every couple months on my route though. You sure you're okay?"

"If someone were here, right where we're standing now, and that person needed to make a phone call, where would they go?"

"I can dial you up anyone you want from inside my truck."

"I'm not talking about myself. I'm talking about someone in general. Assume they didn't have a cell phone. Or car. And there were no other people around. Where would they likely walk to make a call?"

Hands on his hips, the trucker inspects Suddsfield Avenue. "Well you got a Denny's on the main road. But that's all the ways up. Before it you got a few gas stations." He scratches his chin. "I don't think they got pay phones though. I filled up there a bunch, can't remember seeing any pay phones. Like I said I can call anyone in these United States up right from my truck. Then you got a motel. I suppose they'd probably let you use their phone." Dante peers at the signs along the street, stopping on one for the California Gold Inn. He gets back in his sedan. "Sir, you good to drive?"

"You should leave. Don't worry about me. Or the car. And don't call the police. Make sure of that. Do you understand?"

Dante's unfazed demeanor disturbs the man. "Will do."

He slams the Lincoln door, drowning out the thrum of the idling eighteen-wheeler. He drives, moonlight glimmering on the dented grille, not much other damage to the car. He shuts off the music as he nears the inn.

He parks in the lot and enters the lobby, bell dinging above. The attendant lifts her eyes from her *Us Weekly*, lays it down, and asks, "How can I help you?"

"I'm trying to find my nephew. He needs my help. I believe he used your phone before..."

She fixates on his wound, bright lobby lights showcasing the depth of it. "What the hell happened to you?"

"What're you talking about?" She nods at his face. He shakes his head. "I'm fine."

"You ain't look fine."

"I'm fine. My nephew. Was he here?"

"Some kid came by a little while ago bugging me to use the phone, but I wouldn't let him. Motel policy."

"Did you see where he went after he left?"

"Never left. Got a room."

His eyes widen. "He's here? Now?" She nods, her attention still on the grotesque dent in his flesh. "What room?"

"I can't tell you that. Motel policy."

"Yes you can."

"Sorry sir. My hands are tied."

He lingers on her, then peeks out the glass door into the street. Nobody around. He taps his fingers on the counter for about five seconds, deciding whether or not to kill her. He could then go through the booking records himself.

It wouldn't make the most sense he concludes, cops would get involved soon enough, always a problem. Instead he peels a hundred-dollar bill from his wallet and slides it on top of her magazine. She gapes at it.

Sean, still on the bed in room eight, glimpses the antiquated clock on the wall, the second hand quivering a bit after moving to each new notch. Tick. He glances at the phone next to him, quiet. Tick. He looks back at the clock. Tick. Then the phone again. Tick. He's angry with the professor though he assumes his excuse is innocent, sleeping in all likelihood. Tick. Call, come on, call. Nothing.

The bell above the front door chimes as Dante marches out the lobby back into the parking lot. He sticks a key in the Lincoln trunk and unlocks it, a bunch of gear inside, duct tape, crowbars, rags, tools. He fishes out bolt cutters, red metal with black-rubber handles. He throws down the hatch and veers toward the back of the motel, the tool dangling from his right hand a couple inches above the asphalt. He passes the small pool, blue tarp over it for the winter, and shoves open the backdoor.

He strides through the hallway with the nature paintings, approaching room eight. When he gets there he leans the bolt cutters against the wall, grabs his wallet, and slips out his Nevada driver's license. He bends the ID into an L-shape. Pressing the smaller edge above the knob, he sweeps his wrist down, catching the lock with the ID, popping it free with a soft clicking noise.

He sticks the license in his pocket with one hand and clamps the bolt slicers with the other. He cracks the door about an inch, scanning inside, noticing Sean on the foot of the bed. That pre-attack predatory readiness gleams on him. He noses the opened blades through the doorway, around the latch chain. Sean spots the bolt cutters in his periphery. Startled, he breaks focus from the tick of the clock and crawls off the bed.

He falls to the purple carpet, rough fibers scraping his chin, and flees toward the window on all fours. He gropes through the triangle-patterned drapes for the lock and twists it open. He slides the glass up and wiggles his torso through. The cold air hits the top half of his body, feels good, feels like freedom. The bottom half of him, still inside, burns as Dante clenches his bad ankle. Sean screams. The man jerks his leg, Sean's ribs banging against the window casing as he's ripped from the briskness of freedom, chest plummeting back to the coarse rug, *Easy Rider* sunglasses snapping off his collar.

Dante flips and mounts him, Sean getting a flash of those devilish eyes before getting slugged in the jaw, his vision going black for a few seconds, taste of salt in his mouth. Groaning, he tries to break free to no avail. Dante hits him again, Sean choking on saltiness, a crimson stream pouring down his chin. Turning his head, he spits dense, red saliva on the floor.

"What the hell is all this fuss about?" a concerned voice asks outside the door. Dante spins around, spotting an older fellow in a bathrobe in the hallway. He clasps a handful of leather from Sean's jacket, hoisting him to his feet, and lugs him toward the door. The motel guest in the hall steps aside, view on the scene, the bolt cutters by the bed, the severed chain lock, the blood on the rug. He goes from mad to scared as he retreats to room seven, slamming it shut.

Dante hauls Sean past the nature paintings and shoulders open the backdoor. The boy's sore body flops as it gets heaved along the parking lot, blood cascading from his mouth in three streams all over his shirt.

As they pass the pool a police siren rings in the distance, stillness of the country sky interrupted by a colorful, whirling flash. With a hard yank on Sean's arm Dante picks up his pace. Shrill sound intensifying, he rummages around in his pocket for his keys, unlocks the backdoor, and shoves Sean in. He dives in the front seat and starts the engine with a rushed hand. As he sticks the car in drive a Suddsfield police cruiser skids to a halt in front of the only exit.

A baby-faced cop, no more than twenty-five, storms out with a Ruger pistol in front of him. "Freeze right there," he says, tone stern but also excited as if he doesn't get to pull his weapon often in this town. "Come out with your hands up."

A second police cruiser barrels over and another officer, forties, rushes into the lot with the same model gun. The younger approaches the driver's door, the older the passenger's. The junior cop stares into the tinted window, himself and his police lights the only things he can see in the black glass. In about a half-minute the sedan's driver-side door cracks, Dante getting out, hands raised. His expression isn't one of defeat, rather, inconvenience.

Head Up

The professor sleeps next to Aliza in bed, his snoring the only sound in their house, round belly puffing up and down under three layers of covers. A couple bangs at the front door jolt him awake, his right eye opening, then left. He blinks a few times, then peeks at the digital alarm clock on his wife's side of the bed. 2:19 AM.

He swings his feet off the mattress and slides them into his Sharper Image slippers. He grabs his robe, ties it around his tank top and boxer shorts, and heads into the hallway, trying not to disturb Aliza.

He walks down the stairs, terrycloth belt bobbing, and turns into the foyer. Opening the door, he notices two officers from the Pasadena Police Department, a man and woman, the man appearing tired from a long night patrolling, the woman with an alert stare as if her shift just started. "Yes?" the professor asks, perplexed by their presence.

"Is this the home of Steven Merzberg?" the policeman asks.

"That's me. What's this about?"

"Did you rent a Ford Explorer from LAX Airport a few days ago?" It's quiet for a bit, the porch's motion-sensor light shimmering on the municipal building etched into the cop's badge.

"You're coming here at this hour because I put the car in my name? Do you know what time it is?"

"So you did rent it?"

"This is absurd." He adjusts the front flap of his robe, concealing a patch of exposed chest skin.

"Who was driving it earlier this evening?"

"A friend of the family. He was too young to rent a car so I did it for him in my name. I'm sorry. I'll discuss it with you folks tomorrow if you wouldn't mind." He grips the wooden door edge. "Please let me go back to bed."

"That's not why we're here sir."

"I'm not following."

"The vehicle was wrecked tonight."

"Wrecked? When?" His expression morphs from annoyance to concern.

"Probably six hours ago now."

"Where?"

"By the movie theater. The multiplex off Wellmont. No sign of the driver. Which is the purpose of our visit."

"Lord. What happened?"

"We're not sure. It being New Year's, our hunch was that the driver was under the influence, crashed, and fled the scene." He silences a grainy voice from the walkie-talkie on his waist. "Again, just a hunch. We have no proof of that. But statistically...on the holiday...tends to be the case in more instances than not. We were hoping you could help paint a clearer picture for us."

The professor thinks. "The last thing on his mind tonight was celebrating. He was on his way to the airport...to do something very important to him. He needed to get to San Francisco."

"I doubt he made it," the female officer says. The professor looks down at his slippers in a trance, his anxiety kicking in. "Do you have any idea where he might be now?"

"He was supposed to call me when he landed. He didn't earlier. He may have when I went to sleep. Wait here. I'll check." With speed in his step he crosses the foyer into the living room and grabs his phone from the coffee table. He notices a voicemail and missed call from a number in the San Luis Obispo area. Returning to the cops, he says in a hopeful tone, "I have a message. This could be him."

He hits play and holds the speaker to his ear, officers trying to gauge his reaction as he listens. The sound of Sean's distressed voice makes his stomach sink. He does a good job keeping a straight face, heeding the boy's demand not to involve the police.

"Well?" she asks.

Lowering the phone, he tries to appear calm. "He made it to San Francisco. He didn't mention anything about the SUV. Maybe there was a mix-up with the rental reservations? It could be a different Explorer."

"We triple-check things like that, sir," the patrolman says, a bit insulted by the accusation. "Especially at this time of night."

"I wish I had more for you."

They watch him for a while, his unrevealing demeanor still intact except for his eyes, a hint of nervous energy in them. "Okay then," the patrolman says, skeptical. "I'm sure we'll be in touch as we gather more details."

"Anything you need." He forces a grin, his pair of dimples flashing. "You know where I live. Happy New Year." They wander out of the porch-light beam toward their squad car, the professor closing the door behind. Smile faded, he dashes into the den, his left slipper popping off along the way, and flips open his laptop. He Googles "California Gold Inn San Luis Obispo" and selects the top result, a directory of motels in the state's central region. Scrolling through the list, he spots the one he needs, reads the number, and pounds the digits on his phone with shaky fingers.

"I need to speak to a guest urgently," he says into it. "Room eight. Please connect me." He listens for a while, rubbing his bald head. "Is that so?" He taps his left fist on his knee. "The police?" His heartbeat picks up. "Do you have the address of the station?" He hustles into the dark kitchen with the phone, groping around in a drawer until he finds a pen. "Okay." He scribbles on his palm as the information gets recited on the other line. "Thank you." He hangs up.

He runs up to his room, old staircase creaking with his clunky steps. Night-table lamp on, an awoken Aliza gazes at him from bed, eyes half-open, red hair messy. "What's the commotion hon?"

"It's Sean. He's in trouble."

"What happened?"

He wiggles out of his robe and throws open the sliding closet door. "I can't explain now."

"What're you doing?"

He slips into a pair of jeans and tennis sneakers. "I have to head up north."

"It's two thirty in the morning."

He zips a windbreaker over his tank top. "I'll call you from the road."

"Where're you going?"

"I love you." He scurries out.

"Hon?"

Socked

Eyes closed, Sean is slumped on a cold metal bench in a shadowy Suddsfield jail cell, a black semicircle on his swollen right cheek from getting socked in the motel earlier. The authorities are now involved, something he dreaded, a crippling delay. Those metal marbles of thought are clanging around in his skull, Natasha in a hospital bed wondering where he is, her body getting weaker by the minute, no chance for a goodbye before she's gone.

Dante is in a cell to his right, a stream of dry blood running from the wound on his temple to his neck. An old drunk brought in on public intoxication is passed out in a cage to Sean's left.

A ten-foot hallway separates the holding area from the one-room police station, both of the detaining officers inside alone, an American flag in the corner, framed photos of the department softball team on the walls, one for each year starting from 1988.

The younger cop sits at the only desk combing through a three-ring binder, Dante's creased Nevada driver's license and James Crates's Italian ID scattered in front of him among an arrest-report document and a microwavable dinner he's been picking at. The senior officer stands behind, sipping coffee from a styrofoam cup, staring at the bound papers as they turn. "Right there," he says, pointing at something on the page. "Code seven twenty-seven."

"Hell, you don't see one of these every day," he says, reading the description.

"I don't suppose you do."

"And?"

"And what?"

"And what do I do about it?"

The older finishes his drink, then saunters to the coffee pot on a folding table. "Call the State Department in Washington I guess. That's what the binder says doesn't it?" He refills, leaving about a millimeter of space above the hot liquid.

"Does."

He seals the cup with a plastic lid and collects his trench coat from the top of a wooden chair. "When's Jepson getting back?"

He peeks at his watch. "Fifteen minutes or so I'd say."

"You all right by yourself till he gets here?"

"Those boys in there seemed to calm down some."

"That's right they did." The veteran slides an arm in his jacket. "Took 'em long enough." Then the other arm.

"Go home to Maureen. She'll be itching to hear 'bout us nabbing those two. Guns out and all."

"Nah. Makes her nervous, all that."

"Not Shelly. She loves it. Those stories."

"She's a funny girl that Shelly."

"She is."

"Guess that's why you married her."

"I suppose it helped her some." The baby-faced cop looks away with a grin.

"All right. I'll see you tomorrow. Tell Shelly hi. Happy New Year too."

"Same with Maureen."

He leaves, the junior policeman still perusing the text on the sheet. He spoons some peas into his mouth from his microwavable dinner, then pinches the corner of James Crates's ID. He studies it for a bit, then taps its edge on the desk while he assesses the situation. He tosses it on the arrest form, gets up, and moseys down the short passageway into the incarceration area.

Stopping in front of Sean's cell, he says, "Hey boy." He bangs his nightstick between two bars. "Crates."

Sean snaps from his daze. He limps to him, wrapping his hands around a pair of bars. "He kidnapped me," he says in a tired way as if he uttered the same thing a bunch already with no result. "You got to get me out of here. Please. Listen to—"

"We have a deputy in the center of town asking all the right questions to all the right people. He'll straighten the truth from this. Till he does you're sitting tight." He turns to Dante, standing motionless, focusing on the floor. "And that goes for you too." Dante doesn't acknowledge him, light from a lamppost outside pouring through a barred window into his cell, strips of bright and dark alternating over him.

"I have a number for you to call in Los Angeles," Sean says. "A professor. A respected dean at the Southern California Technology Institute. He can confirm the whole thing—"

"For the last time, I told you to quit with all that. I don't know what either of you was really up to yet, kicking around down there." He scratches his chin. "Now, we ran your information and the Spanish-looking fella's through the computer. And between you both you're the only one that raised any flags." He points at Dante with his left index and middle fingers. "He's clean as a whistle. You threw off a code seven two seven. Coming into the country without announcing it to the proper authorities." He scratches his chin again. "The Feds don't take that lightly. You know what the hell this is all about?"

"Please, don't call them. You can't, you can't, you can't."

"I'll call whoever I want, boy." Refastening his nightstick to his belt, he ignores Sean's desperate, pleading expression. "My deputy will be back any minute now with the report. The Feds are getting it whether you approve of it or not. What the hell kind of trouble you been up to giving off a code like that?"

"Hear me out. You can't call them. First—"

"Quiet down with all that. I want to know what mess you been in. Huh?"

"I'll tell you anything you want, but please just let me go for tonight and—"

"No use wasting my time," the cop says to himself. Shaking his head, he disappears up the hall, footsteps softening as he distances.

"Officer. Please." With his good leg Sean boots the bars of his cell, a ding rippling through the detainment space.

The noise snaps the sleeping drunk awake. "What the hell is this?" he asks with a slur, springing to his feet, taking in his surroundings. He squares to Sean, stench of booze floating off him. "Where are we son?"

"Where do you think?" Sean returns to his bench and tilts his head against the brick wall, little muscles by his eyebrows twitching with anxiety.

The jail is hushed for about ten minutes. Then a rustle emerges from Dante's cell. Sean doesn't look over, but the drunk does. He watches Dante slip off his left loafer, remove his Ralph Lauren sock, squeeze it into a compact little ball, and stow it in his jacket pocket. He sees him do the same with the one on his right foot. "What the hell are you doing that for?" the drunk asks, pressing his face between two bars for a better view through the shadows.

Dante locks eyes with him for a moment, then turns his attention back to his shoes, sliding his bare feet inside. Stepping to the front of his cell, he licks his teeth, that predatory calm to him again. "Officer," he says toward the passageway. Sean's eyes open upon hearing the deep, chilling voice. He stares at Dante, wondering what he's doing.

About a minute later the patter of steps carries in, the policeman resurfacing. "Was that you calling on me?" he asks Dante.

"Yes sir."

"Well what the hell is it?"

"Remember earlier when I told you I didn't feel I needed first-aid supplies?"

"I said you were nuts."

"I must admit you may have been right sir. It's not the injury on my temple that concerns me. It's another one. A gash on my abdomen. I just checked it. I believe it's infected. Let me know if you have anything I can put on it."

The officer is still for a few seconds, then nods. He unbuttons his gray jacket, the material billowing around him, the cop fixating on his torso. He begins untucking his white dress shirt, then lets go and thrusts his arm through a pair of bars, clutching a fistful of the young man's collar, slamming his forehead into the metal. He wobbles as blood spills, a three-inch gash across his boyish face.

Dante clamps his shoulders, flips him a hundred eighty degrees, and jerks his back against the cage. He lifts the socks from his pocket, loops them around his throat, and tugs. He leans back with the ends of the socks wrapped tight around his wrists, all his weight on his heels, taut fabric razoring into the cop's flesh. He tries to scream, nothing coming out, the jangle of items on his police belt the only noise in the jail. His cheeks swell from the pressure. The white of his left eye pops red, then his right.

Petrified, Sean backpedals to the corner of his cell while the drunk observes frozen. Sean sees the officer's arms go flaccid, his hands falling from his neck, no energy to resist with anymore. In a bit his whole body stops moving, flesh of his face a ballooned purplish gray. Dante still pulls, the hardened, sharp sock material cutting his wrists, blood trickling down each. The policeman gurgles for a moment, then is quiet.

Dante lets go, the corpse sliding down the rods to the concrete floor. "Holy shit, holy shit, holy shit," Sean says, cowering as far from the scene as the confines of his cage allow.

Kneeling, Dante deposits the bloody socks in his pocket, reaches through the metal bars to the dead man's belt, and frees the gun from his holster. He wedges it in the waist of his suit pants, then unclips the keychain and handcuffs. Standing, he inserts a few keys into his cell lock until he finds a match, then turns, door opening with a squeak.

He exits, latching one end of the cuffs around his left wrist as he steps over the cop's mangled face toward Sean. He unlocks his door in a few attempts and approaches. Backed tight in the corner, Sean kicks at him with his healthy leg and says, "Get away you nut job."

With ease Dante bats his flailing boot to the side, grasps his leather jacket, and rips him off the bench. He slaps the other end of the cuffs on Sean's right wrist, attaching himself to him. "Let's go," he says, dragging the staggering kid out of the cell.

Dante stops a few feet from the drunk's cage. He wraps his fingers around the pistol and aims the barrel between two bars. The drunk's expression turns frantic and his mouth moves to say something, but before he can get a word out a bullet blasts through his right eye, killing him in an instant. Sean almost vomits from the sight, right half of the man's face gone, left eye still open.

Dante whips Sean around the hallway corner and charges into the brightness of the station, gun in front of him, vision hopping around. Nobody there. The old wiring in the overhead light has a soft drone to it, audible now with no voices present. Dante peers out the window, nothing except some passing car beams behind leafless trees in the distance.

He heads to the desk, snatching his license, dropping it in his pocket. He opens a drawer and scours the inside. Then a second. Then a third. He recognizes the feel of the Lincoln keys at the bottom, clutches them, and plops them in the same pocket. He marches ahead, Sean eyeing his out-of-reach James Crates ID on the surface as they move in unison.

Just before they come to the front door it opens, a man in a Suddsfield Police jacket arriving, hunting cap on with the flaps down, confused expression as he absorbs the scene before him. He snags the Ruger firearm on his hip, but it's too late, a round from Dante's weapon piercing the meaty part of his shoulder. He falls on the coffeepot table, tumbling with it to the floor, losing his pistol. Clasping his wound, he flops around, shattered glass from the pot all over, hot liquid searing the skin of his forehead and cheeks.

Looming over him, Dante asks, "What's your name?" He doesn't reply, screaming in pain. "Answer me."

"Daniel."

"Daniel what?"

"Jepson dammit." Fixating on the gunman above him, the deputy stops shouting, the realization he's going to be murdered sinking in. Gut shaking from nerves, he starts weeping. "Please. Please. I have a daughter. She lives in South Carolina. I haven't had a word with her in two years."

A urine spot spreads on the crotch of his beige uniform pants, Dante staring. "Stop doing that."

"Oh God. God help me." He folds his hands, checkered with his own blood, and looks up at the ceiling mumbling a prayer to himself between whimpers.

Dante watches him for a while. "That's not going to help. Whatever it is you're saying. You could've been the best follower of your religion your whole life, but none of it matters now. Because in the real world, in this moment, I'm here and you're there. And I have the gun. It won't work. I promise you. Do you understand?"

"God," the cop says to the sky, ignoring him. "Please God."

"You have a daughter. Is that your only child?" He doesn't respond, still praying. "Is it?" he asks with aggression.

"Yes."

"Instead of focusing on whatever it is you are, focus on what's here. In the world of Daniel Jepson. If you don't have any sons it means the Jepson name ends tonight. Your direct line at least. Since the beginning of humankind there's been a Jepson man on this planet, even before the label existed. Over a hundred thousand years. All those people leading to you. And now to this. And this is how you're going to honor the lineage in its last moments? Crying and wetting your pants? This is how you're going to let all that history culminate after a hundred thousand years?"

"You don't have to—"

"I do. Stop thinking about whether or not it's going to happen and start focusing on making it happen right. Have some respect for yourself and the ones before you." Still crying, the officer wriggles on the floor, urine patch widening, scent of it emanating through the room.

Dante observes him for another half-minute or so, then angles the gun at him. Sean clenches his eyelids and turns his head, his arm stiff as it extends from the gunman's other wrist. Dante moves the firearm in small waves back and forth, watching the cop's frightened eyeballs follow the dark hole at the end, listening to his soft gasps upon each revolution. Then he pulls the trigger. The round enters him through the bridge of the nose, cratering his face, spraying bits of skull and brain into the cheap carpet.

Panting in fear, Sean shields his vision from the dead body with his free hand as Dante lugs him across the stained rug and out the door. They step into the night, quiet other than the scratch of squirrels. Weapon at his side, Dante inspects the Suddsfield municipal complex, library, courthouse, recreation center. All closed.

He makes out the Lincoln in an impound lot behind a chain-link fence about a hundred feet away. Closing in on it, he grabs the police keys from his pocket and releases the cuff on himself. He twists Sean's hands behind his back and tightens the second restraint on him, assuring he can't try to escape again, then opens the rear door of his car and pushes him inside.

He pops the trunk, sifts through all his equipment, and takes out a screwdriver. He slams the hatch, kneels, and removes his back license plate, sticking the screws in his pocket. With the metal rectangle tucked under his arm he struts to the front and detaches the other. He steps to a maroon Ford F-250 pickup, one of four other vehicles in the impound, and unfastens its tags, replacing them with the Lincoln's. He returns to his car and fixes the truck's plates to it.

He gazes around in all directions for movement, the glow from the police-station lamppost illuminating the hole in his head. Nothing, nobody. He climbs in his sedan, turns on the engine, and cruises toward the freeway, picking up his journey where he left it.

No Rite

A lanky seventy-something man is rubbing his body with medical-grade soap inside a shower stall in the hospital in Zurich where Natasha is quarantined. In five minutes or so he shuts off the water and exits into a ten-foot-by-ten-foot vacuum-sealed room with metal walls, tile floors, and no windows. The word "Interaction" is posted on the borders in red letters in multiple languages.

He removes a sterile towel from a stainless steel hook and dries himself off, then drapes it back on the peg, collects unworn sets of underwear and socks from another hook, and slips them on. He turns to his Catholic priest attire, suspended from a hanger. He slides on the black pants, then the shirt of the same color, buttoning it to the top and tucking it in. Bending, he steps into a pair of brand-new shiny dark shoes and laces them.

Catching his reflection in a small mirror, he removes a white clergy collar from a bin and fastens it around his neck. He lifts a comb from the same bin and drags it through his moist white hair. Though he's in good shape for his age, his skin is still old and loose and shakes around his jaw as he sweeps his hand over his scalp. He watches his eyes, flecks of blue remaining in them through the decades but the bulk of their centers gray now. There's a hint of uneasiness to his gaze as if he's harboring a worry but his will to suppress it is winning by a slight margin.

Laying down the comb, he grasps an opaque plastic bag, then walks to a steel door on the far wall. He hits a black button next to it. A loud buzzer rings as the heavy slab frees from its compression lock, a green light flashing as well. A red light emanates from a similar door behind him as it self-seals, assuring both passages can't be open at the same time, guaranteeing no air from the quarantine area can flow backwards into the main supply.

Stepping through the entryway, he progresses to a second small room that appears identical to the last except for its lack of a shower. A blue biohazard suit waits on a metal table in the center. The priest studies it for a moment, the first he's ever seen in person. He peels it off the surface and maneuvers his legs, then arms inside. He secures a zipper and series of clamps stretching across the chest. He grips a rubber glove from the table, holds the base to his lips, and blows inside. Pinching the opening, he checks to see if it retains the air, verifying there are no holes in it that can lead to skin exposure. He does the same with a second glove, then puts both on.

The last item on the surface is an air mask. He straps it on his head, his milky hair curling around the black belts. He puts the hood of the biohazard outfit over himself, a plastic shield now covering his face, the loud huffing of the breathing apparatus coursing through the confines of the airtight suit.

He clutches the opaque plastic bag he carried in with him, then turns to another steel door. He presses its black button, activating a noise and green light from it, in addition to a red one from the self-closing door in the rear. The entrance un-locks and he advances into Natasha's chamber, the opening suctioning shut behind him right away.

He looks around, the bright circular bulbs on the ceil-ing, the six-inch glass over the observation area, the closet of medical paraphernalia. Then the bed. He finds it difficult to view the scene before him. Natasha lies there emaciated, about a dozen pounds stripped off her already-skinny frame, a respirator mask over her mouth and nose, dialysis equip-ment dug into her arm. The pace of his breath increases, crisp close-together puffs consuming the sealed suit.

Her head crawling to the left, she notices him with her weary stare. She doesn't seem fazed by his outfit, all her visi-tors the past few days required to wear the same. She holds her attention on him, the priest stepping closer, less than a foot from the mattress.

The respirator conceals much of her face, but her eyes are exposed, a darker red than they were a few days ago, internal bleeding more extreme now. The priest spots a thin circle of blood around the rim of each eye. He's been among many sick people in the past but the sight of such a young, beautiful girl bleeding from her eyeballs disturbs him in a way he's never experienced in his seventy-plus years. Wanting to evade the image, he moves his focus to a tube extending from her forearm.

"Hi Natasha, I'm Father Beimer," he says in German, his words coming through a voice-transmission device fixed to his air mask. "Nice to meet you." She surveys him with slight movements of her eyes, the rings of blood around them swelling a bit with the motion. "Let's begin my dear."

He reaches into his plastic bag and extracts a vial of olive oil. Bottle in his hand, he makes the sign of the cross over himself, liquid swashing against the glass, then bows his head and says, "Hail Mary, full of grace. The Lord is with thee. Blessed art thou amongst women, and blessed is the fruit of thy womb, Jesus. Holy Mary, Mother of God, pray for us sinners, now and at the hour of our death. Amen." His body heat fogs the plastic shield in front of his face, the girl hazier to him through it now. He removes the cork from the oil receptacle and dribbles some on his rubber-gloved thumb. He spreads it on her brow, the liquid cold, goose bumps running down her neck.

The scent of the oil provokes a reaction in her mind she finds strange in this moment getting her Last Rites read. It triggers memories of meals she enjoyed in Italy, olive oil a staple in Italian dining. A picnic her family went on in Positano. A pasta lunch her mom made her when she had a Tuesday off from school. The dinner she had in Tuscany with her boyfriend James, his aunt Leanne, and her husband Marco.

"Through this holy anointing may the Lord in his love and mercy help you with the grace of the Holy Spirit," the priest says, dabbing more liquid out. Cradling her left hand, he spins his rubbery finger over her palm. He does the same to her right. "May the Lord Who frees you from your sins, save you and raise you up." Making the sign of the cross over himself, he says, "In the name of the Father, and the Son, and of the Holy Spirit. Amen."

While he continues with another prayer, she thinks about all the things she wanted to do in life, see America, go to the moon, get married, have babies, make wine, write music.

He then begins explaining the transition to the afterlife, but her focus is glued to the night table. A Polaroid of her and her boyfriend James leans against the lamp, both of them making funny faces in a booth at the "Happy Dragon," the karaoke bar they went to after the Hotel Vanessa on their first date.

She peers at the slice of space and time in the photo, recalling that piece of her history. She looks so happy in it, detached from the pressure of her classes and the life plan her father expected of her over the next twenty years, in tune with everything, in the moment. Free.

Then she reminds herself in all likelihood she'll never see her boyfriend again and the story of happiness in the image changes to one of despair. In an instant the memory's face morphs into a new one, an ugly one. He's abandoned her and will never share a new experience with her for the rest of her life. He is to exist to her only in the renderings of the past etched in her brain until her brain expires, any minute now. And then she doesn't know what will happen.

Filled with a gust of panic, she can't help but extend her weak hand to the night table and flip the picture over. She glances at the Polaroid's dark backside. Nothing there. No good. No bad. Nothing.

In the Head

Sean blinks in the Lincoln backseat as he peers at 8:34 on the digital clock, numbers blurry to him from lack of sleep, the three digits converging into one multi-shaded green ball. Looking out the window, he sees the Redwood City business district come into view among the morning sky, dozens of modern glass buildings shining over the seaport in the first American sun of the New Year.

Though he's never been in this town he recognizes the body of water and some of the architecture from geographical research he'd done during his *Jeopardy!* era. He recollects from the Colzyne website the company is located here. Things start making sense now, the people behind it all.

He sits up. He wonders how they found out, considering the non-detectable way he hacked into the system. Hank somehow? It doesn't even matter he figures. Not at this point.

In about five minutes the sedan cruises in front of Colzyne Tower, Sean tilting his gaze up at the eighteen-story monolith. Dante hooks around a corner toward a service entrance. He puts the car in park and climbs out. Kneeling, he unlocks the gate with a key and heaves it upward along its tracks, the high-pitched ratcheting sound clashing with the low rumble of the idling engine.

He gets back in the Lincoln and drives through the rectangular opening into a parking garage, Sean scoping a sea of parallel painted white lines, vast majority of the spots empty on the New Year's holiday. His eyeballs burn. He blinks a few times hoping it'll help, but it only makes it worse.

They wind down a few levels, at the center of each a support formation of ten wide columns, a red emergency phone, and an elevator. Sean's been staring with longing at the phones, so close, so distant.

Nosing into a space, Dante kills the engine. He steps out in his sockless loafers, bits of ankle exposed, then opens the rear door and scowls at the beat-up kid in the glow of the interior bulbs. Dante smacks his tongue in his mouth, the pop echoing through the large hollow garage, and says, "Let's go."

Sean takes a deep breath and sets his right boot on the rough concrete, then his left. Wincing from the ankle pain, he tries to transfer as much weight on his good foot as he can. It's difficult to keep balance with his hands clasped behind his back in cuffs. Dehydrated and weak, he topples, his right shoulder grinding against the surface as he attempts to protect his head from the impact.

Dante laughs at him for five seconds or so, then hoists him up from the concrete by the collar, points at an elevator about a hundred feet away, and says, "Come on." Sean coughs a couple times, then approaches the stainless steel entrance with slow, difficult shuffles of his feet. It takes him a solid two minutes to make it over, his shoulder throbbing now just as much as his ankle.

Dante summons the cart, enters, and motions for him to get inside. As Sean drags himself through the gap, his abductor hits "B4." They descend for about thirty seconds in the posh elevator, marble floor, red area rug, mahogany paneling. The doors part. Dante extends his gray-suited arm, signaling for Sean to go first.

He totters out, scenery down here in contrast with the fancy elevator, unadorned cement walls, industrial fans, a chain-link cage with a few hundred stacked Colzyne cardboard boxes inside. He guesses he's in a corporate warehouse. "Follow me," Dante says with a slight grin, gloating in the successful drop-off of his target.

"Where?" he asks, skeptical of each of the five shadowy hallways splitting off from the main branch.

"This isn't the time to ask questions." He bangs his hands and veers into one on the right. Sean hobbles behind with caution, scanning his sides and back every few moments. The darkness grows as they distance from the large overhead lamps by the cardboard boxes.

The corridor is lined with tiny bulbs wedged where the walls meet the ceiling, one every three feet, a faint orangey ripple emitted from them, rest of the hall cloaked in black. Sean's tired eyes do a poor job processing the light, his field of vision dotted with hundreds of little ovals coming and going.

In five minutes or so they reach the end of the hall, stopping at a door with specks of blue paint streaking across the bottom. Dante opens it and holds it in place, Sean peeking inside the tiny square room. Dante unfastens the handcuffs, shoves him in, and slams it shut behind him. Sean hears a click from the other side of the door. Glancing at the knob, he notices it's been reversed so it can lock from the outside in.

His heart bangs. He looks around, no windows, a seat in the middle, a desk in the corner with a single reading lamp on it providing visibility. He assumes the room was empty in the recent past and modified for his expected visit, chair seeming unnatural alone in the center, a desk random down here, the doorknob in all likelihood flipped around just to keep him contained.

He limps to the wooden seat and sinks, freeing the weight on his left leg. The lack of pressure on his ankle is relieving, but he hurts elsewhere, all over, inside and out, his distressed mind having trouble at this point discerning which negative sensations are bodily and which mental, everything blended in an all-encompassing pulse of discomfort.

Dead silence. He stares at the walls, scrapes on them about three feet up, cause unclear, some paint the same color as the kind on the door in tear-shaped dabs on the floor. He wonders if this is where it's going to end for him, this little room with the scuffed walls and drops of blue paint. From the Holy Trinity Hospital in Shipville eighteen years ago to this, some dungeon in the basement of a corrupt medical company.

He shakes his head, trying to snap from the self-destructive spiral he's plummeting down. He realizes the stress, combined with lack of water and sleep, is clouding his thoughts. He tries to fight it, groping for logic. He tells himself if they wanted to kill him they would've done it before, his abductor having a bunch of chances out in the middle of nowhere.

About twenty minutes go by, Sean not moving other than to blink. Then murmurs emerge outside the door, seizing his attention. Inching the chair toward the hallway, he juts out his ear. Footsteps. Voices, four, maybe five.

The door cracks. Colzyne CEO Donald Phlace enters and seals the room behind him, same tailored black suit he had on yesterday morning but without the tie, the reading lamp beaming on his tight, wrinkle-free skin. Arms folded, he surveys the beaten teenager.

Sean recognizes him from an article he read in *Forbes* one day in Italy, Donald Phlace, Wharton undergrad, Wharton again for business school, north of four hundred million dollars in the sale of his genome company to Colzyne when he was thirty-six, vice president at the conglomerate for five years post-merger before being promoted to senior executive VP, CEO next, cutthroat reputation, many say a backstabber, three ex-wives.

Phlace recognizes the kid's face too, battered and all, from the *Jeopardy!* photo on his Wikipedia page, his general look preserved between eleven and eighteen though matured. "You're probably wondering why you're here," Phlace says with a hint of scorn.

"I think I put it together by now," he says glaring, assuming this man is the person keeping him from his dying girlfriend.

"I hear you're a pretty smart kid, so maybe you did put it together. But in case you didn't, let me clarify. You're here because you stole something very important to me." Ten seconds or so go by, Sean not giving him any eye contact. "I've always enjoyed the Holidays. What about you?" He doesn't answer. "New Year's Day, today, is a time to spend with family. My wife and kids should be getting up right about now. I'd prefer not to be here. I'd rather get back to them. Can you help me out? Make this quick? What do you say?"

"I. Don't. Say. Anything."

Phlace links his manicured hands behind his back and begins pacing. "I guess that makes sense. That you wouldn't have much to say about that." He nods a couple times. "I did my research on you. I heard about your parents. What a tragedy. I should've guessed you wouldn't have an opinion on family." He stops walking and leans over, inches from Sean. "Not having one and all."

The kid spits on his forehead. "Fuck you."

He wipes it off with his Brioni suit sleeve and chuckles. "You done acting like an animal? Ready to talk?"

"Fuck you."

"Who has my files?"

"Fuck. You."

"I'm going to ask you again myself. If you don't answer I'll have my new friend Dante come in and ask instead." Leering at Sean, he points an angry finger at the door behind. "Think. Be smart. Make this easy on yourself. Who has my documents?" No reply. "Huh?" Still no response. Enraged, he slaps the kid. Sean's skin hurts, but he doesn't grimace. He bites his tongue and looks the CEO in the eye, defiant. "I'll break you, do you understand that? You're nobody. Do you know who I am? Do you know who we are?" He clenches the leather of his jacket and shakes him. "Who are you selling my Goddamn formula to?"

Sean pushes him off and says with aggression, "Nobody. I'm not selling anything to anybody."

He regains his footing, then snickers. "You don't get to a position like mine in this world if you can't smell bullshit."

"If I wanted to sell your files I would've done it the minute I ripped them from your shitty IT system."

"You just did it for fun then? You really expect me to believe that?"

"I wanted to finish what was there."

"No kidding. To sell to who?"

"To sell to nobody."

"Then why do it?"

"Doesn't matter." They're hushed for some time, the lamp shining on the moon-shaped bruise on Sean's right cheek.

"Well, you can't have it. It's mine."

Sean doesn't speak for a while, then grins. The smile leads to a soft laugh. Phlace is puzzled. "You weren't even close," Sean says, clapping. "It was funny really. You and your engineers and what you were putting in the mixture. It never would've worked." He lets out a sarcastic, mocking sigh. "It was so obvious to me. And you probably spent billions on it. You never would've seen it. Donald Phlace with an army of five thousand scientists and an endless pool of resources never would've been able to see it, even if he looked at it twenty-four hours a day for the rest of his life. Never would've clicked." He snaps his fingers. "Whatever it is you want is in my head. My head. Not yours." He points at his own temple and says with a bark, "My head."

Phlace sits on the desk, his left foot sweeping back and forth. "So you had some luck then? Finishing it." His torso blocks half the glow from the reading light, Sean's body divided before him into white and black.

"I did."

Contemplating, he watches Sean for about ten seconds, the boy's limbs quivering with adrenaline. Phlace slithers off the desk and starts circling the chair. "Did you study business at all? When you were at SoCal Tech?"

"Just business ethics. You know, like not using corporate money to hire psychopaths to kidnap people."

"The first thing they teach you is that the man with the leverage is the most important in the room. Not necessarily the smartest guy. The one with the leverage. Do you know how leverage works?" He stops in front of Sean. "I consider myself a relatively savvy businessman. I do oversee an eighty-billion-dollar public company. I'd say I know a thing or two about it. Most importantly, I can recognize when I have it, and when I don't."

"If you kill me you'll never get what's in my mind. The mixture dies with me."

"As I said, I did my homework on you. Any respectable businessman does before a meeting. And I must say, your credentials are impressive. I bet you did actually finish what we started." He leans forward, his eyeline flat with the seated kid's. "So I'm willing to barter with you."

"How?"

He points at the door. "My chief chemist is standing outside. He's going to come in here in a few minutes and you're going to sit at the desk and diagram out exactly...what's in your mind. And he's going to determine if it's something I can patent, package, and profit from. If it is we escort you upstairs and you're free to go. We forget this ever happened. The cops never find out about your theft."

Distrustful, Sean analyzes his face. "What if I don't do it?"

"Then I don't see a very bright future for you. My chemist is in the hallway, along with my new friend Dante. Both of them ready to do whatever I tell them."

Sean drags his hand through his hair, some windshield bits from the Explorer still sprinkling off. "Dante isn't as good of a friend as you think. I'm sure he didn't relay this to you yet, but he got us arrested down in Suddsfield. Killed two cops after our information was already in the computer system. Shot a witness too. If you did your research on me like you said, you would've learned I died in a car accident four years ago. You know who came up with that little story? The FBI."

Sean nods at Phlace's watch and says, "Right about now I'd say the report from Suddsfield is hitting the desks of the agents who put my identity-protection profile together. If I wind up dead every field operative on the West Coast is gonna be scouring surveillance footage for black Lincoln sedans with dented grilles within a few-hours driving radius of

Suddsfield. It's only a matter of time before they find out one was cruising through Redwood City. And it's only a matter of time from then until they go through today's camera records from the dozens of buildings surrounding this one, and see the car pull right into the Colzyne garage."

Wagging his finger at the CEO, he says, "If I end up dead, and they know he took me here, your picture will be all over the *Wall Street Journal.* It'll be the business story of the year. Whether they could prove you were personally involved or not, you'll be finished in the court of public opinion. With just the two dead cops and one dead witness it'll be easy for the authorities to dismiss…Dante…as some random psycho who hid out in your parking lot while he was fleeing. But me too? Now that raises some questions, especially for a company that works with the same sort of math I dabbled in myself." A pause. "I realize you want to have me shot once I write it down. But you can't. The FBI will piss all over you."

Phlace spends around a half-minute absorbing this, trying to keep a straight face. He puts his hands in his pockets and starts roaming the small space, his athletic frame slicing the reading-light beam as he goes back and forth. "As I mentioned, I'm a businessman. I want to make money off you, not kill you. If you were a businessman too, and I hope you are, sharing the formula is a risk you'd have to be willing to take."

Silence for a while. "Here's my counteroffer."

Phlace chuckles. "Counteroffer?"

A spark of life surges through Sean's drained body. "I give your chemist what you want. But I don't write it down. I'll tell him the ingredients and the portions as he mixes them in front of me. He makes me two doses, with your materials, in your lab. Right now. That I keep.”

"If I give you an actual sample you can send it to a buyer in a heartbeat. It would be out in the world much faster than if you just gave them a diagram on a piece of paper.” Keeping his left hand in his pocket, Phlace rubs his chin with his right.

"Like I said, I’m not selling it to anyone.”

He carries a pensive expression. “Then what do you need two doses for right now?”

"Does it matter? That’s my offer.”

"How do I know you’re not going to hand the final product off today for a boatload of cash?”

"Well, I suppose you don’t.” Sean smirks. “But, if you were a businessman, and I hope you are, it’s a risk you’d have to be willing to take.”

Phlace’s pacing slows, then stops. He stares at Sean. The kid has a fearless determination on him. The CEO stands in silence for around half a minute with a pained demeanor, realizing he doesn’t have any more tricks to play. Head down, he opens the door and walks out.

Sean’s heart pounds with excitement. Phlace has no choice but to get him what he wants. In Sean’s opinion however, a drug as powerful as this should never be in the hands of a firm as bad as Colzyne. He doesn’t want to give them the actual mixture. He thinks of ways he can alter the proportions so it wouldn’t work, while still leaving himself room to modify it on his own so his version would.

He goes through the possibilities in his mind for a while, then has an idea. A certain balance of the chemicals wouldn't be effective on its own, however, if combined with cupric sulfate, a substance common in over-the-counter baby formula, it would be potent for about twenty-four hours, enough time for him to get to Switzerland. He sits up in his seat, a subtle grin on his face.

The Edge of the World

A trim man in his forties, wearing a white lab coat and rubber gloves, inserts a plastic pipette into a test tube, sucks out some liquid, and releases it into a mixing flask. His blue eyes, between his surgical mask and hair cover, are intense and focused. Sean watches him in a connected office behind a thick sheet of glass, the kid's reflection on the surface.

The chemist brings the liquid to the corner of the lab, sliding it inside a slot on a block-shaped silver machine about the size of a bathtub, clicking three buttons. A blue light starts radiating from the opening.

Staring at the shine, Sean notices his translucent reflection enclosing it on the window, shirt spattered in blood, three separate slices in his bottom lip, black half-circle bruise on his swollen right cheek. He ponders the abduction that brought him here, the cause for the battered face he's looking at in the glass. He fixates on something Dante mentioned in the car earlier. He said there's a sense of deviation about the people he's paid to target, none of them fitting into the world's definition of normal.

Sean wonders if he could be considered normal. He assesses all the moments in the past, even before the abduction, that led him here. He goes through them from the most recent to the most distant. He thinks about finishing the formula in Zurich a few days ago, and being in Zurich because Natasha was sick, and caring Natasha was sick because he loved her, and loving her because he met her, and meeting her because he was in Italy, and being in Italy because he had to flee the United States, and fleeing the United States because he solved a problem nobody else could solve, and being able to solve that problem because of the way his mind was wired, and his mind being wired that way because of a mutation in his head when he was littler than a little baby making him different than the six billion others on the planet.

No, he doesn't believe he's normal. He's far from it. But if he were normal he wouldn't have been brought to this lab because there would be nothing to bring him here for. And without him here there would be no blue light shining because there would be nothing for it to shine on. And with nothing for it to shine on his girlfriend wouldn't get the medicine she needs. And without the medicine she needs she'd die. And that makes everything un-normal about his life, all eighteen years of it and the ones to come, okay by him.

The chemist turns off the block-shaped device and extracts the dish of fluid with care, placing it on a stainless steel table. He funnels the orange liquid into a test tube, sealing it with a rubber stopper. He exits, leaving Sean's view for a bit, then enters the attached office he's in.

Pulling down his surgical mask, the chemist hands him the test tube. Cradling it in his palm, the kid gazes at the elixir, Sean Malone's creation. Not James Crates's. Sean Malone's.

The chemist has respect for the person in front of him. He wants to say something, tell Sean how revolutionary his discovery was, but knows his boss is observing from a camera and wouldn't approve of friendliness with the enemy. Admiration in his eyes, he tries to express his feelings with a single nod. Sean can interpret the gratitude, nods back, then advances to the door.

About twenty minutes later Sean's cab is idling in front of a CVS. He dashes out of the store holding a bag filled with a pack of Similac liquid baby formula, a plastic measuring cup, and an eyedropper. "Okay," he says with urgency to the driver, climbing back in. As the vehicle continues toward San Francisco Airport Sean inserts a few drops of the baby formula into the medication's test tube.

A short while later he's settling into a seat on a Swiss Airlines plane, a toiletry kit he purchased in the airport held tight to his stomach, his only possession other than his wallet and passport, both remaining on him since leaving the Merzberg house. To disguise the mysterious orange fluid from the security screeners, he went in a terminal bathroom just before and poured it into one of the toiletry set's travel-sized plastic bottles, the one labeled "Face Soap." The little cylinder is nestled in the see-through vinyl case in his lap among empty ones marked "Conditioner," "Shampoo," and "Body Wash."

While in the men's room he also cleaned up his bloody lips and chin, got rid of his crimson-stained shirt, and put on a fresh one, something he bought at the same shop he got the kit, a touristy blue T-shirt with a graphic of a California license plate, "CALIBOY" the inscription.

"Welcome to your eleven-hour-and-fifteen-minute flight from San Francisco to Zurich," a female voice says over the PA system. The words sound fake to him, like a dream. A little earlier he thought all was lost. He shakes his head a few times making sure he's not imagining this, the elderly Swiss lady next to him throwing him an odd look.

In a few hours he's somewhere over the Atlantic Ocean, observing the scenery in the cabin, tapping his foot. He glances at the other passengers in his area, a couple chatting, a handful eating, a few reading. For some reason his parents have stayed out of his thoughts all flight, something that's never happened on any other plane ride he's taken.

The jet lands on the other side of the world some time later, Sean staring out the window, gray Zurich sky filled with heavy snow, the next afternoon already in Switzerland with the time change.

In a short while he bursts out of the airport toward the taxi line, at least twenty people deep. Consumed with desperation to get to the hospital, he can't bear waiting. He rips a wad of cash from his wallet and extends it to the man at the front, a burly fellow in an overcoat with a blond moustache. "I need this next cab," Sean says in German, antsy. "Please. Take this." The man grips the money in his big hands and counts it. He nods.

The next taxi pulls up and Sean jumps in. "You know where the Luffen Clinic is?" he asks in the local language, sliding across the backseat.

"Yes sir," the wavy-haired cabbie says in German. They start coasting through the snowstorm. They drive for about forty minutes and turn off the main road on a street near Lake Zurich. Car horns outside, the taxi slows, traffic condensing. The man spins to his passenger and says, "Looks like there was an accident. Damn ice."

Sean angles his neck and peeks at the gridlock through the windshield. "I don't have time to sit in this. Let me out here." He unzips the toiletry set, taking out the "Face Soap" bottle, leaving the others on the cushion.

"It's still a ways up. That's a hell of a hike. Especially in this weather. You sure?"

Sean takes some bills from his wallet and hands them to him. "I'm sure." He swings open the door and steps outside, snow dumping, wind moaning. Tightening his left fingers around the plastic soap bottle, he limps up the sidewalk. The gust hits him head-on, his leather jacket and T-shirt flapping up behind, skin of his lower back exposed.

Ignoring the agony in his left ankle, he starts jogging. He goes up a block. The wound is excruciating, but it doesn't matter. Pain is nothing right now, not after all he's been through. He begins sprinting across the icy concrete, arms pumping at his sides.

He covers one more block. Then another. People stare at him. His body aches, but his mind drifts somewhere else, to a place that feels not of this world. Even though he's not the one about to die, his life starts flashing before his eyes as in-dividual slices of space and time. He pictures winding around the furniture in his parents' house with his bare feet when he was a baby, and the way the strands of bulbs wrapped the small plastic Christmas tree his mom used to put in his bedroom in December, and an aerobics video Aunt Mary used to watch in the den when he first moved in with her in her early thirties, and the texture of the pages of an Encyclopedia Britannica set he would read on a daily basis on the kitchen table when he was five, and the tin roof of a tree fort he helped build with some friends on his block in Shipville when he was seven, and the front of the menu at the fancy steakhouse his aunt treated him to the day they found out he was going to be on *Jeopardy!*, and the humming sound of the dining hall at SoCal Tech when it was full of students, and the smell of the grass in the Pasadena baseball park where he played left field next to Kyle in center, and the gem necklace his landlady wore the day he signed the lease for his apartment in Rome, and the scent of paint as it came out of the spray can during all the graffiti runs with Fabrizio, and the first moment he saw Natasha, and how the rug of his hotel room felt against his face when he was lying on it moments after he cured Ebola.

He rushes for twelve blocks, his hair and jacket blanketed in snow, his lungs hot, his skin freezing. Spotting the clinic's black walls and bronze trim, he hooks a right. He bolts inside and across the lobby, his damp boot soles losing footing for a bit. A receptionist shouts something at him.

He advances to the stair shaft, shoving the door open. He ascends a flight. Then another. His injured ankle is numb now from the overload of strain, his left foot just a weight he's dragging at this point. The whole area rings with his heavy footsteps, bottom floor to top. Reaching the fourth, he rams the entrance with his shoulder, a metallic pop filling the hallway.

He flies across the glass-covered bridge, the employee who punched him the other day noticing him and standing. "Security," the man says in German. Grunting, Sean clocks him in the face, then continues through the passageway into the quarantine zone. He heads down the staircase and veers toward pod two.

He opens the "Interaction" door with the biohazard symbol on it, enters the shower room, dashes to the front, and slaps the black button to go into the next room. A green light and buzzer go off as the door frees. He slips into the following room. He spots two furious security guards stomping inside behind him in white shirts with sewn-on Swiss flags. He lunges for the black button in front of him, the next slab releasing. He twists through the entryway into Natasha's chamber, the metal door sealing behind him, guards not making it through in time.

His eyes dart around, stopping on the medical-supply cabinet in the corner. He jerks the handle. Locked. He kicks the cabinet with his good leg. It rattles but doesn't split. He thrusts his foot into it again. Natasha's mother, father, brother, and priest watch in confusion behind the six-inch sheet of glass over the observation area.

He kicks once more, denting the wood but not breaking it. He glances at the entrance, still shut, and figures the guards will need to put on biohazard suits before coming in. He has some time, but not much. Yelling, he boots the cabinet again, deeper imprint, no fracture though. He hits it for a fifth time, caving a small round hole. He punches through and unlatches it from inside.

Yanking it open, he scans the shelves for syringes. He makes them out in the top back corner. He snatches one, then unscrews the cap of the snow-covered soap bottle. He dips the needle inside and sucks up the orange liquid.

He lets out the air bubbles with a squirt, shakes his left arm from his jacket sleeve, and stabs himself with the syringe. Pressing the plastic plunger, he administers half the vaccine, immunizing himself so he can go near her.

He runs to the bed and climbs on top of his brittle girlfriend, his knees digging into the mattress, his breath heavy. Natasha's lifeless, blue-and-crimson eyes fill with a twinkle as she looks at him up-close. He lifts the gown material around her emaciated left shoulder and injects her. "Here sweetheart," he says, brushing some hair from her face with his free hand.

The buzzer blares. He sees the two bulky guards barreling toward him in protective gear. Just as he finishes giving her the last of the dose, they tackle him, the syringe dropping to the floor with a hollow thud. His back crashes to the surface, whole bed frame vibrating above him.

They scream at him in German as they restrain him, but their voices are distant. He's not paying any attention. He gazes at the ceiling light, a warm glow across his beat-up body, wet boots leaning against each other, arms stretched to his sides as they pin him down. He's smiling. They made it. Him and Natasha. Both of them. Free.

Well Then

The next morning Sean's legs are dangling off the stone bridge he was flinging pretzels from a few nights ago. A soft flurry descends in the air. Through the wall of dancing snowflakes, he peers across the water at the gold clock face of the St. Peter Church, over twenty-eight feet wide, Europe's largest. He sits there for a while, the whoosh of cars and trucks behind, his mind pondering what it did the last time he was in the spot. All he is and all he isn't.

In a bit he's in the hospital elevator, some snow in his hair and eyebrows, his reflection peeking back at him in those mirrored walls. He gets off at the fifth level and starts limping down the hallway. This section of the clinic, filled with administrative and executive offices, lacks the secluded, sterile aura of the quarantine area and rather, has a homey ambience, floral paintings in wood-grain frames mounted every few feet against the pinstriped wallpaper, dark-green carpeting and roped trim below.

He stops at a door labeled in German "Dr. Hans Obrecht – Director – Infectious Disease" and knocks. "Come in," the physician says in the same language inside.

Sean enters the room, closing it behind him. He sweeps his eyes over the space, Natasha's family seated on the low black couch he was on the other day, five men in lab coats huddled around the doctor at his desk, Sean's empty "Face Soap" container propped up on it under a powerful magnifying glass. Everyone fixates on him, the mysterious topic of discussion the last day. Dr. Obrecht opens his mouth to speak, then shuts it, unsure how to phrase what he wants to say. Natasha's mom does the same thing.

Sean, discomforted by the eighteen probing eyeballs on him, looks down at that blue rug with the little white circles. He's not ready to field all the intrusive questions just yet. Besides, he has something much more important to do. "Can I see her?" he asks nobody in particular in English.

"She's still sleeping," Dr. Obrecht says in the same language with a heavy Swiss accent, calm water of Lake Zurich outside the window behind him. "It was quite the week for her."

"I can imagine." Sean rubs the back of his neck. "I'll wait for her downstairs. Thanks." He cracks the door and takes a step into the corridor.

"James," the doctor says, rising to his feet, getting Sean's attention before he leaves. Sean turns over his shoulder. "Forgive me, but I think you have some explaining to do."

Sean looks him in the eye. "It's not James."

"Excuse me?"

He's quiet for a few seconds. "It's Sean."

A pause. "Sean. My apologies, I swore it was James." He runs a hand through his silver hair, the strands toward the front touched by the anxious sweat coating his brow. "My colleagues and I performed a blood test on Ms. Vonlanden this morning and well..." He grips the serum's plastic container between his thumb and middle finger and shakes it twice. "What the fuck was in this soap bottle?"

Sean offers a light chuckle. He twists the doorknob a couple times, latch bolt popping in and out with a clink. "I went through a lot the last few days to fill that up. I don't really feel like talking about it now." He glimpses the six men in white lab coats before him, then bends down and rolls up the left hemline of his jeans, exposing his ankle wound. "I'll make a deal with you guys though. I'll tell you all about it later if you can get someone to check this out for me." Balancing on his good foot, he juts his bad one forward.

Stretching his neck, Dr. Obrecht analyzes the gash. "What is it, a laceration?" Sean nods. "I believe we have the expertise on staff to assist with that," the physician says with sarcasm. A couple of his colleagues snicker at his little joke.

"Thanks doc. It's a deal."

"Wait, can you just describe—"

He shakes his head. "We'll chat later." Swinging his eyes toward the doorway, he catches the father's line of vision. They hold their gazes on each other for a few seconds, Mr. Vonlanden's demeanor timid in the presence of the enigmatic healer. Sean recollects the way he screamed at him in this very room a few days ago, called him a nobody. He's certain the father is thinking about the same moment. Sean grins, a subtle smile that says everything it needs to, the ignorant man put in his place, no conversation needed. Sean exits, sealing the office behind him.

Checking out the floral paintings on the walls, he hobbles toward the elevator, a small lamp above each piece of art, a cone-shaped shine emitted along the canvases, brushstroke details brought out. He stops by one that gets his interest, a Peace Lily, five white bulbs on a black background. He stares at it for about a minute, appreciative of its simplicity, then continues up the hall.

About an hour later he's sitting on a folding chair outside a room in the clinic's main zone. He has a blue soft cast on his left foot stretching to mid-calf. As he gulps from a bottle of water, the door opens with a squeak, a nurse stepping into the hallway. He swallows his sip and asks in English, "Hey, is she up?"

She studies him for a while, same probing expression everyone was giving him upstairs. "Are you the one that went in there yesterday with the soap bottle?" He nods, then takes another swig. "What was in there?"

"I'm talking about it with you guys later. I already promised the doctor." He turns to the entryway, trying to peek through a slit. "Right now I just want to see her. Is she up or no?"

"She's a little drowsy still, but yes, she's awake."

"I'm gonna go say hi," he says, standing.

"Yeah. Go ahead." She points at the handle, still gaping at him. He rests his drink on the aluminum seat and grabs a set of crutches against the wall. With the cushioned tops under his armpits, he maneuvers through the doorway.

He notices Natasha's outline behind the sheer privacy curtain circling the bed. He nudges the door closed with his shoulder, then plants his crutches on the tile floor and takes

himself toward her. He flaps the curtain to the side, his girlfriend spinning to the swoosh. Her face lights up when she
sees it's him. "Hey," she says, voice soft and sweet. She pats
the spot of mattress to her right.

He guides the screen closed, a nook forming around them,
rest of the room and rest of the world drowned out. "Hey," he
says with a grin. He nestles on her side, his cast brushing
against her leg.

Her eyes are clear, no more bleeding, but she still appears frail. He knows the remnants of the illness will fade
soon though. The last thing on his mind is her not-yet-healed
surface. His skin remains black and blue and his lip sliced.
But she doesn't seem fazed. The last thing on her mind is his
not-yet-healed surface.

She's not sure what to say, so many thoughts racing, so
many questions unanswered. She squints a bit, watching him
as if she'd encounter something there she never saw before.
He senses what she's doing and finds it kind of amusing. He
can guess how strange this must be for her. He chuckles.
"What?" she asks.

"No. It's just...you're funny. How you're looking at me."
He tilts his head over his shoulder and smiles. "It's still me."

She lies on her side, gazing at him with the pillow under
her right cheek. "What did you give me?"

"Remember when I told you to be strong for a few days?"
She nods, a few blond strands flowing across the white pil-
lowcase. "Well...I was making something for you that would
help."

She lingers on him, hoping he'll explain more. He doesn't, at a loss himself. "They said I'm gonna be okay. It's gone." She pauses. "All of it."

"I know."

She's quiet for a while, inspecting his face again for something she never knew existed. "How did you know?"

"Because I just know certain things." He pats her thigh through the covers. "About stuff like that."

"I don't get what you're saying."

He can't help but find her natural reaction to it cute. He kneels on the mattress and reaches over her, his leather jacket grazing her hip, then grabs her cell phone from the night table. Sitting back down with it in his lap, he scoots closer to her and clicks a couple buttons. "Here. This'll help." A YouTube clip of him on *Jeopardy!* when he was eleven starts playing, screen shining on his "CALIBOY" T-Shirt, yesterday's clothes still on. He passes her the phone.

"What is this?"

"Just watch it."

She sees three contestants behind podiums, the one in the middle about a foot shorter than the other two. "Mayonnaise is an example of this colloidal dispersion of liquid particles in another liquid," a voice says from the speakers.

"What is an emulsion," the little one in the center says.

"Correct."

"General Science for twelve hundred please."

"Earth's crust consists of about forty-six percent oxygen. This element is second most abundant at about twenty-eight percent."

"What is silicon."

"Right."

She holds the phone a couple inches from her face, examining the young contestant's features, detecting traces of her boyfriend James in them. Her attention jumps from the child him to the current him. "This is you?"

He nods. "Yeah."

She watches for another minute or so, trying to piece things together. She lays down the phone, clip still rolling, and looks around their little space for a while, exchange of *Jeopardy!* questions and answers still audible. "What are you, like a genius or something?" He chuckles. Her mouth opens a bit in surprise. "Why didn't you ever tell me?"

He grips a patch of bed sheet, rolling it into a little ball, then unrolling and repeating. "I guess it didn't matter. But then you got sick. And it did." Outside, the snow has subsided, the sun emerging, a wedge of light pouring through the big window on their nook, soft shadows touching the sheer curtain where it bends and billows.

She looks at the podium on the video. "Who's Sean?"

"That's my real name."

"It isn't James?"

He wraps his hand around hers and says in an understanding tone, "This must be really weird for you. Believe me, I get it. Something happened with me in the States and I needed to change my identity. Sounds crazy, I know. I'll explain all of it." He kisses her forehead. "But everything else about me you know. You're the only person in the world I've told any of that other stuff to."

She glimpses his eyes, warm like always. Weighing it all, she stares with folded arms at the silhouettes swaying around their nook for about a minute. The shock of his fake name is a bit unsettling, but then she tries to put it in perspective. Reflecting on what he told her and everything that occurred the last day, she comes to the compelling realization he just cured the world's deadliest disease for her.

Smirking, she pokes his shoulder. Reacting to her playfulness, he smiles back and asks, "What?"

On the show they used to make him wear a lot of hairspray and put him in boxy suits. His personal taste is more casual, and he always hated how they made him look. Being so familiar with him, she assumes this without him even admitting it and decides to have some fun with him. She nods at the YouTube video and says in a taunting way, "Look at you up onstage with your fancy little hair and your fancy little outfit."

His cheeks get red. "Stop."

"Awwwww." She snickers. "What happened to this style? I think I like it better than the one now. Much more refined. Really. You should consider—"

He starts tickling the sides of her belly. "You want to laugh?" he asks with sarcasm. "I'll make you laugh."

Giggling, she tries to push him off. "Stop. Baby." She twists back and forth, bed frame squeaking. "Baby." Her laughter gets louder.

"You asked for it buddy."

She smacks his back. "I'm gonna get you so bad later." They roll around.

I D

A week later a taxicab pulls up to the Rayburn House in Washington, DC, a large Congressional office complex. Sean slips out in a down jacket and beanie, face healed other than a small mark on his cheek, no more cast on his ankle. He gazes at the pillars in front, then crosses the street and climbs the stairs, just a trace of a limp remaining in his step.

He enters and wanders through a hallway bustling with political aides, lawyers, lobbyists, and other federal-government affiliates. Soft streaks of midday February sun spill through the windows on top of the hectic crowd.

He gets on an elevator with three men and two women buttoned up in business attire. As they rise, one of the males starts chatting with one of the females about an article in this morning's *Washington Post* on campaign finance reform. Sean tries to decide if he's hitting on her or not. By the time the cart pauses on his level he thinks yes. He weaves out from the back and walks down a wing filled with all fifty US state flags, each touched by bands of natural light, no two in the exact places.

He stops at a room labeled "Congressman P. Goya – PA – 13th District," opens it, and goes in. Passing a framed photo of the Liberty Bell, he approaches a secretary in a green sweater and pearl necklace. The young woman closes a drawer and tilts her attention up. "Sean?" she asks as if expecting him.

"Yeah. Hey."

"Hold on." She presses a black button on an intercom and says into it, "Hi sir. I have Sean Malone." Smiling, she moves her stare to him. "He'll be just a bit longer. You can have a seat."

"No problem." He settles on a two-person couch against the wall. She returns to her paperwork but glimpses him every few seconds, a dash of intrigue in her eyes, her boss informing her of the kid's lore. He puts on a pair of headphones and listens to music for about ten minutes, a slight bob to his knee.

"Okay," she says to him with a wave, Sean twisting out the earpieces and shifting to her. "You can go right ahead."

"Thanks." He hooks around the reception area to a set of brown double doors, cracks one, and steps into the office, Patrick leaning against his desk in anticipation, palms behind him on the wood surface.

"Jesus Christ, you grew up Sean," the former NSA employee says, taking in the taller, eighteen-year-old version.

"I'm still not used to being called that." Sean shuts the door and walks over. "You look good too Congressman."

"Shit. I'm still not used to being called that either." Patrick chuckles, then holds out his arms. "Good to see you man." They hug. "Sit, sit," he says, pointing at a seat.

Sean descends into it, unzipping his heavy jacket. He flaps it a couple times, trying to get some air on his toasty midsection. Patrick situates himself at his desk across, still has the same ergonomic chair from his NSA days.

Sean spots a framed picture he recalls a few inches from the computer, Patrick with his family at Disney World, two new photos next to it, one of his son, another his daughter, each about Sean's current age in them, both much more mature-looking than as children at Disney World. He also notices a Philadelphia Eagles jersey he remembers, mounted on the wall. He thinks about the last time he saw it, the day he flew to the NSA in the middle of the Traveling Salesman dilemma. He ponders how different his life was then, no graffiti art, no Natasha, no Ebola cure.

He glances at Patrick and says, "Well, you tell me."

"You're positive you want to go through with it?"

"I wouldn't have flown out here if I didn't."

Patrick inches closer, setting his elbows on his desk, folding his hands. "Just so you know, my friend in the FBI isn't thrilled. The program is a one-way deal. Not to mention you did violate the agreement by coming back into the country without notice. He didn't take too fondly to that. He'd be doing me a huge favor." He leans back and rocks a couple times. "That's not to say he won't do it though. If you go through with what we talked about last night."

"I just have to testify, right?"

"Yeah. If you do they'll play ball. They really want to lock this guy up."

Sean bites his lip, a pensive expression building on him. "Man, I still can't believe they caught him…"

Patrick reaches under a heap of scattered documents, fishes out a manila folder, and tosses it to him. "Check it out." The corner hits him in the chest, then it drops to his lap.

Peeling open the cover, he gazes at three mugshots of Dante paper-clipped inside, a look of defeat on him. In the right-profile one Sean can see an oval scar on his face from the whack with the metal rod.

"They found some of his blood in the jail in Suddsfield," Patrick says, tapping his right index finger on his left wrist. "He presumably cut himself on the...apparatus...when he was...handling the first victim. A bunch of the cop's blood was outside the cell, but there were a few drops inside, different person's. One of the officers who arrested you left a few minutes before the attack. He remembers the cells the three of you were in and confirmed this Dante was in fact in the one where the strangling happened."

"How did they track him down once they had his DNA?" he asks, attention still on the black-and-white images of the killer.

"They were able to link the sample to another murder in Oregon from three months ago. He left some blood there as well getting in a physical altercation with the other man before...he broke his neck." He clenches the air with his fingers. "Bare hands. They followed up with some old leads from that incident. The FBI pieced together enough information to get an address on him. Near the Idaho border. It was apparently a battle...but they dragged him in."

"Nuts," Sean says in a subdued tone. He closes the folder, wiping Dante's chilling image from his field of vision, then lobs it on the desk.

"You have no problem providing an ID on him in court? Being a witness?"

"I'll do anything they need to get that monster out of society."

"Perfect. If you help the FBI out on this I don't see it having any issues reversing the identity program it put you in." He loops his fingers around the handle of a mug with the US Congressional seal on it. He has some coffee and asks with a grin, "So you want to bring Sean back from the grave, huh?"

"I always thought zombies had a charm to them."

Shaking his head, Patrick laughs. He has two more sips, finishing the cup. "Let's take a drive over to Bureau headquarters and chat with my pal." He stands and saunters to a brass coat hanger, collecting his wool jacket and scarf.

"What's he gonna need from me?"

"If you put in writing today you'll testify they should make the identity reversal official in the system. Give them a couple more days to transfer your finances and get you new documentation, and after that it'll be like you never left. They of course won't acknowledge they were involved. The responsibility of the disappearance will fall on you. So you'll need to make up a story convincing people why you wanted to play dead for four years."

"Fair enough."

"Don't take this lightly. Assume the media will be all over it. People still remember you from the game show. Journalists will want to cover your...resurrection. You're going to need

something to say. And you obviously can't mention the truth…
anything about the NSA."

"I know, I know. I don't want cyber-crime gangs chasing me now anymore than I did back then. I'll tell them I was
stressed from being in the public eye. With *Jeopardy!* and
everything."

He nods a couple times. "That should work."

"Well, it is true in its own right."

Patrick slips into his coat. "You seem…solid now. You
look…more relaxed than you did the last I saw you. Life good?"

"I can't complain."

"When the press hounds you, just tell them you needed
to get away from it all, and now you're fine. They'll bug
you for a few weeks then let you be. It'll be impossible for
anyone to make a connection back to the NSA if you keep
it at that."

"Speaking of the NSA, what'll happen with all that crap
with Paul Pine?"

"You were gone for a while. Put in enough time to weather
it. New President as you must know. New Cabinet. New
Secretary of Defense. Pine's probably on a golf course somewhere. Fifty pounds heavier. No political reputation to protect anymore. You're not a threat to him. I doubt we'll see
that flabby, pockmarked turkey neck of his ever again." Sean
chuckles. "Hey, they asked me about your aunt too. Is she
staying in the program or not?"

Sean stands and zips his jacket up. "I spoke to her about
it. She's ready to come out of it if I do. She's gonna still live

in Italy with her husband, but would switch back to her real name."

"Shouldn't be an issue. Just make sure she goes along with your story. There can't be any deviations. The media will come at her too."

"She'll be cool."

"All right. FBI time. Let's go." Patrick collects his keys from the edge of his desk, then gestures toward the door.

"I hope they put this psycho behind bars for life," Sean says, walking next to him.

Twisting his maroon scarf around his neck, Patrick asks, "How did you ever go from being in Rome to getting mixed up with some hit man in the mountains of Central California anyway?"

"Colzyne Systems hired him to kidnap me."

"The big pharmaceutical company? With the commercials of the doctor roaming the rainforest in a lab coat?"

"Yup, them. There wouldn't be a paper trail linking them back. But hopefully the hit man gives them up to the Feds."

"Why the hell would they want to kidnap you?"

"I'll be getting to that." He stops walking, Patrick too. "It's the second reason I wanted to fly out here."

"You need something else from me?"

"A small favor."

"What?"

"An introduction."

"Who?"

"The director of the Centers for Disease Control. You know him?"

"Fred Bask. I've met him at a fundraiser before. Why?"

"There's something I want to talk to him about. Something related to Colzyne."

"You can't get on the chief of the CDC's calendar just like that. He's a busy dude."

"Can you reach out to him? He can meet with me when he's free." A few moments pass. "I have a feeling when he finds out what it involves he'll schedule sooner than later."

"I can see what I can do." Patrick puts his hand on the doorknob but doesn't turn yet. "Before I start calling in requests to higher-ups in the federal government you're going to need to tell me what you're…referring to. Why you need him. I don't want to give the impression I'm going to be wasting his time. I'm sure you understand."

"I came up with something." Sean slides his hands in his front jean pockets. "I think he'd want to hear about it. In his possession it can help a lot of people."

"Came up with something?" he asks, surveying him. "What?"

He glances at the chairs back by the desk, then at Patrick. "You might want to sit down."

Under Control

Two days later Sean is waddling down a metal ramp extending from the rear of a U-Haul truck to the pavement below, the top of a dinette table snug against his chest. It's over seventy degrees in Santa Barbara, California this afternoon, the heat combined with the weight of the wood sustaining a coat of sweat on his face.

Once on flat ground he lugs the heavy piece of furniture toward a quaint bungalow home he signed a lease on yesterday, nestled among an overflow of greenery and bright flowers. Behind him in the van's back are four stools, a TV box, a rolled-up area rug, and a lamp, all with their tags still on.

As he heads up the inclined driveway, the property's hilltop view of the coast comes into sight, deep, lush foliage with palm trees peeking out here and there, all set on the backdrop of the Pacific Ocean. The ebb and flow of the vineyards in the distance remind him of the landscape around Marco and Mary's villa in Tuscany.

Arms straining, he guides the table through the propped-open front door and crosses the foyer into the kitchen, where he situates it in an alcove. He lifts his white T-shirt and dabs some moisture around his eyes. He steps into the living room and weaves around eight cardboard boxes toward the rear of the home. Stopping at a window, he scans the deck, a flood of natural light pouring through the glass onto him.

He spots Natasha in a two-piece yellow bathing suit, tanning. He pops the lock on the pane, slides it up, and says with sarcasm, "I don't need any help with the new stuff for my place. Thanks though."

Laughing, she rolls over, a glow to her skin from more than the sun, all signs of her disease gone. "Just give me a little longer." She pinches the curly straw in her cup of iced tea and has a sip.

"I don't care how good you look in that bikini Vonlanden. I need a hand."

"Oh shush mister. You know I'll help. I'm almost done." She sticks her tongue out at him and flips back over on her pink towel. "If I'm gonna move to California I need my California tan," she says squinting up at the bluish-gold sky.

"Five more minutes. I'm timing you." He closes the window. Kneeling, he yanks open a taped cardboard box. As he reaches inside, a knock on the propped-open front door carries into the room.

Turning to the sound, he notices a man on the stoop, gray beard, wide shoulders, lightweight cardigan sweater. "Hi," the visitor says, double-checking the number on a sheet of paper in between his thumb and index finger. "I'm looking for Sean Malone. This was the address I was given."

"You found him." Sean springs up and strides to him. He slaps the dust and sweat from his right hand on his jeans, then locks grips with him. "Nice to meet you."

"Hi Sean. I'm Fred. Fred Bask. Director of the CDC."

"Yes. Of course. Come in, come in."

He enters. "Just moving in?"

"You could tell, huh? Sorry for all the boxes and stuff."

"It's not a problem." The man peruses the empty house, no furniture other than the dinette table in the kitchen. "Do you have somewhere to sit though at least?"

"Yes. One second." He dashes outside. In about a minute he returns with a stool in each arm from the U-Haul, coat of sweat back on his face. He situates them in the living room by the window and gives them a quick wipe with his shirt. "Work?" he asks, catching his breath.

With a shrug the CDC director plops his broad build on one of the seats, cushion squeaking a bit. "Quite comfortable."

Sean climbs onto the other and says with pride, "I bought the whole set for a hundred bucks. Got two more back in the truck."

"Thrifty."

Sean bends, snatches a half-full bottle of water from the white rug, and swigs. "Thanks for making it all the way out from Georgia," he says, blotting the perspiration from his brow with his forearm.

"How could I not after hearing what the Congressman said?"

"Glad we got your interest." He has another gulp. "I think the potential here is...limitless. Let's make it happen."

"I'm going to cut to the chase." He inches forward on his seat. "Mr. Goya filled me in on the overview of your...discovery, and though I'm dying to hear more, I quite frankly can't... believe this really exists."

Sean snickers. "Understandable I guess."

He strokes the whiskers on his gray beard. "In most cases I would dismiss something like this. However, after the Congressman told me about your…history, I can't say I wasn't open to hearing your explanation at least."

"There's nothing to even explain at this point. It's done. I have a formula. I can write it down for you now."

"You have it finalized?"

"Yeah. It's all there."

"Don't get me wrong, a formula would be terrific. I can't even speculate what that would look like. However, with the timeframe you were discussing with Mr. Goya to get it to market, we need proof. Actual case-study proof."

"It's been used before. And worked."

"A real occurrence with a real patient?"

Sean points at the deck through the glass. "Right there."

Brow wrinkled, the CDC director gets off his seat and gazes at the pretty girl in the bikini lounging in the sun. "Her?"

"Her."

"When?"

"Oh, let's see. A little over a week ago."

"She had Ebola?"

"Ebola."

"Ebola?"

"Ebola."

"And now it's gone?"

"And now it's gone."

About fifteen seconds pass, the man's face split among confusion and excitement. "Where did this all occur?"

"Switzerland."

"Is she still being treated by you? What's she doing here?"

"She's my girlfriend. I'm just showing her UC Santa Barbara. She's gonna transfer there next semester and live here with me. It was tough to convince her parents to let her move to the States for school...but I guess they owed me a favor."

"It's completely gone from just a vaccine? All shreds of... Ebola? I don't mean to be rude...but I can't bring myself to trust that. It's impossible."

"You can ask her doctor in Zurich. He saw it work right in front of him. He's been calling me up once a day to pick my brain about it."

"I think I just may," he says, demeanor rigid and contemplative.

"I'll give you his info," Sean says, hopping off his stool. He scoops a black Sharpie marker from the floor he's been labeling boxes with, tears a cardboard flap off one, and starts scribbling on it. He says what he's writing, "Dr. Obrecht. Zurich. Luffen Clinic—"

"Hans Obrecht?"

His hand stops moving. "You know him?"

"Of him. Yes, of course. My office has his number. He's the top infectious disease researcher in Europe. Arguably the world."

"I heard the same thing about him." He flings the cardboard strip and marker on the floor, no need for them anymore.

"And he calls you up every day to pick your brain?"

"Getting kind of annoying really. Nice guy though Hans."

The CDC director takes a few seconds to absorb this. "Tell me more about this medication. How does it specifically work?"

"I'll map the whole thing out for you. But in brief, it alters the way the disease replicates its genetic material."

"Would it prevent infection or can it only be applied to a patient already sick?"

"Both. I'm a real-life case study for prevention. I took a dose. I needed to make myself immune to go near my girl-friend. When she had it."

"Did you experience any side effects?"

"I was a little drowsy. That was it."

He takes some time to process this. "The Congressman informed me it wouldn't just fight Ebola, but other viruses as well. Is that accurate?"

"It should. The underlying way they all build and spread is the same, as I'm sure you know."

"What else can you envision it helping with?"

Hands on his hips, Sean stares into the corner, his head rocking side to side. "Let's see. Malaria. Bird flu. SARS. Typhoid fever. HIV. Even cancer. Those are just the big ones. Others too."

The man rubs his temples. "Can I trouble you for a glass of water?"

"No prob." Sean digs his arm in a pried-open case of Arrowhead bottles by the fireplace, clutches one, and tosses it to him.

He catches it with clumsy hands, bottom banging into his chest, his cardigan twisting to the side. He adjusts his sweater, then unscrews the drink and chugs half. He lets out a long exhale, overwhelmed by everything he's hearing. Silence for a while. "Who's aware of all this other than you?"

"My girlfriend obviously. Her family. Obrecht and some of the people on his staff. Goya. My aunt, my old teacher, his wife. They just know how it interacts with the body. I didn't give them the mixture."

"You haven't provided the mixture to anyone?"

"Technically, a few others."

"Who's a few others?"

"Have you heard of a company called Colzyne?"

"I run the CDC. Yes I've heard of Colzyne."

"Well, them."

The man laughs. "You're telling me you gave a medical blueprint to Colzyne Systems? They probably have their best executives planning out the logistics as we speak."

"Not probably. Definitely."

"How do you expect a government-sponsored operation to compete with a private firm on that level? They specialize in drug production and advertising. The infrastructure is already in place. Not to mention the funding."

"I did give them a version." He pauses. "But it won't work. I'm gonna give you one that does."

"Why won't theirs work?"

"Some of the portions of ingredients are off. They won't even get theirs to clinical trials. I'm assuming once they find out you have the real mixture they'll just quit. And even if they don't, it'll be next to impossible for them to figure out the problem in theirs. I intentionally made it extremely misleading.

And believe me, if I want to make something complicated…I can." He points at the side of his head. "The real formula is here and nowhere else."

"Why'd you share one that's useless? I don't understand the point."

"They're not the type of people who should be in charge of something this powerful."

"Why would you assume that?"

"Let's just say they weren't diplomatic in reaching out to me when they heard I was in possession of this information."

"I see." The CDC director is quiet for a while. "How on earth did you come up with it anyway?"

"I just thought of it."

"My God. How?"

Sean chuckles. "I'm good at stuff like that. I always was."

The man looks around the hollow room for a while, then through the window at the girl, then back at Sean. "I'm obviously going to have my top people vet this. Inside and out. Before we move forward we'll need to go through all the different government units that would be involved, work out manufacturing, distribution, everything. Not to mention interfacing with the FDA. It will at least be a few months before we can make this official and announce it to the public. The fact that this creation even exists. And that's if of course it is what you say it is after we test it. Thoroughly."

He swirls the water inside his bottle for a bit. His expression turns serious, almost grave, and he says, "Now, let's say it all does go smoothly, and we do decide to mass-produce the drug. I must warn you, your entire life is going to change. You being responsible for something of this magnitude, with this level of international impact." He leans forward a couple inches and asks, "Are you ready for that?"

Running a hand through his hair, Sean is quiet for a few seconds. "When I was living in Italy this old man and me got to talking one night by the Pantheon. He told me something I didn't give much thought to at the time. But then a couple days ago, when I was back in the States, I followed up on it for the hell of it. Anyway, he said to check out an experiment with Manx Shearwaters, a type of bird. You ever hear of them?"

"Yes, I'm aware of the species. We studied them in a biology class when I was an undergrad about a thousand years ago."

"So there was a group of these birds who lived on an island by Britain. The researchers took half of them to Boston. The other half they brought to Venice, Italy. They wanted to see how they would react after being moved out of their natural home." A slight grin emerges on his face. "Within two weeks both halves made it back. To their starting location on the island by Britain. Exact place. All the way from Boston and Venice separately. They covered about two hundred fifty miles per day."

"That's impressive."

"You want to hear the most impressive part? That species doesn't fly over land. So it was impossible for them to navigate by memory, you know, looking at points of reference and backtracking. They were traveling over water the whole time.

Blue, unchanging water." Staring out the window, he sweeps his hand across his body, even with the line of the Pacific Ocean in the background. "And they still made it home."

"I can't fathom how that's even possible."

"Neither can I. That's what makes the story so interesting to me. They just had this ability put in them since they were born...to do something like that." Sean folds his arms. "So you want to know if I care about my life changing when this all goes public? A few years ago, yeah, I would've. But now...no. Not at all." He glimpses Natasha, then turns back to the CDC director. "I think if we have something inside of us that's... put there by nature for a reason. We shouldn't repress it. We should listen to what it's saying and not care too much about the consequences."

That Kid Who Cured
All Those Diseases

Six months later Sean is washing his face in a steamy shower at his place in Santa Barbara. He grips a shampoo bottle, squeezes some in his palm, and rubs it through his hair. He rinses and flips the water off. Pulling back the curtain, he steps onto the shaggy blue mat, a small scar on his left ankle from his accident in the Explorer.

He unhooks a towel from the door, dries himself off, and ties it around his waist. Squaring to the sink, he turns on the faucet and wipes some fog from the mirror, revealing his reflection. He opens a cabinet, grabs a razor and shaving cream, then squirts some in his palm. He rubs it in small circles over his stubbled face. With downward strokes he trims off his beard. Jutting out his jaw, he makes sure he didn't miss any spots, then dabs some aftershave on his fingers and pats his skin with it. He puts everything back and heads toward the door.

Feet still a bit moist, he saunters into the connected bedroom, some furniture inside now, a bureau with a Peace Lily plant on top, two night tables with lamps, a full-length mirror, and a bed with a striped comforter. Hanging on the wall above the headboard is the abstract graffiti painting he did of the Hotel Vanessa rooftop, Natasha's Christmas gift.

She has a big duffel bag open on the mattress and is packing it with clothes, a dress and high heels for her, a suit and loafers for him. Noticing him, she says, "If we leave in the next twenty minutes I think we should be okay." She tucks a red necktie in the corner of the bag, then kisses his stubble-free cheek.

"I can make it by then," he says, sliding out a dresser compartment, snagging pairs of socks and underwear. As he slips into them she lunges over and closes the drawer, something he always forgets to do. He strolls into the walk-in closet and collects a T-shirt, jeans, and that leather jacket of his, some scuffs on it from his adventure last winter.

As he changes, his eye catches the Hotel Vanessa painting across the room. Being in an abstract style, the piece doesn't represent the exact appearance of the rooftop the day he saw it, but the shapes and colors he used in it capture the essence of it. For the pool itself he has a figure eight in black graffiti, diving board a tan zigzag, surrounding wall little green squares, sky two shades of blue stripes, and sun a red circle.

Fixating on the images, he reflects on that moment, the slice of space and time he shared up there with Natasha. He remembers he couldn't get a read on her, wasn't sure what she was feeling. It made him tense. But now months later, the moment stands for something different. Above all it represents their first date of many, the beginning of their relationship, the start of something that's been so much already and has the potential to be so much more. In the years to come the association with anxiety will fade to nothing in comparison.

He finds the same is true for all the other events in his life. Perceptions of them tend to change as he does, nothing engraved. Though the universe only allows one instance of our individual experiences, their memories are preserved through our minds alone, and our minds are always morphing as we take on the next set of circumstances nature throws at us. He feels there are no certainties about the moments of our histories. Except one. They're ours.

His motorcycle whips down Southern California's Pacific Coast Highway a while later, Natasha on the backseat in her pink coat with the big black buttons, duffel bag strapped on the bike behind her, towering mountain ridges to their left, endless blue of the Pacific Ocean to their right. The wind hits them head-on, wrapping their skin in a refreshing cool among the warm sun hanging over the water.

He bought a new Triumph bike when he moved back to America, black just like his old one but larger, more space for two. She's used to riding on it by now, her body leaning in a natural way with it as he bends into turns, her golden locks blowing behind her under her helmet, the white one with the pink racing stripes he got for her in Rome.

An hour or so later he cruises into Pasadena, passing by some familiar sights from his days living there. Angling his head back, he comments on some of them to her above the purr of the engine, a baseball field he used to play on, the

Dapper Devil Burrito Shack, his old house. She smiles, enjoying learning about little nuggets from his past.

In a bit he veers into a parking lot behind an auditorium on the SoCal Tech campus, motor still humming even as he slows. News vans for the national networks, NBC, ABC, CBS, all the major cable channels, and a handful of local providers flood the asphalt. A few dozen people circulate with press badges on, a bunch more standing behind a fence along the perimeter.

With his boot heels he guides the motorcycle into a space and turns it off. She hops down with ease, no longer needing his assistance.   They hang their helmets, then he frees the bag of clothing from the rear and slings it over his right shoulder. Now that his face is exposed he's spotted. Ten reporters storm over to him with microphones extended, three policemen jumping in front to block them. The reporters shout his name as they're restrained.

Holding Natasha's hand, he strides toward the back entrance trying not to let the commotion distract him. A security guard in a yellow windbreaker lifts his walkie-talkie from his belt and barks a few commands into it. He refastens the device and waves at Sean. "Mr. Malone," he says, clearing a metal gate out of the way, making a path for him and his girlfriend.

"Hey," Sean says with a grin. "Thanks."

"My pleasure. The changing room they reserved for you two will be the second on your left."

"Got it. Thanks again." He leads Natasha up some stairs, then into the three-story event hall. It's loud, a cross section of voices buzzing on the other side of a tall curtain, a few hundred people behind it at least. They continue down the dim hallway to their door.

About a half hour later Sean is backstage wearing the suit Natasha packed for him, a blue two-button lacking the boxy cut of the old *Jeopardy!* ones, a tailored, modern fit to it. She's to his right in the outfit she brought for herself, a light-yellow sleeveless dress ending just above her knee. She's alluring and tasteful in it at the same time. They're alone behind the curtain, long shadows sweeping across it and over their faces. He guesses more than twice as many people are out there now, the rumble of the voices louder and more intense.

He rocks back and forth in his new loafers, a nervous energy to him. He seems excited but also a tad anxious. Eyeing the floor, he recognizes the tile layout, that glossy beige design with small gray squares he recalls from other areas on campus. He realizes the pattern will be a part of him forever, always reminding him of four major events in his life. His freshman orientation when he first got to this place. The paper-signing session the day he dropped out. The trip he took back here with the professor a few months ago for the chemicals. And above all, this moment right now.

Curious to see what's going on, he nudges some curtain fabric to the side. He glances at the scene, an army of news-camera operators up front, a throng of spectators behind filling every seat on all three levels. Peering through the glare of the hot lights, he makes out Marco and Mary in the front row. The professor and Aliza a few behind. Patrick and his wife a couple chairs over. Kyle on the second-floor balcony chatting with Fabrizio. He tries to only focus on those eight faces among the sea of others.

A fiftyish man in a charcoal suit climbs a small flight of stairs to the stage and situates himself at a podium, the observers hushing in his presence. The CDC director and five others from his organization file behind and huddle around. "Welcome," the man in the charcoal suit says into the microphone, a couple cameras popping. "I'm Phillip Yardley, president of the Southern California Technology Institute." He moves his gaze across the audience. "Today is a historic day. It will stand as the day the world found out about the most significant scientific discovery of our generation. One of the university's own has partnered with the United States Centers for Disease Control and Prevention to produce and distribute a drug that will change human lives forever. Today the CDC's head, Fred Bask, will be announcing the rollout plan for this breakthrough treatment, which will be led by him and the medication's inventor himself. But before we get into the strategy, we at the institute will be awarding the creator with an honorary degree. Doctor of Science. Our highest distinction in the field. Something he deserves more than anyone on this very planet." Clapping, he says with enthusiasm, "Ladies and gentlemen, without any further delay. The mind responsible for this revolutionary achievement. Sean Malone."

The school president turns to the curtain behind him, Sean peeking out through a small split in the material, every camera flashing, whole crowd waiting in anticipation. He looks at Natasha, healthy, radiant, beautiful. He grins. She smiles back. "Here goes," he says taking a deep breath. She leans over, bites his shoulder, then makes the noise of a lion, or a tiger, or something like that.

About the Author

Elixir is Ted Galdi's first novel. He's twenty-nine years old and lives in Los Angeles. He can be contacted at ted@elixirthebook.com.

Author photograph by Scott Witter
Cover art by Carey Conley

www.ingramcontent.com/pod-product-compliance
Lightning Source LLC
Chambersburg PA
CBHW072202130726
47910CB00011B/1777